Spirit of the Blitz

First published in 2020 by
Acorn Books
www.acornbooks.co.uk

Acorn Books is an imprint of
Andrews UK Limited
www.andrewsuk.com

Spirit of the Blitz

Marc Blake

ACORN BOOKS

Contents

Prologue

September 1939

My name is Will Lumley and I live at 14 Henshaw Street in South East London. My dad works in East Lane market. At home there's Gran and Ma and my stupid little sister Aggie, who is eight. I am nearly thirteen.

Our English teacher Mr. Bennett says it's important to keep a record and he made us all start a diary called 'The Day War Broke Out'. When the sirens went off it was a horrible wail like an animal in pain and we all thought we were done for. We marched in quick time to the shelter. There were lights down there strung on a wire and the teachers tried to make us carry on with the lessons but no one could hear a thing in our horrid smelly gas masks. After a while the all-clear sounded and when we got outside it was bright and sunny. No planes in the sky. No clouds of gas.

Dad came to take me home.

'I wasn't scared, not a bit.'

'Good lad.'

We were turning the corner back into our street. I could see the goalposts that he had painted on the wall for us kids.

'Dad, you won't go off to war, will you?'

'We've all got to do our bit son.'

'But you're not going right *now*?'

He squeezed my shoulder.

'No chance. I haven't had me tea yet.'

The Germans didn't come that night, or in the morning, or the day after that. It was all one big false alarm and soon they started calling it the 'Bore War.'

But a month later Dad signed up.

A day later he was gone, leaving me in charge of the Home Front.

Chapter One

September 7th 1940 – Black Saturday

Boom.

A giant stamps all over the East End. Babies wail. Women pray for God to save us.

Boom!

Beckton gone and Silvertown too. Poplar is taking a right thumping. We don't have an Anderson because no one in our street has a back garden, only the WC and a corner for the coal so we're in the communal shelter under the Peabody Estate. There are a hundred and seventy of us cringing and shuddering together.

Boom BOOM.

The jiggling row of storm lights flickers out. When they come on again there is so much dust that we all cough like mad. We huddle under our coats and wait for the world to end. People won't say a word in case it jinxes a direct hit.

Boom BOOM!

It's almost on top of us now. I count like after thunder and before lightening. One… two… someone is saying their prayers over and over but it does no good and I squeeze my eyes as tight shut as I can. The foundations shake and we scramble to get under the benches. I get down as low as possible. I'd get under the ground if I could. I'd burrow right through to the centre of the earth.

Aggie clings to Ma's cardigan and Ma wraps herself round the pair of us. Three… four… suddenly all the air is sucked out. It sounds like the sea pulling back over pebbles. We hold our breath. A new sound, the clanging of fire bells peeling off. The Fire Service and AFS leaping into action. No more pretend war.

BOOM! BOOM! Boom.

The loudest yet but the third one is quieter.

The giant blunders off toward Borough and Lambeth.

We were lucky, people say. An old soldier mutters about having been through it all before and he says that if we do get hit we won't know it. How does he know? When the moaning Minnies went off (that's what we call the sirens now) I ran

1

out with my marbles, a comic and the bloody gas mask. Aggie brought her stupid doll with its cracked face and half the stuffing out. She takes it everywhere. Ma promised we'd be out in a few hours.

It's been more than that.

The first wave has gone over. The ARP warden stationed at the exit says we've to wait until the all-clear. The babies are crying so the Mothers fuss and feed them and people share out what they have. There is bread and butter, some sandwiches and some tinned stuff. There is no tea to drink because no one thought to bring an urn. There are jokes about holding a raffle to send someone out to fetch a kettle but no one is going to risk it. The ARP won't let them.

It was a quarter to five in the afternoon and we had twelve minutes to find shelter. You can go in with your neighbours if they'll have you but you mustn't get caught out because if a firebomb hits you, you will end up like pig crackling. As we ran out down the street I saw them coming over, hundreds of Dorniers and Heinkels in close formation, big black crows filling up the sky, nothing like the dogfights up on Blackheath in the summer. Back then the grass was all turned to straw and the clouds were stacked up like pillows and we watched the vapour trails twisting and turning like ribbons.

You can't get a radio signal underground so we're cut off. My friends Tommo, Jim and Kenneth from Keeton's Road School are here so we play card games. At nine o' clock there's still is no all-clear siren so the children are put to bed and Ma lets Aggie sleep in her lap. It's not an adventure anymore and everyone wants to go home. The bombers pass once more but this time the boom and thump is quieter and steady. It is like when Grandma banged her stick on the ceiling. I was sent up to empty the bucket under her bed. She stopped knocking early this year when they put her in a box in the parlour.

'When's it going to stop?' Asks Ken.

'When they run out of bombs.' Comes Tommo.

'They'll never run out of bombs.' I say.

The old soldier sparks his Player's No. 6. 'It's the big one lads. The Day of Judgment. I hope you've been good.'

'What, like at Christmas?' asks Ken.

'Not much of a present this.' I say, thinking of the things I've left behind. There's a *Just William* story, some penny comics, *Valiant* and *Triumph*, with the new Adventures of Superman in it. We're using my marbles as currency but I've played badly and the best have gone to Tommo. I'll get them back on Monday at...

'Hey, what if the school gets bombed out?'

'No more lessons.' Says Tommo.

'No more Mathematics.'

'No more Mr. Bennett.'

They don't like English like I do. 'Come on 'Itler.' I say. 'Drop one on Keeton's Road.'

'That's enough Will.' Says Ma from across the way.

At ten o' clock they dim the lights. After a while the snores rise and fall like waves.

***

It is Sunday morning and people are rubbing their legs and backs to get the circulation going as they collect up their gas masks and bits and pieces. The ARP men tell everyone to leave in an orderly fashion. I recognise one in his black jacket, white armband and tin helmet. He's one of the caretakers here at the Estate who used to chase us out if we made too much noise or broke a milk bottle. We were too quick for him and as we ran off we'd see him bent over catching his breath. He doesn't look puffed out now, more puffed up, what with having something proper to do.

Outside it's another world, not London, not anyplace. The smoke-filled air smells of burning and everything is singed charcoal black. You can still hear the bells ringing on the fire engines over in Deptford. They have been out all night. Broken glass glitters in the sun. The roads are covered in big black lumps of shrapnel, bricks and masonry. Some of the buildings have collapsed. There are different coloured walls inside, a mantelpiece upstairs, pictures skew-whiff, one of the King. The ARP wardens are getting the bigger boys to clear the roads "in order to re-establish lines of communication." I want to help but Ma grips Aggie and me and marches us home in double time.

When we turn the corner I see straightaway that some of the houses have gone. Mrs. Letchworth from No. 47 is climbing over rubble calling out for her cat. As we approach I start to get an awful sinking feeling.

It's the smoke and rubble we see first, the hole second.

Ma sags and slows, saying over and over, I can't believe it. I can't believe it.

I want to speed up but also I don't. I don't want to see what I have to see.

The bomb crater is next door and our house has fallen into it.

All we can do is stand and look at the smoking pile where Aggie was born and Gran died and where we had to have a bath on Fridays whether we needed one or not. More glass, more shrapnel everywhere, twisted black iron worms. It is horrid.

I want it back the way it was. I keep thinking someone is going to come along, a policeman or an ARP man and pull back a big stage curtain and go, Da-daah! It's a trick to fool the Hun. Look, here's the terrace, the old London Brick, the higgledy-piggledy chimney, the sagging window sills, the lines of washing, the goal we painted on the wall. Here it is! But it's not a disappearing trick. It really has gone, leaving bricks and rafters and the spine of our house sticking out. I can't even see our little bedroom anymore. Mrs. Eversholt from opposite is standing at our front post in her pinafore dress with her arms folded.

'We was in the cupboard under the stairs. We come out when the fire engines turned up. Figured lightning doesn't strike twice. Guess you were unlucky Mrs. L.'

Ma does not answer.

'They come and checked for gas. Said if it had fallen in the street we'd have all gone up sky high. Be thankful for small mercies.'

Ma offers a pinched smile.

'If there's anything I can do…'

'No thank you Mrs. Eversholt.'

'Where is my dolly going to live?' sobs Aggie.

'We can't take no one in.' Mrs. Eversholt is still saying things even though we have not asked her to. 'I've three as is it and father's poorly.'

Ma puts a face on. 'We'll be perfectly fine, thank you. We've relatives in Lee Green.'

'Who's that Ma?' I ask,

'Your Auntie Joan.'

'But we haven't seen her for –'

'William. Go and see what we can salvage.'

She has our ID cards and Ration books and all the valuables. She had them in the shelter, kept safe, but what's in the house? What's left? I climb up over the roof where it has fallen in. I find one of my football boots. No good. Everything is all messed up together with broken furniture and tiles and bits of brick. I start to cough and pull my jumper up over my mouth. Ma calls out to me to find any clothes that can be of use. Aggie is sitting down crying. Ma is trying to stop her by saying 'Love, please don't', but she's saying it more to stop herself from joining in.

'You're not supposed to go in 'til its declared safe.' Calls out Mrs. Eversholt.

Ma leaves Aggie with her and climbs up to where the bedroom was. In the remains of the dresser I manage to pull open a drawer and get out her jewellery. 'Paste', she mutters and leaves it there. Together we wedge open one of the wardrobe doors and pull out some of Aggie's clothes and some bedding. We find some twine to tie up a broken suitcase and put the rest of the clothes in a bundle. Once we have everything piled up in the street I look back at the house.

'Are we going to go, Ma?'

'I don't see what else we can do.'

'We could get some tarpaulin and put it over the top and live underneath?'

'It's not safe.' She says.

'But it's our *home*.'

'Not anymore it isn't.'

I can see the Pye radio in the parlour, its wire netting bent and the valves smashed to smithereens. Ma goes about piling things on Aggie's old pram.

'There. Now we're Romany's.'

'What's a Romany, Ma?'

'Gypsy. We'll have to find shelter for when this happens again.'

Aggie starts up. 'Isn't this the finish of it?'

'I'm sorry love. There's more to come… so its chop, chop and off we go. We'd best go find shelter for tonight.'

Aggie bursts into tears. Ma tries to ignore her. We're half way up the street before she gives in. Ma is strict and sensible with us when she needs to be and like Dad she doesn't like anyone wasting her time.

'Come on Aggie. I know you're scared. We're all scared.'

She's got tears and snot all over her face.

'H-how will Dad find us when he comes back?'

'He'll find a way.'

'But there's no house.'

I have an idea. 'We could leave a note.'

For a moment I think she's going to lose her temper. She doesn't usually, not properly unless I have really done something wrong like broken a window or taken something off a market stall and then it's Dad who delivers the walloping. Aggie is brightening.

'We could leave it in a milk bottle on the step.'

'The milkman will have it.'

'We'll just leave it in the door then.'

Ma lets out a long sigh and leans against a wall while I tear out a piece of paper from this diary and write to Dad. Aggie and I argue about what to say and Ma goes off to knock up some of the neighbours to ask about where to stay. She comes back puzzled, saying there's no one in.

'They'll be at church.' I say.

She claps her hands together. 'Well done Will.'

'For what?'

'That's where we'll go.'

We put "St Peter's" as our new address on the letter and I fold up the paper and Aggie puts it half in and half out of our letterbox so Dad will find it there. I write his name carefully on the front. Corporal Joe Lumley.

***

The streets are still hot from the fires. Brick dust hangs in the air like mist and makes us cough. There are firemen with hoses shouting out about damping down the roads and buildings. A black car with its bell ringing passes us on its way to check out a gas leak. The East End is still on fire over the river. People pass

5

on information. Thameside is a wall of flame from London Bridge to Woolwich. Beckton Gasworks gone. Silvertown, Stepney Green and Canning Town bearing the brunt. No one knows how many dead. Thousands have been injured.

The Jerries' didn't get the church. It's odd being here when it's not Christmas. St. Peter's is full of people sleeping along the pews, wrapped in blankets or playing cards and smoking. There are families like us and tots running around. I recognise a couple of kids from Keeton's Road School. Tommo, Jim and Ken must have got lucky. Two men in long black dresses are putting up trestle tables with a clack-clack noise like a gas rattle. Ma seems lost.

'What's up Ma?'

'I don't know who to tell we're here.'

'It's God's house isn't it?'

She gives me a thin smile. 'I don't think he's in, love.'

'Maybe he's out fighting the Jerries?'

'I should blooming well hope so.'

Her laugh is low and throaty and comes out when she's had a stout or joining in with a singsong. She finds a friendly woman who shows us to a place where we can put our stuff. They are giving out broth. A big tureen is put on the tables. There is bread too. Hot loaves. Women are slicing it up in white pinafores. At the smell of it, we all start to move forwards but the vicar stands and speaks in a posh voice.

'As in the parable of the loaves and fishes, we will try to accommodate you all. Do please line up in the aisle. In the interest of ensuring everyone has a hot meal we will say grace now.'

People take off their caps or kneel in the pews. Ma pushes my head down.

'For what we are about to receive may the Lord God make us truly thankful.'

'Airmen.' Say all the people,

The queue shuffles forwards and we get our soup, which tastes of vegetables and soil but with bread and butter it isn't too bad. At least it fills our tummies after a day of not eating. Then the moaning Minnies go off again and we take cover down in the crypt. It's even more crowded with hundreds of people on mattresses and camp beds and deckchairs. The stink of the Elsan toilets is awful. More and more stream in from outside until there is no room for all of us. Ma wrinkles up her nose and takes us back up to the church proper but this is full too. The vicar doesn't look as though he is going to stop anyone but the verger says something to him and they close the big doors. We find a space at the end of a cold hard pew.

I lay on my back and look up at the black beam roof. If that gets hit and comes down then we're done for. I can hear the lazy drone of a Heinkel. The explosions come closer as they search out their targets. The women are praying out loud and crossing their hands over their chests and Aggie is frightened so Ma has to pull a blanket over her head. It gets dark and the walls grow red and orange from the fires. One bomb comes so close it makes people scream.

At eight o' clock the bombers pass over and I smell smoke. The all-clear is followed by clanging fire bells and people start talking all at once, saying, "That's the docks done for. Deptford's got it." Aggie wants to go somewhere quieter but Ma says it's safe here. People light the big church candles and it feels better, Christmassy.

I offer to do a recce to find somewhere better to sleep. Ma says okay.

There's a dark space beside the organ. As I approach, I see it is a narrow passage. It smells damp, old as a grave. As my eyes get used to the dark I make out a flight of high stone steps curving up and round in a spiral. I feel around with my fingers on the cold stone and start to climb. There is barely room and I'm not big. It leads steeply up behind the organ and with each high step it becomes darker until it is pitch black. Around and up I go until I can just see the top of the brass pipes and the church roof beams. I emerge near the curved ceiling onto a short wooden balcony, maybe twelve feet long. There are big sacks lying on the floor, too big for sandbags, maybe it's food – potatoes or something. My first step onto the old floorboard makes it creak. I clamber carefully over the first sack. If I move them all up to the end there might be room enough for us all to bed down. We could use the sacks as pillows. It will be quiet up here. I reach out to the sack and it moves!

A horrible head emerges, a skull with old skin stretched over it and thin wispy hair. It has a horrid shrunken face, a ratty beard and nasty brown stained teeth. A bony hand shoots out and grabs my wrist. I smell its breath, rank and stale with drink.

'Bugger off out of it, Cowson.'

I am terrified. I try to shake my hand free. It holds me in a tight grip and hard yellow eyes stare back at me. A line of drool loops out of its stinky mouth and clings to his beard.

'I sleep up here. If I catch you again I'll bleedin' well throw you off.'

No time to think. I kick at the sack as hard as I can. Breaking free of his grip, I scurry back downstairs so fast that I nearly fall. My heart is going nineteen to the dozen and I don't stop until I am out and back among all the people out in the open.

I throw myself down on a pew and gulp in fresh air. All around me sleepers are wrestling their nightmares. I just had one. My heart is going fast. I let it slow and then find Ma with Aggie curled up in her lap like a cat.

'Find anywhere?' She asks sleepily.

I shake my head.

'We'll stop here tonight but tomorrow I have to get back to work.'

'What about us?'

'You best take Aggie to school, then go yourself.'

'What if the Jerries come again in the day?'

She yawns. 'You'll use the school shelter. Now try to get some kip.'

I lie down and shut my eyes. I can't imagine how we are going to carry on after what we've been through. Our house is gone, half the street blown up, everyone screaming like the devil. I tuck my face into my elbow. Soon my shirt is wet and my throat hurts. Ma must have heard because her hand begins stroking my hair, long soft strokes from the top of my head to my neck and soon I am shivering like a dog with its tummy tickled. She whispers.

'We're not staying here another night, Will. I'm not putting up with this.'

'Where will we go?'

Where *can* you go when you have fallen off the end of the world?

Chapter Two

September 9th

Ma works in Swan & Edgar department store at 49 Regent Street as a seamstress altering clothes for the customers. She doesn't deal with them directly. The clothes are brought down to her and the other girls at the back of the shop. After Dad went off to war she was lucky to get the job and came home smelling of ladies' perfume. She starts at eight o' clock and does not get home until teatime. She says there'll be nice things at Christmas if they keep her on. Since Aggie started going to school proper she has someone to collect her afterwards, but now that we are homeless I will have to do it.

The bus makes a detour around new holes in the roads. I deliver her to her school before turning back to Keeton's Road. The school building is still standing even though there are plumes of smoke billowing up from fires all around. The bell is ringing for Assembly and boys are running to get inside before Mr. Willkie catches us. He hits harder than the others, despite his age.

We line up for prayers and class registers. Mr. Samuels reads out the names until he gets to Tommo Brown. There is nothing. Some of us crane our necks to see if he's not paying attention as usual. I can't see him. Mr. Samuels repeats his surname and when no one else gives an excuse he moves on. John Price is present but Little Kenneth Fields isn't there either and nor are the Cooper brothers. The register is short because a lot of the boys who were evacuated are still away. It feels a bit like end of term, but not in an exciting way. The Headmaster says a few words about keeping our chins up and carrying on as normal but the hymn is a serious one and the younger boys begin to snivel. I was looking forward to telling everybody about our house being hit by a bomb and about the horrid old man in the church but it doesn't seem like such a good idea anymore.

When we get to class, I ask our form teacher Mr. Bennett what would happen if a bomb hit the school? He takes off his glasses and sets about cleaning them with a little cloth.

'Arrangements will be made to continue your education.'

'But Sir, if there ain't a school, where do we go?'

'If there *weren't* a school, then you would be schooled privately.'

'How do you mean Sir?'

'Those who have premises would be called upon to do their bit.'

'Sir does that mean we'd go to school round *your* house?'

'I'd be delighted. Fifteen mucky little tykes tramping dirt all through my vestibule. Oh, what an absolute joy that would be.' He replaces his specs and glowers at us. 'Not in a month of Sundays.'

He winks as he says it, but before we can push him further the wailing Winnies go and we put on our stinky gas masks and march to the playground shelter. Because of this we miss Mathematics, so there is some advantage to the bombings after all.

***

I pick Aggie up from her school, as we are going to meet Ma at Piccadilly Circus. She's given me a shilling for fares to go up West. The Number 12 has netting on the windows in case of bomb blast so you can't see much except the buildings being pulled down near Waterloo. There's a notice outside Lambeth North Underground forbidding anyone from sleeping on the platforms. I tell Aggie it would be safer than in a mouldy old church but she's chatting on about things she drew at school so instead I listen to the grown-ups grumbling. "That 'Itler, says one. Mass murder that's what it is. If he could see what he's done to old London town he'd soon stop". Another says he'll stop at nothing to get what he wants. They talk about Mr. Churchill, who everybody loves. I wonder when I'll next get to hear the radio or go to the Cinema. I hope they haven't hit the Rialto because every Saturday it's Roy Rodgers and Tom Mix. Someone makes a remark about the King and Queen. "All right for them in their Palace, says a man with a rolled-up cigarette. Tickety-boo for them while we get it in the neck."

We come over the river with all its swaying barrage balloons, up along Whitehall past Trafalgar Square. More people get on so I move Aggie along the aisle and down the steep stairs. I want to jump off the back as usual but I can't with *her* here, so we get off properly at the bottom of Lower Regent Street.

The newspaper sellers have the *Evening News* early edition. Our Winnie is pictured in the East End. Colombia Road. There is a story that says a crowd of people broke the padlocks at Stepney Green Underground and are going to go down and sleep for the night whether Mr. Morrison wants them to or not. Bully for them.

Hundreds of people are being sucked into the Underground entrances round the Dilly. All the lights are off but you can see the words where the bulbs were and the billboards for the theatre shows. The statue is all boxed up 'for the duration' and there are posters on it about the war. Swan & Edgar has big picture windows cris-crossed with brown tape and where the crosses meet it makes little brown stars. There are sandbags piled up in front and signs for the public shelters. The policeman have to direct traffic because all road lines have been painted out and when it gets dark there mustn't be any light at all. We come to one of the big front doors but it won't budge. Suddenly I am scared. Are we too late? I don't want Aggie grizzling all over me but she's asking questions.

'Where's Ma? What if we can't find her? What'll we do?'

'We hide somewhere.'

'What if we're out here when the bombs come?'

'We'll find another way in. Come on. Chin up.'

Dad says that. He puts his big knuckles under my chin and whisks them away as a joke. As I pull her along, I can see Aggie's face creasing up and I think she's going to cry and that makes me cross.

'Don't do your stupid crying act with me. We'll find her.'

We come to another pair of brass doors and I knock hard on them. As I do, I hear the first chilling wail. We used to grumble about it last year. Here come the moaning Minnies, the wailing Winnies – now it's dead serious. Air Raid. People start moving as more sirens join in. The sound joins up like the crying babies last night. Even the big barrage balloons bumping together in the sky are pressing down on us. Get inside. Keep safe. Don't delay.

At last there is a return knock on the other side and through the glass I make out a man in a porter's uniform. His mouth is moving but I can't hear him. He points to his left and nods his head in that direction. We bolt for the next set of doors. They have big brass fittings and handles that are too heavy to budge. The Porter pushes one open and warm perfumed air drifts out.

'I can't let you in.'

'But my Ma works here.'

'Get round the back then. Hop it. She'll be down in our shelter.'

We dash along the pavement until we see a line of people disappearing into an entrance in the wall. Aggie yells out for Ma.

'Will. Aggie!'

We rush to her and she squeezes the stuffing out of Ag.

'I thought I'd lost the pair of you.'

'What's this place?' I ask.

'Their own shelter.' She winks at me. 'I let a few people know about our situation.'

We troop to the basement. It's a lot better than in that church. There are several storerooms off a main corridor lit by storm lights and it's clean, not dusty or smelly. Everybody speaks proper and is polite about offering room to others. There are long rolls of fabric to use as emergency blankets and old camp beds and an inside flush toilet - not like last night when I had to go on the side of the church. Once we have settled down, a fat man in a pin stripe suit with a clipboard comes round checking off names. He has square rimmed glasses that make him look comical but I'm guessing he's important by the way everyone fusses over him.

'Ma – who's that?'

'Mr. Watson – one of the under managers. He's from Carshalton but he's staying here on weeknights 'til 'Itler gives up. We reckon he can't bear to go home.'

'Perhaps he's got a rotten wife?'

'Will!' says Ma, but not like she's upset.

Mr. Watson hovers above us. Aggie is playing with her dollies, oblivious to it all.

'Mrs. Lumley isn't it, hmm?' He asks, as if Ma had done something wrong.

She sits up, all prim and proper. 'That's right Mr. Watson.'

'These your two then?'

'William and Agatha. Say hello Will.'

I put out my hand as I have been told to but he does not shake it and instead licks a pencil before writing something on his sheet.

'I understand you have been billeted here under… extenuating circumstances.'

He makes a sort of humming noise at the end of each sentence.

'We've been bombed out.' Ma says, straight, because you can't argue with that.

'Not the only ones. You're welcome to stay the night but for future reference there are plenty of *public* shelters.'

'I do *work* here Mr. Watson', says Ma, reddening.

'Indeed, but we are terribly crowded and there are several senior members of staff in need. We can't just go letting *any*one in, can we, hmm?'

'What do you mean by anyone, Mr. Watson?'

He gives a little chuckle. 'Well, we're not Communists.'

Ma says nothing. I don't know what this means but I will ask her when he's gone.

'Jolly good. Well, help yourself when the trolley comes round. We start at the usual time tomorrow. Eight o clock sharp.'

'Yes of course.'

'And I shan't expect to be seeing you in the queue tomorrow, Mm?'

Without waiting for a reply he turns smartly. The heels of his shiny shoes crunch against the concrete floor as he goes off to check the next group of refugees.

'What's a Communist Ma?'

'The opposite of 'Itler.'

'I don't understand.'

Her eyes are still on him, a fat man full of food.

12

'Mister Watson doesn't want just *any*one staying here. He doesn't think we're good enough to... she pauses to think... he's letting us stay on a dispensation.'

'So we have to go somewhere else again?'

She nods and closes her eyes but not because she is tired.

'But you work here. Don't you have a right?'

'Seems not.'

'But that's not fair.' She says nothing. 'Ma. It isn't fair!'

'Will. Stop asking questions. If life was fair our home would be standing and your dad would be here safe and sound and there wouldn't be a war on. Life isn't fair.'

I get out my *Valiant* comic but I only stare at the pictures. If Dad was here he'd know what to do.

A bit later, a trolley comes round and there is food from the kitchens and oranges and a cuppa for everyone from the urn, which they brought down in the goods lift. We go to bed full up, though you can still hear the boom and thud of the bombs and the tube trains shuddering underneath us. Tomorrow, we are homeless again.

September 13th

Aggie and I are not going to school. Instead, we are spending the day queuing outside the public shelter near Dover Street Underground. Ma says I have to be the man of the house even though I said we don't have a house and she looked at me fiercely and said it's my job to protect our family. The big letter S in the street indicates there is room for eighty people. We have sandwiches and an orange each and have promised to be there when she comes out after work. It is a warm day with a blue sky and Aggie wants to go play in the Green Park. I tell her she can't, even though we can see the masses of the tall plane trees past the Ritz hotel. She gets insistent but before I have a chance to do anything the sirens go off and we march in. It is dank and disused and soon, hot and smelly. We are all crushed up and Ag clings to my shirt. I hear the bombers screaming right over our heads. A daylight raid. I hope our boys are up there in Spitfires shooting them all down. The building shakes above us. Must be a direct hit near Trafalgar Square. Aggie grips tighter and then, BANG. The air is sucked out of the room like opening a pair of giant bellows.

'Close one.' Someone calls out.

'Them bloody Germans couldn't hit a barn door.' Says another.

I don't think this is funny because my house and friends are gone but I know he's just trying to keep up spirits. I soothe Aggie, making all kinds of promises to her about playing in the park or going to Buckingham Palace.

After an hour the all-clear sounds and we're allowed out. There are columns of smoke rising on all sides. St James' church has been hit and there's a big hole in its roof. In Piccadilly the buses and cars begin to wind back to life like clockwork toys. One driver who crawled under his car slithers out and dusts himself down. Everything is frosted in glass. The lorries move off and people carry on and here come the bells and fire engines to tell us it's properly over.

'Let's go.' says Aggie, pulling me along.

'Where to?'

'The Palace. You promised.'

'Did I – when?'

'Back in there. You said.'

'But we have to stay here.'

'You *prom*ised.'

She starts skipping along once we get into the Park, making up a stupid song about going to see the King and Queen. I've never seen the Royals, only on the Newsreels. The trees have fat wide trunks with great hunks of green and brown bark and there are crinkly yellow-green leaves the size of your hand. There are soldiers and Nannies pushing prams and a big billow of white smoke in the direction we are going. I shout after Aggie, telling her to wait but I have to run after her before she gets to the Mall. The palace is smoking. They've been hit. There is a crowd and a van with a camera on it to make a film for the cinema news. A bomb has made a big hole in the North Palace wall. Aggie and I thread our way through the people and because we are short they let us in and we get right up near the front.

A huge cheer goes up as the King and Queen come out. George the Sixth is a short man in a military uniform and the Queen is dowdy with a determined expression and a hat. They hold up a bit of bomb casing and show it to the camera. Someone says its been checked by the bomb disposal squad. "We can't have the King and Queen going up in a puff of smoke, now can we?" There are lots of pressmen in big suits and the news comes back that the Queen says we are all in the same boat together. The King has been on a tour of Shoreditch but I don't see how that helps. They shake hands then go back inside and the camera crew packs up and drives off.

Ag is giddy with excitement about what we are going to tell Ma and how we can make a joke of it, maybe tell her that the Queen says we can go and live with her in the Palace. We eat our sandwiches and play by the lake and I make a paper boat out of pages from the *London Evening Standard* and watch it go off on the twinkling surface of the water and we doze off, grateful for the kip.

We wake up feeling chilly and I hurry us to the shelter. When we get there my heart grows heavy. The queue is all the way to the end of the street and around the corner. I count up and there are more than eighty here even without those who are saving places. I tell Aggie we had better join the back anyway because that's where Ma is supposed to meet us. We stand there, quiet and miserable, dreading what she will say. All the fun of a day off school has seeped away. I think of what to tell her and I know she will know I am lying. Dad says, just be honest and you can't go far wrong. I decide that is what I will do.

She arrives at six but instead of being upset or angry she takes one look at the queue and says,

'Right. No room at the Inn. We'll be off then.'

'Where are we going Ma?'

She points to Piccadilly Circus Underground. 'Home – or as near as.'

We're thrilled to bits. She buys three Penny tickets and we go down the wooden escalator to the platform and take the Bakerloo Line to Elephant and Castle. Ma's eyes widen as Aggie tells her about seeing the King and Queen and as we draw to a halt, she shakes her head and chuckles.

'You have been busy, Christopher Robin.'

'What does that mean Ma?'

'A story about a boy who went to Buckingham Palace.'

'Am I in it?' Aggie asks.

'If you want to be.'

When we get off at the Elephant, Ma sits us down on one of the heavy slatted wooden benches attached to the wall.

'We're stopping here for the night.'

'Right here?'

'We've got tickets. They can't throw us out.' She shows me the stubs of cardboard. Valid for travel – it says.

'But we'll be sleeping not travelling?'

She crinkles her nose. 'The girls at work are saying it's inevitable people will come down here. Anyways, it's safer than that church—'

'With all the mad people.'

'Old Watson's marked my card too.'

'Are we going to live like mice?' Asks Aggie.

'For tonight.'

I've an idea. 'But what about when the station closes? Won't they clear us out?'

She folds her arms. 'We'll have to see about that. Let's see if they want to throw a woman and two children out into an air raid in the middle of the night, eh?'

We sit and watch as waves of people in hats and coats pile off the tube trains and go up to the lifts. I hear the machinery clanking up and down. When it gets quieter Ma produces a boiled egg and a buttered bun for each of us. I eat but without interest because I know it will soon be time for the bombs and sure enough the eight o clock siren goes. But then the lift doors open and people start to arrive in two's and three's, then whole families with blankets and bedding and cardboard suitcases. They've had the same idea as us. They mass onto the platform, swirling out like a flood. Some are saying that they forced their way in as the Elephant and Borough are being hit heavily. They start to settle down to smoke and play cards.

Presently, the stationmaster marches along and stops halfway along the platform where everyone can see him. He's dressed in a blue serge suit and has a whistle and a moustache and he is what Ma calls 'one of us.' He clears his throat and announces.

'Evenin' Ladies and Gents. Now, London Transport doesn't condone this sort of thing. In fact the Ministry of Home Security says it's downright illegal.'

A chorus of catcalls and shouts of 'what are they going to do about it?' until he holds up a hand for silence. I feel warm and strong.

'However, we can't get the police to throw you all out so I'm going to turn a blind eye. A very *big* blind eye. As you know, the rails are extremely dangerous so I want the lot of you to please move at least three feet back from the platform edge.'

It is like when we have been given permission at school and everyone obediently shuffles back against the tunnel wall. I thought he might get out a yardstick but once he is satisfied the arms and legs are all in he speaks again and there's relief in his voice because we have all done as he says and there are lots more of us than him.

'There are no ablution facilities here so for the greater good the best we can do under the circumstances is to rig up a latrine at the northbound end of the platform.'

Two guards walk smartly toward the tunnel at the end. One carries a fire bucket in each hand; the other has a short ladder and a roll of hessian cloth and together they proceed to hang it up to make a curtain.

'The power will be switched off at ten thirty prompt. Do not in any circumstances go down on the rails. We've enough trouble with Jerry wiping us out from the sky without anyone getting fried down here and all.'

We give him a big round of applause. Once he has gone and we all spread out again but in general we keep to the rule. Everyone seems happy to be under the ground even though the bombs up top means the Walworth and Old Kent Road are being hit something awful. I come across another boy from school called Daniel who has a Happy Families set of cards with evacuees on it and other war people. We play until Ma says it is time for bed. I write my diary until they dim the lights. I will try to sleep using my coat for a pillow, but it's hard on the concrete.

***

A noise. It is Aggie, whispering in my ear that she needs to go to the WC. Mum is spark out so can I take her? We pick our way through the people to the end of the platform where the curtain is. I pull it back and there's a nasty stink. The buckets are full to the brim. Aggie looks at me pitifully.

'Nothing I can do.' I say. One's or two's?'

She holds up a finger.

'Just go then.'

'What if it goes over the edge?'

'Let it.'

She stares at the horrid smelly bucket. 'All right, but don't look.'

'No fear.'

I let the curtain fall and gaze into the tunnel. Under the arch it is darker than any sky at night, darker than any London sky full of flames and soot. I stare at the blackness and wonder when my eyes will start to get used to it.

Slowly, I begin to *sense*. I can't say what it is but I think there is something *in* there. I get goose pimples on my forearms and the back of my neck is tingling. Behind me, the wavy snores rise and fall, but the tunnel seems to have a breath and a rank smell all of its own, as if something is dying in all that inky blackness. I don't like it. I don't like this one little bit. I think the tunnel knows. It knows I am here and it is waiting for me. I want to turn round and run and hide but the black hole under the arch seems to draw me toward it. I am rooted to the spot, terrified. I press down onto the platform to stop myself floating up into the air and being swallowed up by all that blackness.

Suddenly, there is a hand on my hand. I jump and the spell is broken. It's Aggie. She has finished and is pulling at me to go back. I spin round and we scuttle back to our places among the shelterers and bury ourselves in our clothes.

There is something evil in there.

Chapter Three

September 17th

Ma made us wash in the public conveniences then took us to Saturday morning pictures at the Rialto and left us while she went to queue for food. After we watched Merrie Melodies there was a Newsreel showing the King at Buckingham Palace. He looked taller and more important than when we saw him and Aggie and I strained to see if we were in the film but we weren't. The Queen said she intended to visit the East End to see the damage first hand and got a cheer for that, though some of the kids in the picture house blew raspberries as they'd had their flats and houses bombed out like us. Then it was Roy Rodgers and five minutes in, the sign we dreaded came up on the big screen.

Air Raid in progress.

This released sighs from us older boys. We knew it was probably a false alarm and only some put on the gas masks. Aggie didn't want to and neither did I but there wasn't time to get to a public shelter so we stayed put while the ushers whispered urgently with an ARP. The daylight raids are less dangerous, what with random bombs falling in the oddest places. The picture house was as still as a game of Grandmother's footsteps. I watched the dust dance in the light of the projector and waited and counted. One, two, three, miles. No boom. Five, six seven. Is Ma safe? She'll have found shelter. She can run when she needs to. Aggie has some sweets. I nudge her to give me one and when she says no I pry open her fingers to get at them. After a while I hear a telephone trilling high up in the projector room. Then there is the sound of whirring machinery, which produces a massive cheer as the all-clear message comes up. On come the Cowboys. Yee-hah.

Ma meets us outside with a bundle of our clothes, which she has managed to wash, including Aggie's doll. The shellac is cracked and an eye is missing but she is delighted to have it back and hugs it for dear life. I miss my Meccano set. We want a spot at the Elephant tonight so we join the queue outside, passing a headline on the newsstand: "80 Tube stations to be opened up." The *Daily Mirror*

18

says public pressure has been brought to bear on the Government and that it is Mr. Churchill's work. I think I was just scared the other night. I will stay with Ma and keep away from the tunnels.

3pm is the new official time when you can put your bedding down and get your space. It costs a penny each and Ma has one each for both of us to give to the man at the booking office. It's good to have the sun on my face. Other than reading or playing marbles with Aggie there's not much to do but watch the buses and cars with their lizard slit headlamps and beetle-black windows, all the noisy military trucks, lorries and horses and carts. The women chat away and the men are in shirtsleeves, smoking, coats folded over their arms. This war is a seesaw; one moment blind panic, the next we are all standing enjoying the sunshine like it's a street party.

A man slips out of the station entrance and starts working the queue. As he gets closer I see he's not much more than a boy, maybe fifteen or so. He is slender like a weasel up on its hind legs: a boy in a suit with a smudge of hair on his upper lip and a trilby hat to give him a bit of age. I don't recognise him from round here. Perhaps he's Lambeth. He natters to the people. He's got a patter with a rhythm to it.

'Places. Clean and dry. Best on the platform. All reserved. Get 'em before they go.'

'Who's that man Ma?'

She folds her arms. 'A spiv.'

'What's that?'

'VIP spelled back to front. Someone who'll get hold of things.'

'What sort of things?'

An old man behind us speaks up, rotten brown teeth moving about in his mouth.

'He's a dropper. They pull a fast one and get down here before the official opening time. Saw him here yesterday on a crutch saying he'd come out of hospital. He'll get hold of several spaces and charge the earth. There's always those who'll pay.'

The Spiv's eyes are on fire, black like my best marble. He sidles right up to Ma.

'Sleeping ticket love? Half a crown?'

'Half a crown to sleep on the platform? It only costs a penny.'

The Spiv's words spill out like they're afraid of being caught in his mouth. 'We're all sleeping on the ground love, whole of London; you want to end up on the steps, the stairs, the escalators? Uncomfortable. Not dignified. I got a lad down there pegging out places with a blanket. Good spots marked out. Keep you and the kiddies dry.'

'I am not a kiddie,' I say out loud.

He shows his teeth but it isn't a grin. 'Good for you son.'

'I'm not your son either.'

He turns to Ma, ignoring me. 'You want it or not?'

Ma purses her lips. 'Do I look like a mug?'

He sniffs. 'Your loss. You'll be begging for these in a couple of days.'

He fans out the platform tickets but in a flash they're gone and he moves on down the line, slippery smooth. He spots a woman with her purse out and the business is done in quick time. I'm cross. He can't be more than a couple of years older than me. I don't want to be called a kid by someone in a stupid chalk-lined suit. I bet it's second hand. I bet it's his dad's – if he's even *got* a dad.

The old man next to us is talking at Ma. We'll have company tonight.

'Some of them wait on the platforms pretending to be foreign.'

You should tell someone.' Says Ma, looking ahead and not at him.

The old fellow is in the know, tapping his nose. 'I got a mate in the *South London Press*. Get him to do a report on the dropper's game.' He looks round at the queue, accusation in his eyes. 'Brings out the worst in people, all this.'

∗∗∗

Three o clock. The gates open and we surge down to the booking office to get our tickets. Some run down the spiral stairs with damp bedding you can smell as they go past. Ma pays the money and when we get to the bottom it is chaos, people staked out, not a square foot of ground and angry voices.

'What time did you get here you sod?'

'Don't go leaving any space, will you?'

'Come on you lot, budge up a bit.'

Aggie sucks her thumb as Ma looks about in dismay. Behind us, people keep coming. We move along, caught up in the rush. People are standing, sitting, a thousand of them, maybe more, right up to the platform edge and shouting back at the others. Stop shoving. Give us a bit of room. Oy, there are children here. We are swallowed by overcoats and greatcoats and the light is mopped up except for the lamp overhead. Aggie holds onto Ma for dear life. A tube blows a loud honking whistle as it comes into the station. You can't see anyone through the blackout windows but when the doors judder open Ma forces us toward them.

'We'll have to get on. Go somewhere else. We can't be doing with this.'

'Where?'

'Back up West.'

'Won't that be full up too?'

She bustles us into the corner. Ma comforts Aggie while I am crushed up against a man reading the *Daily Worker*. It's right in front of my face so I read that the newspaper had sent a deputation to a Shelter under the Savoy Hotel. When they got there they found they had waiter service. They refused to move and made a bit of a stink in drawing attention to the differences between the posh people and those East and South of the river who were being hammered every night. Then they ordered tea and bread and butter until the all-clear to show them they were just as good as anybody. I let out a chuckle. The man looked down at me and winked.

'Stuff 'em all, eh?'

It's ages before the engine whines back into life. The doors close, the rubber strips bounce hard together. Another long blast on the whistle and we move off, juddering into the tunnel. Lambeth North is full. Same story at Waterloo, Charing Cross and Oxford Circus, where Ma decides enough is enough.

'Let's get off and try going west.'

We pick our way through the crowd toward the Central line. Voices around us sound foreign.

'Ma – I whisper – these are *Germans.*'

'There's refugees from all over Europe. They got out once 'Itler started making it tough for everyone. They might be Polish.'

'But they sound *German.* We're fighting the Germans.'

'Not all of them.'

I don't understand. We are still six deep on the platform and well beyond pleases and excuse me's. With grim determination Ma gets us on the next train.

Bond Street.

Marble Arch.

Lancaster Gate. The crowd begins to thin.

We get off at the Queen's Road where there are only sixty or so sitting along the platform. Two long white lines have been painted down it, one two yards from the edge, the other one yard away. Another new rule. We have to keep behind the first line until 7.30 pm because of the rush hour. After that we can move forward to the next line. Ma finds us a spot and gives us our tea. We eat sandwiches and watch the people. They are quite different here, men in bowler hats, women in fur coats and high heels. One of them, a lady with a dead fox hanging round her neck, looks at us and says "Shocking" then walks off, click clack.

Ma stares with her mouth open.

'Why did she say that? "

'Never you mind. Eat up and don't get crumbs down your front and for goodness sake pull your socks up.'

I do what she says. There are other people like the posh lady and one of them even bends down and puts a tuppenny piece in Ma's hand.

She gets up and gives it right back to her.

The siren goes at eight as usual and more people stop with us as they get off trains. Shop girls from Kensington wearing lipstick and stockings and people in pearls and dinner jackets. By half past, people are knitting or playing cards or reading and we hear from our neighbours that there are no trains because they aren't going overground at Shepherd's Bush. Aggie, who has been playing quietly, suddenly sits up and stares at the eastbound tunnel.

'What is it Ag?'

She points at the black hole. I stand and look but cannot see anything except for the rails gleaming. After a moment I began to feel empty in my stomach, a sort of strangled cry, like a surprise. My ears are buzzing and my mouth is dry. I feel Ma pulling at my sleeve and then a thousand people breathe in at once. BOOM! The whole station shakes. The overhead lights rattle and one or two blow out and the rails sing and women scream as a searing hot blast of air comes right out of the tunnel and rolls right over us. Glass breaks in the lamps and babies began to cry and everyone covers their faces. I don't have time to cover up and I fall backwards, hitting my head.

When I come to, Ma is holding my hand and a nurse is feeling the back of my head saying it is a bump, no damage, I'll be fine. Am I able to sit up? I do so quickly, as I can. I don't like being looked at. I hear voices around me.

'Must be Lancaster Gate.'

'Gone through the tunnel roof.'

'Some of them leave a crater fifty feet deep.'

'How many, do you think?'

The Stationmaster makes an announcement. There won't be any more trains coming through tonight. A few brave souls go to ask for any more information. They try to keep it from us, but the news trickles back, a ripple of whispers kept afloat above the kiddies. Marble Arch Station, direct hit. Twenty killed.

September 20th

6.30am. We are woken by the first tube train of the day, screeching out of the tunnel as the lights go on along the platform. The staff move people's arms and legs out of the way. Wakey, wakey, rise and shine, they shout. Everyone clambers to their feet, some getting on the first train hoping to grab a seat and get straight back to sleep. You can go round in a circle but London Transport won't allow anyone to kip on the tube trains overnight. They want us out of the stations for the rush hour and we are happy to oblige because everybody needs the ablutions. There's a tea van that goes round in the mornings stopping at station entrances and you can get soft doughy buns that taste like a hot cloud.

There's a pecking order among the stations. Bond St and Aldwych are good addresses to get bombed in but it's first come, first served. Last night we were lumbered with Oxford Street and hardly got a wink because of all the foreigners playing noisy games of cards and arguing over nothing. The newspapers say a hundred thousand are sleeping rough and most of them are right next to us with their stinky smelly feet. There is to be a proper platform ticket issued soon at a penny-halfpenny a place. I hope they hurry up.

Outside, the cold stings my bare legs and wraps Ma's coat tight round her. John Lewis, Selfridges and Peter Robinson have been hit. Bourne & Hollingsworth took a few but they are open again with Union Flags on the front. Someone has written on a big board "Even more open than usual." We walk down past Robinson & Cleaver. Aggie drags as we reach William Hamley's. 'No money for sweets', admonishes Ma, as she hurries us on. We come round the wide canyon curve into the Dilly and she kisses us goodbye at the entrance to Swan & Edgar and digs out a promise to carry our gas masks at all times.

As fast as they can put up a sign – danger Unexploded Bomb – another one gets found in a shop or lodged somewhere dangerous. The firemen are still at work and there are snaking coils of hose everywhere and great sprays of water catching the sun. We take the Number 12 and I drop Aggie off and walk to school. Boys are collecting shrapnel but I can't see the point in gathering up the twisted bits of metal that destroyed our home. We don't talk about who isn't there and the register takes no time at all.

***

Tonight at Holborn we are lucky enough to get in before the siren. They are sealing off the line and are going to board over the tracks. Urns are brought out and hot sweet tea is a penny a cuppa. I have a book from school called "William and the Evacuees" by Richmal Crompton but he's a bit posh. Aggie tries to catch one of the tube mice with a bit of bread and Ma is not impressed when one of them runs over her hand. The air is hot and smelly and everyone is stinky. I wish they wouldn't take their shoes and socks off. I put the peel from an orange under my nose to cover the smell but after a while it stops working so I put my gas mask on.

'What are you doing Will?' Asks Ma.

I shrug. The big eyeholes are misted up. The rubber respirator makes a farting noise.

'Take it off.'

I shake my head.

'Be like that then.' She carries on knitting. I sit up and fold my arms. No one cares. I lie down and try to go to sleep but my face is hot and itchy so I take off the mask. People are wheezing or making horrid clucking noises with their noses. I lie with my head on the hard stone and listen to the vibrations of the bombs as they land. Thud, thump, thump. I close my eyes and hear people rolling over, scraping suitcases and shoes and, fainter, the scrabbling of rats: tiny noises you would normally never notice. When a tube train comes I can hear it from a hundred feet away. I am Kemosabe. A scout with super-hearing.

At ten thirty, a prayer is said over the Tannoy and the lights are dimmed and it is time for everyone to go to sleep. Some people have other ways of passing the time and you can hear them spooning, covered in a blanket. They don't even care when you step over them to go to the toilet. I look away and stare at the tiled walls or the posters for the musical cabaret. Applesauce with Max Miller, the Cheeky Chappie. I tug at Ma's sleeve.

'How much longer are we going to be down here with all these stinky people?'

'I don't know Will.'

'I'd rather be bombed than this.'

'You'll just have to get used to it.' She mumbles, sleep lapping at her.

'No I won't… I won't.'

She is too tired to argue. I get up and play hopscotch between the people and war workers, clambering over all the gnarled white feet. The papers are calling us the 'great mass of humanity'. At the bottom of the escalators there are more of them, washed up as if the Thames had flooded and left them stranded, crooked on the steps or diagonal on the slopes. I start to climb. It takes an age to get to the booking hall, pulling myself over the scarp of snores and quiet weeping. At the top the shutters are locked with chains and a big padlock. No use rattling them. No police or ARP will let you out.

Outside I can hear the thud of masonry falling, the crackle of fire. I smell cinder and ash. They can't put anti aircraft guns in the centre of town. I think of Dad in his rough khaki, his big pockets, his brass and buttons, webbing, engulfed in dirty green. I imagine him assembling his rifle or polishing his boots with that hard rhythm he uses to clean out the grate. Dad never lets a moment go by without making some improvement. Even with the wireless on he'd be laying down the paper for shoe cleaning. He was always doing things. *Never let a moment go to waste*, he says.

***

When I get back Ma takes my hand and squeezes it. I try to sleep and when I can't I stare at the tunnel entrance, black, round and empty like a dead mouth. I lay my head on one side, closing one eye, then the other.

I sense something again.

It can't be here – we're a mile or so away from Lambeth North.

From out of the tunnel a shadow begins to creep over the sleeping people. It has impossibly long talon-like fingers. They are like claws. I look for a pigeon that might have got trapped down here but there is nothing. No bird, just darkness coming out of darkness. I get to my feet and creep along the platform edge. Arms and legs are splayed out like tree roots, suitcases and shoes in the way. It's easier to get down onto the track, into the suicide pit. Dimly, I can just make out a grey shape in the tunnel. It is ever so faint. It is a… a face hanging in the air.

An upside down triangle framing two dark circles for eyes. There's no nose or mouth, like a skull. A skull with a round hole where its jaw ought to be. No, it's a gas mask, high up, floating towards me. I take a step backwards and my foot strikes a tin someone dropped. The mask disappears, enveloped in pitch-black gloom.

There is silence for a minute and then an awful skittering as three big black rats run right out over my feet. I let out a yelp – and immediately another one as I am pulled back by my collar onto the ledge.

'What's all this then?'

It's an old man of fifty. He has grey hair flattened to his scalp and a lined careworn face. He wears a stationmaster's uniform.

'Cat got your tongue, Sonny Jim?'

'No but the rats nearly did.'

'Well you don't want to go disturbing them then, do you.'

I scramble to my feet.

'What were you playing at?' He sounds annoyed but keeps his voice low so as not to wake anyone.

'Thought I heard something.'

'That'd be the fluffers.'

I pull a face.

'The rails don't clean themselves lad. We've gangs of Railway workers in the tunnels at night.'

I don't think cleaners would be wearing gas masks. The man has a badge. Mr. Sands. Station Supervisor. Shelter Marshal.

'What's your name?'

'Will, Sir. Lumley.'

'Been our guest for long?'

'Only tonight, but we've stopped down the Elephant, the Dilly and Queen's Road.'

'Tourist eh – who's we?'

'My Ma and sister, they're over there.'

He looks away then back at me. He has a kind face with an honest mouth and lines going up to a fat nose, a twinkle in his eyes. He taps his nose with a long finger and produces a satchel. Inside it is a bun. He breaks it in two and hands one half to me.

'Hungry?'

'Thank you, sir.'

'Call me Sands. Now listen to me. You don't want to go creeping about and here's for why. It's a warren in there. You'd never be seen again. Once you're off the tracks there's sewers, abandoned tunnels, ghost stations.'

'It's haunted?'

'Wouldn't be surprised. It's the oldest Underground network in the world.'

'How long have you worked here?'

His voice rises. 'I'm not *that* ancient. First tube was Pddington to Farringdon Road. Eighteen sixty-three. A *bit* before my time. Been here sixteen years. Seen things that would make your hair curl. Suicides, stabbings, you name it.'

He produces a flask of tea. 'Sip?'

He swivels open the top and pours hot liquid into his cup and passes it over. His rough old hand is twice the size of mine and there is a slight shake to it.

'Under here is London's history – Roman, Medieval. Think of all them bodies buried under the City – all the old consecrated grounds. When they was digging, sometimes they'd go under a cemetery and the bones would shower down on the men'. He pauses, takes the cup. 'Old curses, sacred ground. Plenty died in the making of the Underground. Tunnels collapsed, people trapped under machines, things your Metropolitan Railways Company doesn't want people knowing about. But the spirits don't rest.'

He takes a sip of tea and stares into the black tunnel.

'London is a thousand years of rotten deeds. When it rains it seeps into the ground. All the blood from murders and cutpurses, tuppenny ha'penny thieves… all swept down into the sewers. Mother Thames does her best to wash it away, but she can't keep it clean so all that evil ends up in the tunnels, seeps into the brick – it's all around you.' He drains the cup and twists it firmly back on the flask.

'Why did the rats run? What were they scared of?'

'You more than anything. I'm surprised they've not come out more, what with all the extra food.' He gestures to the sleeping mass.

'How big can they get?'

He holds his hands a foot apart, then moves them wider still, a yard.

'No.'

He playfully puts his fist to my cheek. 'Get out of it.'

He rises; knees crackling like Rice Krispies as he massages his lower back with his thumbs. 'Now off you go – and stay out them tunnels.'

'Will I see you here again?'

He sniffs. 'I expect so. Nighty, night.'

'Good night Sands.'

I go back to Ma and Aggie and for the first night since the Blitzkrieg began, I sleep like a log. I'm glad of it because later on that night, things get worse.

A boy has gone AWOL. He has been taken.

Chapter Four

March 1940

It's Dad's first leave after Basic Training. He's at a camp somewhere in the North but he can't say where. He says he doesn't mind the Army because they get up later than he does for East Lane market. He doesn't like Army food and he reckons the cooks are more likely to kill us than the Germans. He says all the road signs have been painted out so that if the Germans do invade then they will get lost. He says there was a rumour they might parachute in and come dressed as Nuns and that they had to question one of them – a nun, not a Hun.

After tea, Dad and I went for a kick-about in Burgess Park with the old cracked leather ball. I used to play in the street but the moaning Minnies were going off so often we've been forbidden to play out. He showed me a trick called the back foot, which meant he let the ball go when he was tackled, but he was *actually* putting it in position so his other foot could pass it across. I never saw it coming.

We went to see Charlton play at the Valley against West Ham, the last game of the season. Dad was in uniform and some of the old men saluted him. *My dad!*

'They won't stop the football, will they? I asked, once we were up on the terrace.

'No chance. The day England gives up football, it's all over.'

'We are going to win, aren't we?'

'Yeah, Two-one, I reckon.'

'No Dad. I mean the war.'

'England Three, Germany Two.' He said, winking.

And we did win, Charlton that is.

That evening, the best day of my life turned into the worst. After Aggie and I listened to a programme on the Home Service, Dad sat us down and sparked up a Craven A. Mum stood behind his armchair, fussing with the bit of cloth on top.

'There's this thing called evacuation. You heard about it at School?'

I had, but I didn't want to say.

'They reckon it's not safe here in London so the idea is you kids go out to the country. Be nice, fields and cows and horses and all that.'

Aggie squeaked. 'Will we have to live with the aminals?'

'No love, you'll live with people.' Said Ma.

'And with you.'

Ma opened her mouth but nothing came out.

Dad said. 'Your Ma has to stay here and work and there's your Gran to consider. She's not getting any better.'

Gran had helped with peeling and preparing the vegetables but it was enough for her and she had gone to bed, wheezing. She was always in bed before us now.

'I want to stay with you!' bleated Aggie, her eyes brimming with tears.

Dad put on his stern voice. 'It's for your safety. The war's going to get worse.' The Germans have been sending planes over. There are dogfights over Kent and Sussex.

'Where are we going to go?'

'I don't know yet son.'

'Is it a law?'

'Not yet.'

I swelled with relief. 'Then we don't have to. You won't make us. Not if we don't want to. We can't leave our school and friends.'

'I think you'll find they're going and all.' Ma said.

Dad reached up and took her hand, which was pale against the smoky brown fabric. I had the idea that all the mums and dads had been speaking about this like at last Christmas when someone broke three windows at Keeton's Road and no one owned up to it. Ma started to use her persuading voice, all singsong.

'You'll love it – fresh air and fields, new friends, adventures, all kinds. Aggie – you love animals. And Will, it'll be just like in all them books you read.'

'How long for?' I asked.

'A few weeks, maybe a month or so.'

'How many months?'

Dad's face was clouding over. 'We don't know son. No one knows.'

I went hot and red and my fists did not know what to do. 'You want to get rid of us so you can fight your stupid war. We live here in London, and I'm not going.'

In a flash Dad was up out of the chair ready to give me a clip round the ear but Ma stopped him and said I should just go to bed. I stamped up the stairs.

'What have I done to deserve this? Nothing! Stupid bloody war!'

Dad stood by the post at the foot of the stairs and said something but I didn't hear him because I slammed the door. In our box bedroom I found a canvas bag and put my books and socks and a vest and a map of London in it. I had no idea where I was going but I knew I would need food. For now I got into bed in my clothes and made plans. It wasn't long before Ma brought Aggie up and tucked her into bed. I guessed they had promised her sweets or dolls to keep her quiet. I

28

was turned to the wall and when Ma tried to touch me on the shoulder, I shook her off. She said something about all of us making sacrifices but I wanted to say that if you love us then don't send us away but I knew silence was better so I lay still until she went. The floorboards released a creak as she looked in on Gran before going downstairs.

Music drifted up from the front room for some time, then I heard the stairs go again as Ma and Dad came up. The light went out under the door and I counted to fifty before getting out of bed. I drew out my bag and crept past Aggie to rest my hand on the door handle. I turned it slowly until it gave and with a sharp tug the door came open. I held my breath. The bedside light in Dad and Ma's room was still on. I held my shoes in my hand as I began to creep down. Gran let out a harsh hacking cough. I froze. At eye level I could see light under Dad and Ma's door. There was the iron leg of the bed and one of Dad's army boots tipped over on its side. Now or never, I thought, and, waiting for Gran's next big cough, I used it as cover and padded down into the kitchen.

I got out the bread and jam and cut some sandwiches with the big flat knife with the bone handle. I took a tin of corned beef from the pantry and thought about putting a pint of milk in as well, but I reckoned I would be able to get one off any doorstep come the morning. The shiny back door key was always left it in the lock so I turned it like a safebreaker and slipped out. The night air was fresh and smelled of freedom. I slipped the latch on the gate and tiptoed down the thin alley between the houses. They looked like cutouts against the navy blue sky and a quarter moon threw milky shadows.

Southwark Park has guns in it and they would be manned so I headed for Burgess Park. The streets were deserted. It was my night playground. I felt like a burglar or a dog on the prowl. They've told us to have domestic pets put down but everyone thinks this is a terrible idea. We aren't going to kill our cats and dogs because of the Germans. As it got to midnight it was dead silent, as the church bells aren't allowed to ring out anymore. I reached the Park gates, heaved myself up over the railing and strode across the grass. I saw a couple of foxes with long bushy tails, sniffing for food. They didn't seem bothered by me – I suppose we're neighbours. I found one of my favourite spots from the summer, a hillock with bushes where you can't be seen. I climbed up behind and lay on my back and ate a jam sandwich and gazed at the stars. The barrage balloons were black bubbles, like speech balloons in the comics. It was as if they were talking to each other.

"Jerries coming yet?"

"I'll blooming well stop them if they do Captain!"

When the moon came out, the light dabbed the rooftops and outlined the chimneypots. You wouldn't get this in the stupid countryside.

I must have dozed off because when I came awake I felt damp and sniffly. I tucked my legs up under my coat and buttoned it over my knees. It was still dark, though there was a faint light in the sky over in the east toward Deptford. I looked across the wide area of grass and saw the strangest thing, a man standing dead in the middle, not moving. I couldn't see his face, but as my eyes grew accustomed, I made out an Army greatcoat. Military Police? The bushes hid me well enough but even so the man started to walk in my direction. I prayed he had not seen me. He looked about, first to his left then to his right, as if hunting for a lost ball. As he came to the bottom of the hillock I leant back out of his sight. My heart was bashing like a fist against my ribs. I flattened down under the bushes hoping he would go away. I listened as hard as I could but I heard nothing. Had he gone? After a moment there was a faint scratching sound, then the smell of cordite. A match. I risked a glimpse. He was sitting right there on a bench, having a smoke. His face was rimmed by orange light. I saw his nose, his stubble, and tired eyes.

When I joined him, he put his arm around me.

'How did you know I'd be here?'

'Where else was you going to go? China?'

We sat in silence as his cigarette smoke curled up and away. He put it out on his boot.

'Ready for the off?'

I nodded and we began to walk home.

'You're getting a bit old for speeches Will. I can't tell you what's what, but if I say you're to do something then there's a good reason for it.'

'You going to tell Ma about this?'

'What – and wake her from her beauty sleep?'

'We don't want both of us in trouble.' I said, smiling.

He chuckled. 'You have to look after her and your sister while I'm away.'

'How can I do that if I've been sent away?'

'Always the smart one. I don't know where you get it from.'

'The milkman?'

He gave me a playful swipe and ruffled my hair. 'I got to be up in three hours. Got a war to win.'

'You better.'

'I'll do me best Son.'

I hesitated. 'I'll miss you, Dad.'

'Likewise.' He stopped in the middle of the road, our little row of terraces stretching away each side. 'But remember, I'll always be with you.' He thumped his chest. 'In here. Right, soldier?'

I saluted and he saluted back, his boot heels crunching loose stones on the tar macadam.

***

In the morning Dad had gone. Ma put us in our Sunday best and marched us to the Community Hall. It was noisy and bustling and there were lots of children there – some from Keeton's Road, some from Aggie's school. We'd all been made to wear our cleanest clothes and line up while some posh women inspected us. I had an idea.

'Aggie. We've got to look scruffy.'

'Why?'

'Cause if we look a sight, we won't get picked and we won't have to go.'

We messed up our hair and I told her to scratch her head like she had nits. When the women came I could see they weren't impressed and I even dribbled a bit as if I was stupid like Timmy Mullins in our class who will eat anything for a dare. If this had been the Children's Parade we would have been on a charge. The tweedy women went off and spoke to the mothers who came to collect us and give us our billets. Ma had a perplexed look on her face and told us it was a place called Wales, which we had never heard of. Before we knew it – we hadn't thought it would be *that day* – we were packed onto trains at Paddington Station with all the mothers crying and waving hankies at us like there was no tomorrow. Once we pulled out, we sat back silently on the uncomfortable horsehair seats and watched out the window. Prisoners, all of us.

When we arrived, I realized my plan had backfired because we got the worst billet, a Farm where the farmer and his wife used us as free labour in continual pouring rain. A couple of weeks later I was given a stamp and paper and allowed to write a letter to Ma. I wrote two. One was polite and that one I read out loud to Mr. Price and his wife. The second letter I slipped in with the first before sealing it when he took me to town to post. This one said:

Dearest Ma.

It is horrible hard work here. We get up at six in the morning and feed the pigs that *stink* to high heaven in the muddy sty. Then we have to carry milk from the cows and pour it into big churns. We get a big breakfast but that's about all until night-time except some dry funny-tasting bread and cheese. There is no school except chapel on Sundays. The day is spent digging and planting and fetching and carrying until my hands are red raw. I don't understand most of what the farmer tells me but he pushes or slaps me until I get it. Aggie helps with cooking and making preserves in the big kitchen so at least she is inside for most of the time. The Price's have big red faces and no children themselves and I can see why, because if I were theirs I would run off or kill myself. Aggie cries all the time and isn't allowed any dolls or anything like that. When I come in from the field there is some stew but it's full of grizzle and I have to hide bits of it under the table in my hankie and feed it to the big dogs later. We sleep in the same bed in a freezing room and Aggie always has a cold. Can I please come back to the war?

Your loving son,

William Lumley

The letter took a week to get to her and two days more for her to scrape together the money for the train fare. Ma turned up one afternoon and introduced herself to Mr. and Mrs. Price and went to talk to them in their parlour. Aggie was still jumping up and down when Ma turned the air blue and told us to go and get our things. I threw everything into my cardboard case and all three of us were a way down the muddy track before she stopped and nearly hugged us both to death. Ma produced some biscuits from the Peek Frean factory in Bermondsey and even some chocolate once we boarded the steam train. The miserable hills and valleys were all smudged and running with endless teeming rain.

'Worse than 'Itler.' muttered Ma.

Chapter Five

September 22ⁿᵈ

Ma pays the conductor and we grip the rail as we climb up the steep stairs of double-decker. We are going to see Auntie Joan in Lee Green. Aggie insists on the top deck even though you can't see much through the netting. Many of the old Victorian houses on the Walworth Road have been hit and it looks like a row of gap teeth. People are nattering and you cannot help but overhear. Peckham, Deptford and Bermondsey had it worse than anyone except the docks. The Minister of Home security, Mr. Morrison, is touring disused tunnels and Air Raid shelters in the Borough with the Mayor of Southwark. Making provision, he says. I wish he'd make us a new home.

We change at Lewisham Bus Garage. You can't miss Auntie Joan because her hair is done up and she wears bright red lipstick and odd clothes. She looks like a film star. Ma lets out a delighted shriek.

'What *are* you wearing?'

Joan does a twirl. 'Trousers. I'm in the WVS.'

Her legs are ever so long and she is wearing high-heeled shoes. With her is her daughter Evie who I remember is nearly a year older than me. Last time I saw her she ignored me completely even when her Ma asked her to play with me. She looks too old for play now. She has long reddish brown hair under an odd sort of cap and a blue coat with a belt with a huge buckle on it. Her face is very pretty, with a freckled nose and wicked green eyes that seem to be on the lookout for mischief. She's taller than me now but I notice that like her Ma she is wearing shoes with heels. She seems very grown up. True to form she ignores me, making friends with Aggie by talking to her about her doll. I think she's a bit stuck-up. When we get the next bus she sits next to Aggie and Ma sits with Auntie Joan, which makes me glad because it isn't right me being with all these women. I sit up front and after a while I hear Evie and Aggie giggling. I turn round to glare at them but they put on fixed expressions of innocence. I pull a face and turn back but they carry on being stupid. In the end I turn round to Evie.

'What's that thing on your head?'

'Don't you know anything?'

'Not about hats. Why should I?'

'It's a Berry. I'm supporting the Free French.'

'I think you're wearing it because your hair is dirty.'

'My hair is perfectly clean thank you. Lot more than I can say for you.'

'What do you mean?'

She pinches her nose.

'Have *you* been sleeping down in the Underground every night because your home was blown up?'

'No.'

'Well shut up then.'

'Don't be rude Will.' Ma says. Auntie Joan laughs.

I turn back, having won that one. The bus makes its way up to Blackheath village. You wouldn't think there was a war on up here. Greenwich got off lightly. We stop at a pub and Joan gets drinks – a ginger ale for me – which we take to the garden with a view of the pond. Aggie goes off with Evie to look at the ducks. I am happy to sit on a bench and watch people. It's lovely and warm with hardly a cloud and after a while the sun seems to strip away the dirt and damp smell of the tunnels. Ma produces food from a wicker shopping basket and lays it out on the garden table.

'Ma. Won't we be a target for the bombers, sitting out here like this?'

'We'll spot them if they come.'

'You can be our scout, says Joan. 'You see one Messy shit and we'll pack up and go.'

'It's *Messerschmitt.*' I say. 'And they're fighter planes. The bombers are Heinkels and Dorniers.'

Ma tweaks my cheek. 'He's so serious – like his old man.'

'There IS a war on.' I say.

Joan lights a cigarette. 'No reason not to have a little fun.'

While Dad is away fighting for us all and there's a boy gone missing underground.

'Go call Evie and Aggie, Ma says. Time to eat.'

There is a pasty each and hardboiled eggs then cake for afters. Evie pesters her Mum to try her gin but she won't let her. Afterwards, Joan produces some sweets. I tell her I am full and I don't want any, though I do really.

"Where did you get them?' Asks Ma.

'I know someone who knows someone. Get you jam, tickets.'

'A spiv.' I say.

Joan purses her red lips. 'That's right.'

Evie stares at me from under her berry. I don't know any French but I could tell her about the top speed of a Spitfire or how to strip down an Enfield rifle or the Charlton scores in the last five games before they stopped the football but I don't think she'd be interested. She and Aggie go off again.

A couple of men sidle over to us. They are wearing worker's gear, heavy boots, thick trousers and sweaters and smell of drink. Each has a brown frothy pint of ale. They have strong accents. I don't know where from.

'Afternoon Ladies. Enjoying the day?' Asks one.

'Very pleasant I'm sure.' Says Ma in her please-go-away voice.

'You two sisters?' asks the other.

Auntie Joan smiles brightly.

'I'd not have guessed – youse two look quite different.' He says to her. Ma frowns.

'You after some company?' asks the first.

Ma says. 'We were having a private conversation. '

The second man looks at Auntie Joan. 'What are you wearing there?'

'Haven't you ever seen a woman wearing trousers?'

'No', they chorus.

'It's part of my job. Women have to work now there's a war on.'

'Will wonders never cease?'

'Aren't you in the Services?' asks Ma still pretending to be polite.

'Someone has to dig the roads.' Says the first one. He seems angry about something. The second one whispers to him. 'I'd like to get her out of them trousers.'

'Nah.' says the first. 'She's one of them.'

'One of *what*?' Says Joan.

There's no immediate answer and Ma looks cross. I think Auntie Joan was enjoying it before but now there is an edge of menace. Am I supposed to do something?

'Ah, one of them *trousered* Ladies we've heard so much about.'

This breaks the ice with Auntie Joan and she allows them to buy her a drink. Ma refuses at first but they go on about it and she agrees to a half of stout. She scowls at Auntie Joan as they go in to get the drinks because we are stuck with them. It turns out they are from Ireland and they make bad jokes and after a couple of general question they ignore me. Ma drinks her drink as fast as she can and asks me to go get Evie and Aggie from over on the heath. I'm glad to be out of there.

***

'Ma wants us back.'

'Why?' Asks Evie.

'She just does.'

Reluctantly they come and stand beside the table. Once the men see the girls the temperature drops and they make their excuses and leave, tipping their caps in an exaggerated way at Ma, who they have decided is above her station, which is funny because her job at Swan & Edgar is the lowest of the low.

'Come on – we're off for a walk.' Ma says.

We gather up our things and stroll across the wide Heath. You could land a fighter squadron on it. The grass is still parched from the long hot summer. To our right there are hillocks and clumps of brush – it's said they are old plague pits. Ma is in a bit of a grump. Auntie Joan says it was all a bit of fun, but Ma says it was a bit of fun that landed her in her predicament in the first place and those men were Irish and the Irish were bombing us only last year. One bomb went off at an Electricity Substation in Southwark and it could have been them. Auntie Joan tells her not to be ridiculous and furiously smokes a cigarette. She says things are different now and we can talk to who we want when we want and we shouldn't keep to the old rules. If Dad were here he would have seen those two off.

We pass through the great stone gates of Greenwich Park and go along a straight road that leads to the Observatory. The big leaves on the plane trees are turning crisp, orange and yellow. Aggie collects the fallen ones and Evie helps her and the war seems a thousand miles away until we reach the end and see the view down in front of us. The docks are gone, destroyed. Most of the warehouses and factories are burnt out or still on fire and there are great big gaps where streets used to be like missing clues in a crossword puzzle. Hundreds of smoke plumes rise in the distance. It's a vision of hell, says Ma. It seems so silly for us to be fighting when the Jerries have done all this. She and Joan hug each other. We are about to turn back when I see twin trails of white smoke in the sky. A dogfight.

A Spitfire and a German plane, twisting, turning, swooping like birds, the German chasing the Spitfire who – to a rousing cheer from me – loops the loop and comes back on him, bearing down and using his eight machine guns to fire at the slower craft. Daka daka daka. The German plane turns tail and flies off towards Chatham. I am so excited I could jump up and down. 'He got him. He got him, didn't he Ma.'

'I think so.'

'I know so.'

'You boys, says Evie. It's all death and destruction.'

'If we don't fight, we'll get invaded. Is that what you want?'

'Calm down Will.' Says Ma. 'We all want an end to it.'

'We have to kill them before they kill us.'

'That's the only answer is it?' Says Evie.

'Yes, you stupid girl.'

'Will!' exclaims Ma.

Evie laughs. I want to kick her.

Ma says. 'Will – apologise to your cousin.'

'Why?'

Evie is still smiling. I haven't done anything except say the truth. We have to fight, all of us. If you don't want to fight then you're a traitor.

'Because I'm telling you to.'

I walk away, kicking twigs across the road.

'Will.' Ma calls, with her warning voice.

I turn back, my face hot. 'I don't care what any of you say. I'm going to kill every bloody German in the world as soon as I'm old enough to join up.'

'Good for you.' Evie says and gives a little clap. 'My little soldier.'

They laugh. Why do women think it's funny when they haven't even made a proper joke? It's not funny. It's war - and that's no joke.

***

Tonight we are staying in Auntie Joan's room in Lee Green. When she found out we were sleeping underground she insisted on it, even though she isn't allowed visitors and she and Evie sleep in the same bed. Ma says that when Evie was little (and no less horrid I bet) Joan worked in the laundry at the Workhouse, but now she's in a Home for Unwed Mothers. It is a big white house with bay windows divided into rooms. Mrs. Halstrom, a fat lady in pearls, runs it and we had to stand in the parlour while she and Joan had an argument. Ma was ready to leave but Aggie was crying from tiredness and this made the lady agree to let us stay in the end.

'We are not,' she said, in a shrill voice, 'setting a precedent. We shan't be taking in waifs and strays. There simply isn't room.'

I didn't think this was fair because it was Auntie Joan's idea and Ma had to stand there and be insulted. Once she left, Joan pulled a face but Ma said.

'I've been insulted by better than her. Not bigger though.'

Joan snorted with laughter. 'Enormous isn't she? Nothing's on the ration for her.'

'Anyway, water off a duck's back.' Ma says.

Joan leads us up the stairs and we follow her navy blue trousers and wiggly bottom.

It's a big room with a cast iron bed, a tin bath, a mantelpiece and a fireplace that doesn't look used. There is a picture of the King and Queen above the bed and a big oak wardrobe with suitcases on top. Joan pulls out a camp bed to give to Evie. Me, Ma and Aggie are getting the double bed and Joan is going to sleep in the big armchair. We have our tea in the kitchen at the back, which is fish paste sandwiches and a tall glass of milk. Ma looks up as the big black and white clock chimes six.

'I'm all done in. Tell 'Itler to give it a rest for tonight.'

We troop back upstairs and the moment I slip under the eiderdown I fall asleep.

***

The Air Raid comes late at ten o' clock. Bleary-eyed, we traipse out into the garden with our bedding to the Anderson Shelter. It is horrid and damp underfoot and the place smells of old wax and paraffin. The corrugated iron roof is slimy to the touch. Some of the other women from the house are there too and I realise I am the only boy. Ma takes care of Aggie and I try to get to the top bunk at the back so I can wrap myself up in my coat. Evie finds me and clambers up there too.

'Hey soldier-boy. Aren't you going to protect me?'

'You don't need protecting.'

'Yes I do. Budge up.'

She wriggles close. She has a nightdress under her coat and she puts her stockinged feet on my legs.

'Get off. Your feet are freezing.'

'I'm warming them up on you, aren't I?'

'Is it always this cold and damp in here?'

'Yes. Brrr.' She is shivering but exaggerating it. Our bodies come together and after a while there is a little warmth. I feel sort of funny. She turns away so we are spooning. Her hair smells of something like lemon or rose, not carbolic like when we have to wash ours. I wriggle closer up.

'Oy watch out, you'll have me off.'

'Don't you ever stop complaining?'

She doesn't say anything for a bit and we listen to the hum of bombers overhead. Everyone holds their breath. It is a clear night, which is called a bomber's moon. It means the moonlight on the river is like a silver snake leading them right to the Docks. If the anti-Aircraft guns in the countryside don't get them it's a clear run. The hum begins to fade as they turn toward Deptford and start in on Southwark. The giant starts up again. BOOM, boom, boom. The women in the shelter start talking among themselves.

'What's it like sleeping in the Underground?' Asks Evie.

'Hot and smelly. The people are friendly but they don't half pong.'

'If you live underground for a long time you'll get so used to it you won't want to come up again.'

'Don't think so.' I don't want to tell her about what I saw. Not yet.

'You might live there forever, catching train passengers and eating them.'

'How would I cook them?'

'You could make a fire.'

'People would see.'

'You could find a secret tunnel.'

'In the dark?'

'Take a paraffin lamp.'

'I don't know how to cook.'

'No one knows how to cook people. You make it up as you go along.' She giggles.

'You're mad. Anyway, we won't be down there forever.'

'You can't stay with us.'

'No one wants us to stay with them. We're gypsies.'

She lies quiet in the bunk. My arm is on top of her. I pull my coat over us.

'Sometimes I go inside under the stairs.' Whispers Evie.

'Your mum doesn't mind?'

'Long as I'm safe.'

'Is there room in there?'

'It's drier than here. And a lot warmer.'

Suddenly, Evie is gripping my hand and pulling me down.

'Come on, Let's go.'

I put my feet in my shoes and we make our way out past the others. Ma has Aggie all wrapped up and doesn't notice when we dash out across the back garden, which is all dug up for vegetables. There are silvery blue tubers with great fat leaves in rows. Evie pulls open the back door and we go through the kitchen and into the hall where she undoes the little triangular door to the cupboard under the stairs.

'We'll be safe in here.'

We're in the dark, close together. It is dusty and there are mops and things. I want to say something but I don't know what. There is hardly enough room for two so she sits right up close, in my arms and with her face almost touching mine.

'Put your hand here.' She whispers.

She takes my hand and puts it on her chest over her nightdress. There is a little bump and a tiny hard knob in the centre. I cannot breathe. I move my hand around so the bump is under my palm. It doesn't feel too bad. She shudders a little.

'Are you cold?'

'No. Now the other one, slowly.'

This is a game where I don't know the rules and I don't know what I am supposed to win. She makes a little snuffling sound and puts her face right next to mine. Her lips touch my cheek and find their way to my mouth. She kisses me.

'I thought you hated me.' I manage to say. My heart is beating very fast.

'I do.'

'Then—' My words are cut off when she kisses me again, her lips on mine, moving around. Her lips are softer than bread, wet like a boiled sweet. We breathe in and out through our noses. After a long time, she pulls away and rests her head on my shoulder. I make out a thin line of moonlight around the door.

39

'What happened to your dad?' I ask.

She's sleepy. I hear it in her voice. 'There is no dad.'

'He died?'

'Never was.'

'My dad's a corporal.'

We fall silent, hearing the bombs fall. The sky will be red and orange all night and people will be dead, dying or injured but here we're safe. I don't want it to end. I want to stay crouched in this cupboard with nice smelling Evie until the war is over then Dad and Ma will open the door and we will pop out and get married.

Her arm goes around my waist and she dozes off on me as I protect her from the raining bombs and 'Itler and his blooming Luftwaffe.

Chapter Six

September 25th

It was the middle of the night when the wailing started up along the platform. It was a woman calling out, making us writhe awake under our blankets. Her boy had gone AWOL. A pair of ARP wardens arrived to assure her that no one could go missing down here but she was hysterical and she kept calling. 'Sammy. Sammy.' They couldn't stop her so a posse was formed, a dark huddle of men clustered up at the end of the Central line, Westbound toward Tottenham Court Road. One of them broke away and came past. I asked what was going on.

'We're getting torches, checking the tube tunnels.'

'Why would he go in there?'

He shrugs. 'You're a kid – you tell me.'

I didn't say anything, having seen that awful ghostly face in the mask. Perhaps the boy saw it too? The ARP man came back with his tin helmet and they marched off into the dark. Torch beams cris-crossed the arched roof and died out when they disappeared round a bend. The woman sobbed quietly. Others in the search party, who had gone to look around all the tunnels and platforms in the station, soon returned, shaking heads, offering reassurances: He'll turn up. Can't have gone far. Someone will fetch him back. We tried to get back to sleep.

An hour later the torches came back and the footsteps of the men grew louder. They were dirty like miners as they clambered back on to the platform edge. No sign, they said to a policeman. They had been all the way to the next station and back. They separated and the policeman crouched down next to the mother of the boy. She was wide-eyed, her tear-stricken face collapsed.

'Could you have perhaps left him with someone and forgotten about it?'

She shook her head. 'No, never.'

He said that so long as the boy was down here somewhere he was a lot safer than up top – what Dad would call a bit of nous – and that once the station opened in the morning she was to go to West End Central Police station and file a missing persons report. She burst into tears again and he looked anxious.

Other people were dog-tired and the war workers needed some kip. He signalled to two other men and she allowed herself to be led away. They seemed glad of something to do. I looked back at the tunnel. The black mouth had swallowed its prey.

September 26th

The Underground stations are so crowded now. You know it's going to be a struggle when you come down the escalators, which have been turned off for safety, and there are already people lying on them in blankets. The tunnels are full and when you get to the platforms there is no room. Police officers and ARP wardens are on patrol and most of the stations have the painted lines to show you where you can and can't go. As the trains come in, the commuters have a hard time wading through the sleepers. There is some jostling but it is good-natured, especially at the weekend. At Leicester Square they like a singsong, all the favourites like 'London Pride' and 'Maybe its because I'm a Londoner'. There is an American band lead by a man called Glenn Miller who had to decamp at Marble Arch during a raid. They put on an impromptu concert down there and everyone got up and waltzed to the music as it floated through the corridors and the tunnels.

I wonder if the dead people like to dance as well.

September 30th

People are saying some of the bombed out houses might be fit to live in. There is no gas or electricity or anything, but it would be nice to have a roof over our heads.

Martin Cowell and his family were killed last night. Martin used to play football with us and we went to see the Cup Final last year at Wembley with our dads. Wolverhampton Wanderers played Portsmouth, who won 4-1. An incendiary bomb started a fire and they were still in their house. They tried to use the bucket and water extinguishers but the fire was too strong. Martin's Mum was always saying she would rather die in her own bed than in a dug out outhouse and she got her wish. We had a minute's silence and then fire drill in the playground. Later on there was another daylight raid and we all had to go to the bunker and sit inside until it was over. I made sure I was last out and I took the torch. I feel bad because batteries are scarce but what I am going to do is for the good of all of us.

I have a plan.

In the WC I unscrew the torch and two plump batteries fall out. I test them by putting them on my tongue and the metallic tingle makes me shudder. I don't have to pick up Aggie from school today, as she is with Ma at Swan & Edgar. Mr. Watson relented, under 'public pressure' says Ma. He says so long as she is well-behaved, she will be allowed to stay under the table where Ma does her dressmaking.

Fat chance of that.

When we arrive at Aldwych the station entrance is so full we don't stand a chance of getting in. I look in vain for Mr. Sands by the metal gates but there is no sign of him. Ma hurries us through the streets to Strand station. This messes up my plan.

'Ma, can we take a train back to Aldwych once we get in?'

'We'll stop wherever we can.'

'But I like that one.'

'You changed your tune.'

'Can we?'

She frowns at me and hurries Aggie along. 'We'll stop where we can.'

It's not fair. *I'm* supposed to be the man of this family.

Everywhere is the same story. Too crowded. We take the Northern Line up past Goodge Street to Euston and Camden Town. Ma dozes off and we carry on out to the suburbs, travelling mile after mile overground with the wheels rattling and people peeling off at each stop. I sit and fume.

Someone needs to investigate, to see what's going on.

We pass places I'd never heard of. East Finchley. Woodside Park. Aggie asks if we are going to the seaside. The tube train ends at a place called High Barnet where the train empties and the engine whines down and dies. Ma wakes with a start. She seems utterly lost.

'It's the end of the line Ma.'

The guard is coming along, making sure everyone has alighted. Ma ushers us out into a glass walled waiting room where we sit on fat wooden seats.

'Are we going to live out here now?' asks Aggie.

'I have no idea.'

'I've been on look out, I said. There's no fires up this far.'

The waiting room has a heater under the seats. We would be warm and dry.

'We could stay here.'

'We'll just wait and see.' Says Ma, producing bread and butter with a trace of jam she has managed to get from someone at work. Aggie and I devour it while we watch the tube go out again, empty. As eight o clock approaches I hunch up ready for the siren, but when it sounds it is miles away. Through the glass wall we watch searchlights play on the undersides of purple clouds and on the barrage balloons. Moments later we hear footsteps and the Stationmaster rattles the doorknob. He is a bit stooped, maybe because he is embarrassed about being so tall.

'What are you doing here?'

'Sheltering.' Says Ma.

He looks at us suspiciously. 'You can't stay here, you know.'

'There wasn't time to get to a public shelter.'

'Have you got tickets?'

Ma shows them to him.

'These were issued at Leicester Square. You live in Barnet, do you?'

Ma folds her arms. 'We've not been through yet. These tickets are valid.'

'For travel.' says the man. 'Not for kipping out in the waiting room. I'm sorry but I can't be accountable to London Underground or the ARP if a bomb fell on you here. You'll have to take the next tube back into town.'

'You'd rather we were bombed in the City.'

'I didn't say that Madam.'

'It's what you meant.'

'I don't want any trouble.'

Ma gets very reasonable with difficult people, especially official types like Mr. Watson. When they are in the wrong and she is right, she won't budge. I guess Ma won't win this argument but I admire her for trying.

'We aren't being any trouble.'

'You can't sleep here Madam.'

He says 'Madam' as if it was an insult.

'We've been bombed out. Where do you expect us to sleep?'

'Can't stay on LT property unless authorized. There are eighty stations underground in the central area.'

'We know.' I chip in. 'We've slept in most of 'em.'

The hooded lights of a tube snake towards the platform. 'You'll have to get on this one, says the Stationmaster, or I'll have to call the police.'

'We'd be safer in the cells.' Says Ma.

'You probably would… if that's what you want.'

'A woman and two children who have done nothing wrong but try to survive.'

She glares at him, her eyes hard. He looks away and fumbles for the door. 'It goes out in eight minutes.' He goes out, leaving the door open so the cold seeps in.

A few minutes later we are travelling back to the fires and bombs and death and destruction. If that is North London you can keep it.

***

After several stops and starts and changes we *do* manage to get back to Aldwych, which we are beginning to think of as home. When we decamp onto the platform Ma recognises a couple of women from the night before and they budge up and make room. When she tells them about the dictator in Barnet they huff and puff like the wolf in the Three Little Pigs story and Ma comes out something of a hero.

My plan is on again.

Aggie plays and I pretend to read, but I am really waiting for lights out. I have been thinking a lot about that mask in the tunnel, about its dead eyeholes. Thinking about the way it hung there, watching, waiting. One kiddie has gone for sure and who knows if there aren't others? When the grown-ups talk among themselves there is always one who uses the words madness, bedlam, lunacy. A city collapsing, the sky raining bombs, streets on fire, hell on earth. There are mad stories that never make the newspapers, such as the one about scores of people taken to shelter in a school, which got bombed the next night. The casualty numbers are changed so it looks as though we're doing better than we are. There are Spivs out for anything they can get, a black market starting up, plenty going on in the blackout.

After lights out there are a steady stream of people using the ablution buckets but it slowly diminishes. I wait an extra half hour to be on the safe side.

The hands on the clock above the platform came together.

It's midnight. I'm ready.

I creep to the end of the platform and drop down into the gulley. I stop to listen. Gentle snoring. I move forward step by step as the sooty blackness gathers round me. The tunnel is carbon black.

I hear rustling, a mouse scuttling around. I am enclosed in the dark tunnel. Behind me the platform shrinks to a crescent of dirty orange. I lift out the torch, press the switch and the beam reveals dirty old bricks and crumbling mortar. I turn it to the tunnel and the beam is lost in inky black. There is a slight recess on the left wall, a bricked in arch. Cables run along the floor. The mice avoid the glare – no rats tonight. I shuffle forwards. In the beam there is nothing but tunnel, bricks and rails…

I hear something. I hoist the beam around. Nothing.

I kill the light. I can hear breathing.

It is a long, low, intermittent wheeze. Each inhalation is laboured, a fight for breath. It is in front of me, off to the left. I aim the torch and flip the switch. As the light appears I feel a sharp blow to my wrist. For a second there is a hooded shape, the glint of shiny metal, the eye ring of a gas mask and then the torch is broken in two with its precious batteries rolling off. Suddenly, I am running back, dignity abandoned. I scurry toward the light, to the safety of people. My heart booms like the bombs in my ears as I clamber up onto the lip of the platform.

I turn away from the tunnel too fast and in my haste I kick metal and something wet slops all over my feet. Oh god. It's the ablution bucket. Its contents pour out onto the rails. It is such a horrid stench that I want to be sick. I step away, retching, then, breathing fast and hard through my nose I grab some pieces of the newspaper left on a nail. I wipe what I can off my shoes and socks.

The tunnel is silent. I was stupid, a stupid scared little boy.

No one was woken when I panicked, not a good sign. Thoughts tumble into my head. How many were there? Was it one or more? It was *waiting*. It didn't want to be seen. A bomb goes off in my mind.

Germans.

What better place for them to hide, right here in the Underground? They could find their way around down in here and no one would know. Why did he have a gas mask on? Because he doesn't speak English.

***

Through square panes of glass I see Sands asleep in the little booking office. His hand is pressed to his face making his cheeks pillow out around his mouth. He snores gently. I creep in and shake him awake and he makes a noise like a donkey.

'Sands. Could the Germans get into the tunnels and start an invasion from there?'

'You what?'

'I think I saw one.'

'You've got an overactive imagination. Get back to sleep lad.'

'Is it possible for a German to get into the tunnels?'

He rubs his pouchy eyes, which makes them baggier and redder, then reaches for a metal teacup. He takes a sip of cold tea, winces, chews it around in his mouth and swallows it. He clears his throat then speaks in a way that sounds as if he is reading from a London Underground Transport leaflet.

'We took preventative measures against the tunnels being breached under the river last year. We plugged a few with concrete, which is why some of the lines are closed for the duration. You seen how if there's an air raid the trains stop before they go under the river down at Charing Cross?'

I nod.

'We put in flood barriers. Remote controlled. Great big steel doors. Water tight.'

'What's that got to do with the Jerries? I can see how it makes us safe from the bombing but—'

'We've had that many people working down here, there ain't no room for the Hun.'

'But that was before the war.'

He produces a pipe and starts thumbing tobacco out of a pouch.

'I saw someone.'

'Where?'

'In the tu—'

'What were you doing in there when I told you *not* to?'

'I was just near it.' I lie.

'You don't half pong and all.'

'I kicked the ablution bucket by accident.'

'Oh that's good. That's helping the war effort.'

'Sorry Sands.'

'You best get yourself washed up. You can catch diseases. There's a tap on the westbound platform 3. Rinse it off proper and use the carbolic.'

I turn to go but he grabs my sleeve.

'Will – *If* the Jerries come, they aren't getting in down here. And if they did try anything they'd have to get through you and me first – all right?'

I grin. "All right.'

'We're the last line of defence, right?'

I salute him and go off to clean up.

But if it is not a Jerry then what is it?

Chapter Seven

October 10th

This morning the Luftwaffe answered our prayers and bombed out the school. When I got there it was a smouldering wreck with half its brick face torn off and the roof fallen in and exercise books fluttering about madly as if on strings. The younger kids were skipping for joy as teachers herded them away from the building. Fireman were spraying the gable end and making rainbows in the sunshine. I am free to do as I please. No job and no school, but also no friends. Tommo and Jimmy got evacuated out of London. Little Kenneth didn't do so well as his family bought it too. A direct hit on their shelter.

So I walk the streets. Borough and Bermondsey are rubble. Bits of bomb casing and chunks of fused iron lie everywhere like black slugs. Where there was a gas tank, a shop or a municipal building there's just white sky. The roof beams stick out like that game of 'here's the church' when you turn your hands inside out and waggle your fingers for the congregation. London is disappearing. It's like doing a jigsaw puzzle backwards.

I find myself back at our house. What *was* our house. It's sagged in on itself now, given up the ghost. The note I wrote to Dad is still in the letterbox but it's all soggy and when I pull it, it comes apart. I tear out another page of diary and write another, telling Dad to come to Swan & Edgar or to Holborn Underground Station. I try to remember his face but all I can think of are things we did together like the football or him showing me how to stack fruit so the best of it sells quick. I climb up into the house over the roof and get down into their bedroom. I've seen the Rescue squads do it and they're careful not to dislodge anything. Being small I can get between the joists. Opening the wardrobe, I find Dad's old coat, the one he always wore on the stall. It is a great thick black woollen one for hard winters with deep pockets on the outside. It still has the smell of him. I put it on and do up the big buttons. It's much too big and comes down almost to my knees but it lovely and warm and I will never take it off.

October 14th

Trafalgar Square has been hit, along with the Horse Guards parade, the Admiralty Building and The National Gallery. The newspapers say that the paintings are in storage so the Nation has no need to worry – so that's all right then.

I'm riding the tube from Elephant and Castle towards Morden. I am sick and tired of looking after Aggie. I go past Stockwell and Clapham North where they are planning to dig a deep shelter under the common. There are signs everywhere, telling us what to do and where to go. Ma and I have had a falling out. I hate Aggie because she hangs around asking non-stop questions and wants to play stupid games. She carries that doll everywhere, with its broken eye and dirty dress and talks to it like a mad person.

Clapham South.

Mr. Watson has decided that Aggie is not allowed to stay with Ma all day. Setting a precedent, he says. If he allows one child in, then all the other staff will have the right to bring their children in to work with them and that just won't be right, will it? Ma goes on about this to anyone who will listen down in the Underground and I hate mister bloody Watson because it's his fault that I am stuck with Aggie.

I check my reflection in the blacked out windows. I look serious and old but that's good. She will like that. Evie.

Balham, Trinity Road.

I alight at Tooting Broadway and walk up Mitcham Lane towards the Amen corner. It's a dull afternoon, the sky a thick slab of grey. There are brick terraced houses with sawtooth roofs and russet red trees lining the pavements. You wouldn't think there was a war on here. Evie told me before that she moves around a lot with her mother. Even though she lives over in Lee, the LCC said she has to stay at her old school in Balham. I'm going to surprise her by meeting her at the gates. The street is a long road stretching down a hill with a few cars in it. I go up to the iron school railings. They won't last long. A lot of metal is being melted down for the war effort. I take up a position opposite the main gates, leaning against the red brick wall. I hope I'll spot her when she comes out. A copper cycles past and for a moment I think he's going to stop but he doesn't. My plan is to accompany her home on the bus. I won't try to kiss her or anything. I'll just sit with her and talk. I know she won't be able to invite me in, not with that horrid landlady and anyway I don't want Auntie Joan to see us. I'll ask her to Saturday morning pictures and we'll stay until the proper film comes on in the afternoon. There's one on called Gaslight, which sounds grown up so she might like that.

Women start to arrive in hats and coats, all chatting away. Soon there is a cluster of them around the entrance and there isn't room to see as the schoolgirls pour out. I keep my eyes peeled but although my heart goes in fits and starts she does not appear. I cross the street and come closer. She will be in her uniform. She will have a satchel, her long legs in stockings and her hair will be done in plaits. I'm glad of my dad's coat because I have the collar up and I can stuff my hands in the deep pockets. There are flakes of loose tobacco in one of them. I rub it on my fingers. She'll come out soon. There will be a moment when she can't place me. One of her friends will whisper to her, a giggle, then she will see me. What are you doing here Will Lumley? Come to accompany you home. A gentleman, one will say. My brave cousin from Southwark, she'll announce. He's had it worse off than us, bombed out in the first week and still he thinks of me. She'll take my arm and off we'll go with her smiling at the thought of the others gossiping about us.

The flow becomes a trickle. I'm worried now. Did I get the wrong school? I could ask someone if they know her but the older girls have all gone. Perhaps she is doing something after school? It's getting dark. I am heavy and cross. A gaggle emerges, eyeing me as they turn away and go up the road. Then a girl comes right across to me. She is skinny with an oval face and lank brown hair.

'What you doing here?'

'Waiting for someone.'

'Who?'

'Evie Wilde. Do you know her? '

Her lips form a little bud. 'Hang on.'

She dashes off back inside to her friends, who congregate in a coven. After a moment another girl comes out. She is a little bit fat but has a pleasant face.

'Evie's gone.'

My heart sinks. How did I miss her? A wasted trip on the tube and where did that get me? I wanted Evie's company: anything to be away from Ma and Aggie for a bit. I mumble thanks and start walking up the road, but the girl comes running alongside.

'She's gone round her friend's house. Jennifer Sway.'

I feel light again. 'D'you know where that is?'

'I'll take you, if you like?'

She takes my hand, which is a bit strange, but what can I do? We zigzag between grey streets and brown houses in the gloom. There are rows of Anderson shelters in the back gardens, people turning over the earth to be made into allotments: 'Digging for Victory' says the posters. Mist is forming and clinging to the piled up mounds of earth. The girl tells me she is called Deborah and she is full of questions about my adventures in the Blitzkrieg. We come to a house and wipe our feet as Deborah rings the bell. Another girl invites us into the parlour where there is a fire in the grate.

'What's your name then?'

'Will Lumley. Where's Evie?'

'She had to run an errand. I'm Jennifer. You want to wait?'

I nod.

'Sit down then. Cuppa tea?'

The two girls go off together. I sit down, enveloped in a big hairy armchair. There's pictures on the mantelpiece and a big wooden radio with a grille on the front like the one we had at home. It makes me sad. If this were my house I could play with my planes or Meccano or read comics on the floor as the heat from the fire warmed my face and sides. The girls bustle in with a tray and Deborah makes that bud with her mouth again. 'You all right Will Lumley?'

'Yes of course.'

'Not too hot in that coat?'

'I'm fine, ta.'

'You sure? Your face is bright red.'

'I'm fine.'

They pour out the tea and even have a couple of malted milk biscuits.

'Why don't you take that big coat off?' says Jennifer.

'Don't want to. Where's Evie gone?'

'Are you her bloke?'

'I'm her cousin.'

Deborah slips off her shoes and wraps her stockinged toes around the brass rail on the fireguard. 'So why are you here to see her? Not *serious* is it?'

'I just thought I'd come and see her, that's all.'

'That's all.' Echoes Jennifer Sway.

'What do you want to play?' Deborah asks.

'Don't mind.'

We play Happy Families but it's boring, so Jennifer gets out a proper set of cards and we play pontoon and gin rummy. The fire makes me sleepy and I don't mind when they suggest that we sit and play on the floor and bit-by-bit we get tangled up on the carpet. When the clock chimes six, I look up.

'When is Evie coming back?'

'She should be here by now. Maybe she's at Amy's house?' Says Jennifer.

'Oh yes,' adds Deborah, but not very convincingly, 'She could be there.'

'You said she was coming *here.*'

'She was.' Deborah says.

'Was?'

'Is.'

I get up. 'She isn't coming at all, is she?'

Jennifer smiles in an annoying way. 'She'll be at Amy's. Her mum picks her up in a van from there sometimes, now she's in the WVS.'

'Can you take me over to Amy's?'

The girls look at one another.

'For a kiss.'

I had to kiss her and Deborah, who then put on her shoes and coat and led me back toward the Station. It was past seven. I tried to hurry but she liked to dawdle and I wanted to push her. We came to a parade of shops and she rang a bell in a door set in between a Haberdasher's and a Bicycle repair shop. A frumpy woman answered in a pinafore and curlers and told us that Evie had taken the tube a quarter of an hour ago. I ran for Tooting Broadway. I paid at the turnstile and rushed down to the northbound platform. It was busy with people in uniform and shelterers. A quarter to eight. Evie will have gone up to Clapham to get a bus. Why did those stupid girls keep me waiting?

The tube shudders in. A whistle peeps, the doors clang shut and off we go. We get to Clapham South and I hear the wail of the Minnies. We stop and wait in the tunnel as the engine winds down. We sit in silence, the women all knitting, clickety-clack. There is a loud *whoof* and a bang from somewhere. I was wrong; they are bombing down here. The giant is back. Maybe they should just drop one right on my head. Evie doesn't even care if I exist. She's so much older. Cleverer. I don't know anything except comic books and football and what they made us learn at school and even *that's* gone now. There is a sort of high-pitched whining in my ears. I swallow but it won't go away. I am odd, itchy and hot. I want to pant like a dog. I move my jaw around making it click. I cannot stay in my seat. I go to the double doors and peek out at the dark. I hear a strangled cry and… *whoosh!* The doors vibrate and there is a huge suction and everyone is pulled this way and that, losing their balance or dropping things. My stomach is full of wasps. I smell water, which is wrong, here under the ground. I look at my hands and they are shaking. I close my eyes trying to make everything go away until the train moves again.

At Clapham Common we cannot get out, as there is a raid still on. I hunt for Evie on the platform but it's hopeless. I give up. I'll never find her. I take the next Northern Line train to Tottenham Court Road and change. There are so many stoppages now. They come with hardly a moment's notice and everyone buckles down and gets on with it because what can you do? Ask 'Itler to stop sending his bloody Dorniers and Heinkels to kill everyone? I'm hungry. I spent my money on train tickets. Ma will have food. She magics it out of nowhere.

***

When I get to Aldwych I find them in the eastbound tunnel. Aggie is asleep, a lump under a blanket. Ma grabs my arm, belts me round the head and then drags me off into a corner.

"William, we was worried sick. Where you been?"

'I was just travelling round.'

'Getting into trouble no doubt. You eaten?'

I shake my head. At the end of the platform a makeshift WVS canteen has been put up to serve teas and cakes. We join the short queue and Ma hisses at me.

'Aggie and me were beside ourselves.'

'She doesn't care.'

'She loves you very much.'

I fold my arms.

'She's your flesh and blood and you have to look after her. You're the man now.'

'No I'm not. I'm just a babysitter.'

Ma produces a cigarette and hunts around in her bag for matches.

'Ma – you don't smoke.'

She isn't listening. 'Watson won't have her in the shop. What am I supposed to do? Her school's been closed for the duration.'

I have a brilliant idea.

'How about leaving her with Auntie Joan?' I could take and fetch her from Lee.'

And get a chance to see Evie proper.

'Joan's working – and they won't have Aggie where she's staying.'

'You sure?'

She finds a match, lights up and blows out the smoke.

'You aren't smoking properly.'

'Don't you tell me what to do Will Lumley.'

'You're supposed to breathe it in.'

'I'm getting used to it.'

'You could at least hold it right. It's not a tea cup.'

I take the ciggie and turn it round.

'You do it like this.' I hold it between my thumb and first finger so the red tip is hidden in my palm. Third light, Dad said. First light, the sniper sees you. Second light, as you pass it to the next bloke, the sniper takes aim. Third light. Bang, you're dead. Ma takes it and tries it and gets smoke in her eyes and when she squints I have to laugh. She orders teas and a sandwich for me.

'There's talk that they're going to open up a hostel under Swan & Edgar. We'll have a proper place to stay.'

'What about Mr. Watson?'

'It'll be run by the ARP. He'll not get a look in.' She blows out more smoke. 'Until then, you've got to do your bit. Ok?'

I wolf down the food.

'Is that your dad's coat?'

'I went back to the house.'

She strokes the lapel. 'It's much too big.'

'I'll grow into it.'

She rummages round in her bag. 'Aggie found this, she thought you might like it.'

It is a Dinky Toys Royal Tank Corps Medium Tank set. Brilliant.

'Where did she find it?'

'In the street, she said.'

'Did she now?'

I play with the tank for a bit before bedtime. It really is a good one. Ag is always finding things, probably because she is closer to the ground.

***

A bomb hit the northbound tunnel of Balham tube station at two minutes past eight. It was a 1400-kilogram semi armour piercing shell. The tunnel collapsed and a bus fell into the hole, fracturing a water main. The water flooded the tunnels all the way to where I was in the train, a hundred yards short of Clapham South. I learned this from the newspapers and from people who knew what was going on, on the Home Front, the Station Marshals and ARP wardens. The police are helpful but strict but you don't like to ask them for anything because they have so much to do all the time. There was so much water released from the split main pipe that it filled the northbound tunnel then went round the other way and filled the southbound one as well. Everybody drowned: Men, women and children. Sixty-eight killed and another seventy injured. In the newspaper there was a picture of the bus tipped over into the hole. It took a crane to hoist it out but that section of the line will be closed for a long time. I pray Evie wasn't there. but I think that what with all the lies her friends told me, she probably wasn't. When it's your time, you can't do nothing about it, that's what people keep saying.

I don't think its Evie's time yet. She's not the sort to go getting killed by a bomb.

There are posters of the missing boy on the tube tunnel walls.

They have been there for over a week and no one pays any attention. Who's going to notice one missing child in the middle of all this?

***

I keep an eye on the tunnel entrance until lights out. Afterwards I keep watching the black tunnel and after a while I think I see the shape of the mask floating there, but when I move to look more closely there is nothing. I lie back and go to sleep.

In the morning, my tank set is missing.

54

Chapter Eight

October 16th

We are at Charing Cross tonight. There's a lot of bustle and good-natured joshing as we clatter down the stairs. At the bottom there is a rush for spaces because you don't want to let the good ones go. A lot of people are getting coughs and colds because of it being so nippy outside but stuffy in here and when one person starts sneezing the next night there are five of them. "Coughs and sneezes spread diseases, trap the germs in your handkerchief", says the poster. The fat man in the drawing has the look of Mr. Watson.

Because I went to Balham on my own, Ma has decided on a curfew. In the day I have to queue up for hours with her ration book and I am not allowed to go off at night. She says this is what Dad would have done in the situation and I can't argue. I think a lot about the thing in the tunnel but the problem is I have no proof. All I have is what I saw and my missing tank set, but that could have been thieved. There is a lot of laughter and 'camaraderie' at the grown-ups' end of the platform. Because we are in the middle of Theatre land, a lot of the actors come down after the shows and there is talk of getting a Music Hall act to do a turn. The women actors are very glamorous in their fox furs and silk dresses and they make a lot of fuss of the little kids. Other than that it's all a bore.

I can't even go and see Sands because he is over at Aldwych.

We are thirty-three nights into the Blitz.

October 18th

Adventure!

I had just settled down on the newspapers I put out to insulate myself from the ground when a warm breeze ruffled them as a tube train drew in. The doors opened and I saw three boys. They were making fun of one of their crew, a lad in short trousers who ran out along the edge of the platform. He had a slight limp; Rickets, I'd guess. He dropped down, grabbed something and then disappeared back into the tube carriage. The other one was tall, leaning against the open door. It was that lanky Spiv who had been selling platform spaces a couple of weeks ago. He looked right at me and put a finger to his lips.

His accomplice, a short fat boy, bundled his friend back on and the littlest one held his trophy aloft. As the doors slid shut, the Spiv made a beckoning gesture. 'Join us', he seemed to be saying. As the tube rattled off, a man, who had been sitting where the boy ran past, started patting the pockets of his coat as if he was on fire.

'Me tin. Where's me baccy?'

My heart started to beat fast. I saw but should I say? What good would it do now they'd gone? This bloke was one of the worst snorers on the platform and no one likes him for it. What is a grown man doing down here anyway? There is always a question about men sleeping here. There's a poster. *Be a Man and leave it to them.* They are supposed to allow spaces for women and children but the refugees and foreigners in the West End don't take any notice, can't even read, some of them. Why isn't he fire fighting or being an ARP or doing war work?

He started accosting people. 'You see anything? I had it right here. Someone must have it.'

One woman didn't like his 'tone of voice'.

'It's a Balkan Sobranie tin. I ought to get you ruddy lot to turn out your pockets.'

'You certainly won't.' Said the woman.

Dad says if you start a fight be sure you can finish it.

'Come on – who's had it?' He tries to laugh as if it's a joke, but it's not really.

There are shrugs.

'Could have dropped it on your way down here.' Says someone.

'I had it right with me.'

All this fuss caused by one boy. Baccy that isn't worth half a nicker.

'Don't think the war's stopped them.' Said an old man in a manner of speaking that suggested he had a lot to say and didn't mind who heard it. 'I seen 'em, spivs and pickpockets making profit out the war.'

This opened up the conversation to a general discussion about the rationing and the price of food in the shops and people who name their price for things. The old man carried the baton onto British spirit and fair play for all except when it suited them.

'It's everyone for themselves.' Said a haughty woman, sniffing the air.

We can take it! Is what they say on the Pathé Newsreel but down here there is nothing but grumbling, sneezing and stealing. I wonder if those boys will come again?

October 19th

Ma has a shift on a mobile refreshment canteen over in Stepney Green and she's taking Aggie with her. I've to keep our places and that means I've got the whole time free until half past ten.

At half past eight I am standing at the same place as last night, watching and waiting as each train comes in. I don't know what to expect. Maybe they won't come tonight? Five to nine. Five past. I am about to give up when a train pulls up and two pairs of hands reach out and whisk me onto the tube train. There aren't many passengers inside. The runt who did the thieving and the boy with a bit of weight on him push me down onto one of the rough fabric seats.

Opposite sits the Spiv in his slick suit, sizing me up. He is so pale, almost white. There are hairs on his upper lip above a cruel thin mouth. He has a spotty forehead, a slightly bent nose and eyebrows that slant in towards deep-set eyes that give nothing away. I'd guess he was sixteen, seventeen. He's smoking and he stares at me long enough to make me feel uncomfortable.

'What's your name then?'

'Will Lumley.'

He nods at each boy in turn. 'That's Ollie, that's Johnny.' Ollie has his top shirt button undone and his tie loose. He wheezes a bit and breathes in and out of his nose; Johnny is the boy who had had the tin off the war worker. He has sticking out front teeth, small eyes and hair that sticks up in tufts, a bit like a rat.

'I'm Perce. Where you from, son?'

'The Elephant.'

'The Elephant where?'

'Keeton's Road School, but it was bombed out. Where's yours?'

They laugh. Johnny's is a high-pitched giggle.

'Do we look like we bothered with school?' Perce says.

I can't see him doing sums, handing in his homework or cheeking a teacher.

'There's a *war* on.' Says Ollie in a sarcastic way. 'Schools can't keep records and the LCC don't have enough truant officers to chase everyone.'

Johnny squirms, gripping the shiny armrest. 'We do what we like, when we like.'

'So what *do* you do?'

'Oh, we got plenty to occupy us.' Says Perce, stretching his arms out along the back of the seats. 'Here's a little lesson for you, schoolboy. Look and learn.'

We pull into St James Park. The evening crowd gets on, posh people in furs or shiny black shoes going to a dance or a nightclub, the Pigalle or Café de Paris. *The Evening Standard* says these are the safest restaurants in town and that the clubs in St James, Pall Mall and Berkeley Square are thriving. It's another world.

The eyes of the gang dart over the prizes; a clutch bag in a Ladies lap, a man using a flint lighter to light his cigarette, another checking his fob watch. More get on at Victoria and Sloane Square. Perce stands to offer his seat to a Lady. We follow suit. I catch Johnny's gaze. It's filled with rage and I don't know why.

South Kensington comes and goes.

Butterflies in my stomach. I watch the straphangers, men in uniform or tails, faces dull and drink weary, wanting to be home in their beds. The last time I slept in a bed was at Auntie Joan's and that wasn't for long. I think about Evie for a moment then cram that thought away, deep down. Johnny is pulling at my arm to get me off at Earl's Court. The moment the doors open, Perce and Ollie sprint between the shelterers and head off towards the surface. We regroup up on the eastbound platform.

Earl's Court is a big shed and the four platforms have a glass roof. There is no raid on but the blackout is in full force and no one is risking sleeping here. It's almost empty. We huddle by the waiting room and I am amazed when Ollie produces a fob watch and Perce a crisp white five-pound note, displaying it 'for our edification' before folding it away into a pocket. Johnny has a bracelet. How did they do it? Their faces are in shadow but I sense the excitement, the energy boiling off them. Dippers, that old man called them.

'How did you do it?'

Perce. 'I gave up my seat, didn't I? Help the Lady, brush against the husband, bob's your uncle.'

Ollie, with his sarcastic voice. 'Terribly sorry Guv. Bumping into you like that.'

Johnny is almost skipping around in glee. Dad set me straight once on stealing when I made a grab for some penny chews in the local tobacconists. I could barely sit down for two days.

'D'you ever get caught?' I ask.

Perce shakes his head. 'The trick is not to do too much, just keep your hand in.'

Ollie and Johnny snigger.

'We don't it regular. We have other sources of income. That was a demonstration. To show you what we want.'

I wilt at the heat of their gazes.

'What d'you mean?'

'Why d'you think you're here.' Says Ollie.

'We're recruiting.' Perce says, quiet.

'Why me?'

'Why you indeed, Sonny Jim?' Perce seems old beyond his years.

'That's what you got to prove.' Says Johnny. 'If you want to join.'

My heart creeps up my chest. 'What do I have to do?'

Perce leans in. 'something of value, that's all. You have to lift something decent, no cabbage.'

'When?'

An Eastbound District line train lumbers in like a black slender snake.

'Now's as good a time as any.'

'But I don't know how?' My voice goes up high.

'Keep calm, act fast. You see it, you take it, you pocket it. That's all there is to it. If you need a diversion we'll oblige. You pick the mark and tip us the wink.'

'But I've never done anything like this before.'

'Oh well bugger off then.'

'No...'

They surround me, saying nothing, knowing that my hesitation means I'm interested but just scared. Before I can say any more, Perce pulls me onto the tube and the others get in at either end of the carriage. I feel as heavy as lead.

It is quiet and dim, as if they were holding a séance on board the tube. There are a few passengers seated, reading in low light from the almost blacked out bulbs. That will help but as I look around there doesn't seem to be anyone displaying anything I could risk taking. What if I get caught? I'd have to tell the police where Ma works and she'd get the sack and then we'd have nothing and nowhere to go and she wouldn't want me and nor would Dad. They would send me to prison and that would be the end of it all. My hands are hot in my pockets. My mouth is dry and my face is all sweaty. I should make a run for it at the next stop. The gang is strap hanging, like apes, watching me.

We pull in at Gloucester Road and Perce whispers in my ear.

'You've got four stops.'

Ollie is suddenly at my side. 'Don't let us down and don't run, 'cos we'll find you.'

The doors shudder shut and we move on. There are more people on the platform than on the train and I figure that if I have a chance at all it will be among them. I'll do what Johnny did – drop out and grab something because than at least I'm not trapped in the tube. Victoria is the interchange for the main line services. I can hear every breath inside my head, as if I were wearing my gas mask.

South Kensington.

Sloane Square.

Victoria. We pull into the long curved platform like sheathing a knife. The moment the doors open I bolt, weaving in and out of the crowd. I see a middle-aged woman with her purse open. Without thinking I make a grab for it but, as I think I am away, I feel her talons grip on my sleeve. The bright red fingernails are digging into me, bunching the material. I see steely determination in her powdered face. She is not going to let go without a fight. She doesn't scream out, instead her mouth is a grimace, a jagged shard. I do not know how to win this. Her grip tightens and I release a yelp, but luckily it is covered by the platform announcement. "Mind the Gap." I let go her bag but her hand is still clasping Dad's coat, tugging at it, at me.

There is nothing for it but to shrug it off and let my arm slide out of the sleeve. I do this and she is left with the coat as I leap back on the carriage. The doors close. I put my back to them and squeeze my eyes tight shut, praying she hasn't raised the alarm or managed to get hold of a guard. My heart is thumping as hard as the Giant. Boom, boom, BOOM. The doors rattle in their grooves but far too slowly. I am screaming inside, go, go, please GO.

Finally, we pull into dark enveloping blackness.

When I open my eyes I am surrounded. Perce gives a mirthless laugh, like a comedian poking fun at his audience.

'At least you tried. Other's haven't.'

Ollie. 'I thought she was going to have your bloody arm off.'

Johnny. 'You lost your coat.'

'It was my dad's.' I feel rotten and hollow and stupid.

'He won't miss it.' Says Ollie.

Perce. 'We're supposed to steal from the rich, not give it them.'

'I don't suppose she'll leave it there so I can go back and get it?'

Laughter.

Perce. 'I expect she'll have it cleaned and pressed for you.'

I'm in shirtsleeves and tank top. Luckily I didn't have anything much in the pockets. 'What about her giving it to Lost Property?'

More laughter. Ollie puts on a posh voice, pretending to be on the telephone. 'Hello. I would like to claim my coat please. An old lady was trying to steal it off me. "What's that? Would I care to talk to the police?" '

'I still need something to wear for the cold.' I say, angry and upset.

Perce says. 'We'll sort you out.'

I suppose stealing a coat is about the easiest thing you can do down here when we're all lying wrapped up in them. I feel really bad. I care more about that coat than joining this stupid gang. What's Ma going to say? Before we get back to Charing Cross we change trains a couple of times and as we are moving through endless crowded tunnels full of sleepers Ollie stops us and presents me with an overcoat.

'It's red.' I say, indignantly.

'No it's not. It's scarlet. Anyway, beggars can't be choosers.'

As he unfurls it, I think of Evie once more, the day we went to Blackheath.

'It's a girl's coat.'

Johnny laughs in a cruel way. 'Put it on anyway.'

'I don't want to.'

Ollie, threatening. 'It's a gift.'

'It's stolen. That means it's not a gift.'

Perce stands, armed folded and leaning against the wall. 'Just put it on.'

I struggle to get into the sleeves. They find it hilarious and Johnny calls me little Red Riding Hood and for a terrible moment I think they are going to give me that as a nickname. Another tube pulls in.

'Can I join then?' I ask.

Perce shakes his head.

'You want your ears cleaning. Still have to prove yourself. Tomorrow night we'll meet you at Tottenham Court – Northern Line northbound. You better have some stuff you've nicked or forget it.'

They get on board. I get one foot on and Johnny pushes me back out, hard, right in the chest. I fall back and the doors close in my face. Perce points to his wrist as they move off.

The tube slides into the dark and hot stifling air blows all around, rustling newspapers and blowing up dust, which gets in my eyes. I try to blink it away and, as I look back at the dark crescent of the tunnel I see a shape at the other end of the platform.

It is tall, black and not human, almost like a giant bird with a huge black beak.

I rub my eyes and stare at it again but it has gone.

It was there for only a matter of seconds, an oily thing, dark and sleek.

My heart slowly slows.

I didn't imagine it.

I tear off the coat and throw it crossly to the ground. I look at it there, no use to anyone. I don't want it – but where is its owner? I figure Ollie took it a couple of corridors back so I dog leg back the way we came, up and over the Piccadilly line. The people are mostly asleep. I ask if anyone has lost a coat. I get no English from the foreigners, grunts from the rest. I leave it.

***

I reach our space in time to see Ma and Aggie getting off the refreshment canteen train. Aggie is sleepy as she has been given hot milk, but Ma is suspicious.

'Where's your dad's coat?'

'I lost it.'

'You're supposed to have been here all night.'

I really don't want this interrogation.

'I was. Someone must have took it when I went to the loo.'

I can't leave you alone for a minute without something getting stolen or lost. You've got to buck up your ideas William. You've been sitting here all night doing sweet bugger all while I'm working a full day *and* a night shift.'

My voice is loud and quivery. 'I'm more upset about this than you are. I loved that coat. Now I've got nothing.'

'Whose fault's that then? You've got to look after everything with the kinds of people you get down here.'

61

I go quiet and stare at a patch of shiny concrete until I cannot hear her and my only thoughts are that Dad would know what to do and he's not bloody here either and I hate everyone and everything and most of all the bloody giant for burying London right on top of us. Eventually my wet eyes come into focus and I see something being held out I front of me. It is a slice of bread and butter.

'You hungry?'

I'm starving. I am always starving hungry. I don't think I will ever get used to having nothing in my stomach. I grab the slice and wolf it down. Ma cuddles up to me and produces a small misshapen pie.

'I had this away for you. They gave it me, but I kept the half.'

'Thanks Ma.' I say, starting in on it.

While I'm enjoying it, she rummages around in her big case and throws something at me. It is my old coat.

October 20th

Forty-four nights, no let up. At six am they turn up the lights. There is a crackle then on the Tannoy, an official voice saying 'would all shelterers please make your way to the exits. Please move in an orderly fashion.' If it's Sands, he'll add a cheery 'Wakey waa-key. Rise and shi-ine.' The rails go on and electricity sings through them. The escalators grind into action, heavy wooden teeth going round and ferrying us to the surface. The chains and padlocks are uncoupled and the big slatted metal doors are pushed back.

Ma has found someone at work that also has a kid. Her mother is going to look after Aggie up in Camden so I am free to roam. It is a foggy autumn morning and you can't see anything except the criss-cross windows in the buildings. Cars loom out of nowhere and buses and trucks growl past, resentful of the cold. There is a thick layer of ash on everything, like dirty snow. There is always shattered glass, buildings down, holes in the roads, diversions, UXBs. The plane trees have shed their leaves. Burrs and twigs lie everywhere on the ground amidst the rubble. Fire department crews finish their shifts and the demolition teams come in, pulling down shops and offices. People queue at the public conveniences to wash or shave; others get on the first tube of the day and grab another hour's shut-eye before rush hour.

Debenham & Freebody has been hit so bad it will have to come down. Bourne & Hollingsworth has gone and broken Mannequins litter the street. The early arriving staff are sweeping up and collecting what they can. There is no one in charge, just people mucking in. As I come to John Lewis I see the front windows are blasted out. There's no one around. Inside, the wooden sales desks are splintered and a fallen girder has almost cut the place in half. There are bright silk scarves and perfume in fancy crystal bottles. The escalator has a hole in it, ruining it, but there is room to scramble past and to climb up to the first floor. I have an idea.

Upstairs it is still and silent, colder than in the street.

More sales desks run the length of the walls. I start to fill my pockets, grabbing what I can, three wristwatches and a cigarette case then, like a magpie, anything silver, bright or small. In they go, a bottle stop, some silver spoons and some things I don't even know what they are called or what they are for. My pockets bulge with loot. My breath billows in the cold air. I try not to tread on broken glass or to make any unnecessary noise but as I dart along I begin to get a sense that someone is here in the building. I do up my coat, folding tongues of fabric over the pockets, disguising the loot.

Standing by the window is a man, not moving. The fog has lifted and he is haloed in sunlight. It could be a dummy. No, I don't think so. He wears a smart black suit. He must be a floor manager, someone who makes sure the staff do their jobs properly and that the customers are satisfied. His hair is combed back, balding. He looks asleep or drunk. His eyes are heavy lidded, his mouth half open. I take a couple of paces backwards and my shoe catches a tipped over clothes rail. He comes to life – a toy wound up, folding his hands over each other as he moves toward me. There is a ring on his third finger and he worries it with his other hand.

'May I help you sir?'

He keeps on coming. I look behind me at the blown out escalator. I might be able to jump down across the gap but if I fall it's a good twenty feet into rubble, concrete and sharp pieces of wrought iron. If I grip the rail, I might make it.

'Help you Sir?'

He starts to pace, shoes crackling on broken glass. I trot down the stairs as fast as I can, gripping the handrail and launching myself across the space to get a foothold on the other side. A tread gives way but I have the handrail in my grasp. I swing onto the tread. Once I am on the lower steps I clatter down and it's not until I'm at the bottom that I risk a look back. He's still up there, gazing down at me with a sorrowful look, a head up on a parapet. There is a rumbling and a movement in the supports and pillars. I had better get out. He had better get out. Should I call out to him? Surely he must have heard? No time. I dash across the shop floor in sight of the day staff gathered outside.

'Oy, you – out of here.' Calls one.

I tear off out past him and dash along to Marshal & Snelgrove. I slow up, taking great gulps of air. I go inside the big shop, playing the innocent, a boy looking for the lavvy. I ask someone and locate the WC's, then find a stall and close the heavy oak door behind me.

I sit on the seat to count the loot. I have six watches and a cigarette case, which will come in handy when I learn how to smoke. I have tiepins, a bottle opener and a stopper and two lighters. I have done well. I stuff it back inside my pocket and wrap my hankie around it before sauntering out from a different exit. My heart is still beating nineteen to the dozen.

The day's work has started. People are making repairs and putting up sawhorses as diversions for buses. Others are going to work, as if there had been no bombing at all. It's like they're playing a trick on 'Itler and the Luftwaffe. No, nothing's happened. We're all just going about our business. What bombing? No idea mate.

I feel like a criminal and that everyone can see. Are they looking at me differently? Will Ma and Aggie know? I find I've walked for ten minutes without thinking and it has brought me back in sight of John Lewis. I've only gone and returned to the scene of the crime.

There has been a collapse on the first and second floors. Rescue Squads are hard at work and there are Firemen and an Ambulance crew. A small crowd of workers gather round. I loiter close enough to hear their chat. There is a shelter under the shop. Stretcher-bearers are bringing out a body under a blanket. One of the staff steps forward to take a look at the face. He gives a curt nod. One of the dead man's arms slips out and hangs out below the stretcher. I see a hand with a wedding ring. My blood turns to ice. I cannot move. I hear the rest as if underwater. Mr. Treadwell, a floor manager, a dedicated employee and widower. Always first up from the shelter, looking after the stock. He never missed a day of work in his life, loyal to the last.

I have seen my first ghost.

I somehow manage to get my legs to move and find an alleyway. My mouth won't stay shut. My tears are salty and they make my collar damp.

Chapter Nine

The night-time siren goes off as usual. As we parade down into Aldwych Underground station I come across Mr. Sands, who is collecting tickets.

'Seen any more Jerries Sonny Jim?'

I shake my head.

'Told you so. Where you been lately?'

'Charing Cross, the District and Bakerloo lines.'

He nods over at Ma in her WVS outfit. 'See you're not wanting for anything?'

'Ma's on the canteens.'

'Good to have you back. Your usual suite?' he jokes.

'Yes please – and breakfast at six. Will I see you later?'

'Where else am I going to be?'

I try to hold back but Ma starts going on about saving a good space. I want to talk to Sands but there's an ARP man hanging round him. It's busy and bustling and I catch only a few words. 'You heard? Another one gone'. Sands face clouds over and I notice that his hand is trembling as he takes tickets.

The posters beside the escalator say *Grow Your Own Food, Women Come to the Factories* and *Be Like Dad, Keep Mum.* We have to keep secrets and not let things out because there may be spies. We all know that the papers and Newsreels don't tell the whole truth about casualties or where the bombers have been or the real extent of the damage but we just have to knuckle down. It's all for the war effort.

And people to go missing and no one does anything about it.

We get our spot. As soon as Ma has taken Aggie off on her rounds I get the tube to Tottenham Court Road. I've thought of a number of ways of displaying my booty including wearing all the watches on one arm but I decide to play it cool.

Nine o' clock comes and goes and at twenty past Johnny appears off a train.

'Success?' He asks.

'Maybe.'

'Yes or no?'

I nod.

'Come with me then.'

He walks fast, trying to make up for his limp. We go up one stop to Goodge Street and instead of taking the lift we go along the corridor to the round emergency staircase exit. Before we go up he ducks under the stairwell. The walls are painted iron with thick chunky rivets. Although it's dim under there I can make out a metal door in the wall. It has no handle but he slips a shiny brass key out of his sleeve. In a moment we're inside and in total darkness. My eyes refuse to get used to it and I feel around with my hands, touching pipes and wire mesh. I bang my shins on something sharp and let out a yelp.

'Johnny – I can't see.'

He doesn't answer. I go hand over hand along the curved wall. Suddenly a series of storm lights blink on over my head. We are in a long tunnel, a storage area full of workmen's things, rolls of wire, cable and pipes. Johnny is at the far end, grinning.

'Come on then, slowcoach.'

He disappears round a corner. There is barely enough room to stand upright and I have to stoop low as we go down a short metal spiral flight into a brick tunnel. There is no need for tiles here. This goes off at an angle and, as we go deeper in, I can tell it's not been used for decades. It's musty and the crumbling mortar has squeezed through the cracks in the bricks. The floor is rough and all broken up. We go down again, a short flight of stairs to the bottom where there is black water.

Johnny produces a torch and shines it right in my eyes. I splash through cold water, soaking my school shoes and socks as I follow him. This had better not be a wild goose chase. Another turn leads to a long straight tunnel, which is vertically chopped in half by a breezeblock wall. Behind it I hear trains thundering past. Up ahead I make out a faint waxy light. As we approach, a small door comes into view and I hear laughter within. Three steps down and we enter a small storeroom full of boxes. Perce and Ollie are sat on palliasses, smoking.

'Where's your red coat?" Ollie asks.

'Lost it.'

Perce blows a smoke ring. 'What you got for us then?'

'It better be good.' Says Ollie.

I lower my head and look a bit hopeless, as if I'd failed.

Johnny is outraged, shouting and pulling at my clothes.

'You said you had stuff. Bloody lying bastard, bloody sod.'

Perce doesn't seem so concerned. 'You didn't check?'

'No I didn't. He told me.'

'Did I?'

Johnny balls up his fists. I like seeing Johnny squirm so I wait until Ollie moves angrily toward me before I produce my treasure, a handful of watches out of my pockets and the rest. They fall on it, gawping at the watches and fingering them grubbily.

'Pretty good this, fetch a few bob.'

'Couple of quid more like.'

'Quality.'

I look around, seeing grown-up magazines, boxes of cigarettes, matches, and food in tins. 'Are those chocolate bars?'

Perce tosses one at me. I break off a piece and savour the hardness as I bite, then the soft cloying taste, that stickiness in my mouth. It is wonderful. I'm about to break off another big mouthful when Perce grabs my hand.

'Not so fast.'

Between the boxes in the centre of the cave is an intricate wooden octagonal table, Egyptian or Indian perhaps. On it are three fat flickering candles with stalactites of wax dripping off the edge. I can see dirty depressions where the boys have been pressing matches and fingers into the wax, making puddles and allowing the rivulets to flow. Johnny turns out the main storm light and they form a circle round the table. Their faces look hollow, skull-like.

'All new members got to be initiated.' Says Perce.

He holds out his hand and places it, palm down, right over the flame. I wince but he does not flinch. His eyes flicker to mine.

'Ten seconds.' He says solemnly.

I watch in awe as he holds it there for five, seven, ten seconds before whipping it away. Fear shoots through my bowels. He plunges his hand into a water bucket beside him. I hear it sizzle. I'm sure I can smell burning flesh. On this signal the others say nothing but slowly lift up their hands. On each palm they have identical dark black patches where they too have burned themselves in the name of the cause. I doubt I will last three seconds, much less ten. It was bad enough that I went looting this morning and that man died – but this? My legs are moving on their own, itchy, wanting to be away. Johnny grabs my wrist tight and holds it between the candles.

'You got the bottle?'

Dad says never be a coward – or if you are one, never show it. What he's doing, fighting the war proper, is a lot braver than this.

Maybe if I hold it high enough? Maybe to one side?

'Do it.' Says Perce, with an evil grin. 'Go on.'

I put my hand over the candle and the pain is immediate and intense. My first instinct is to pull away but somehow I hold it there. It is a sharp agonizing pain. I can feel the skin on my palm puckering and blistering. Johnny's face is alive with childish glee. Ollie snorts and a bubble of snot comes out of his nostril. Perce is silent, watching. I cannot take it anymore. I don't know how many seconds have passed. I stuff my hand under my armpit. It burns. The pain bites into me, sending shock waves through my body. Perce grabs my hand and plunges it into the ice-cold water. It is instantly relieving, but not much. I grit my teeth and stare up at the ceiling until the first wave of pain has abated.

'Six seconds. Not bad.' Says Perce.

'Am I in then?'

'You're in.'

I allow myself a smile. When I look back at them, Perce is holding up his right hand to show his palm. It is unmarked. I don't get it. Grinning now, the other two hold up their hands like Red Indians in the Cowboy films. They spit on their palms and rub off the smudges, the smuts of charcoal. I get it.

'You bloody tricked me.'

'Go deeper in the bucket, you berk.' Perce laughs properly for the first time.

I scrabble about and find a round object. I fish it out. A thick half a crown, which fitted neatly into his palm. They dissolve into helpless laughter.

'You rotten lot.'

'You can do better than that.' Says Ollie.

'You buggers. You bloody bastard buggers.'

They cheer.

'That's it' says Perce, producing a beer bottle. 'Right, we're off up the Tilbury.'

***

The Tilbury Shelter in Stepney off the Commercial Road is the most disgusting and unhygienic place I have ever seen. It's notorious as being the worst shelter of all, housing up to fourteen thousand people some nights. One side is vaults and stores and the other a goods yard. There is a big surface building, a kind of warehouse, then endless railway arches. Everywhere, there are gigantic bales of newsprint; it's a whole village with alleys and gunnels and roadways ankle deep in filth and human waste, and all of it trodden into the blankets people are trying to sleep on. They're all colours and creeds, Jews, Muslims, Slavs and Hindus. A rancid stink makes me want to puke. Ollie, who has wrapped his face in a scarf, says it's hundreds of cartons of sour margarine that got fouled. There are only twelve latrines behind cloth curtains and buckets for the kids. There are prostitutes everywhere and sailors on leave and army types and fights breaking out and couples courting and Hawkers selling cold greasy fried fish. Perce buys some for us.

'It used to be a shelter in the first war, so the old folks knew of it as a place to go.'

'It's bloody horrible.'

'It's business.'

Ollie and Johnny paw at the fried fish. I take some too. There are fires burning in braziers and people stood around drinking. It's like how London must have been a hundred years ago. I see a procession of people that don't fit, dressed too well, huddled together, nervous. I nudge Perce.

'Who are they?'

'Sightseers from up West – come here on poor tours. Ollie, Johnny, get to work.'

Wiping their greasy fingers on their clothes, off they go, dipping and dropping. Perce produces a bottle of beer and offers some to me. It tastes horrid but it makes you warm inside.

'You done well. Didn't think you was much of a prospect at the start. You keep the Den a secret. You never speak to the rozzers about anything. Clear?'

'Clear.'

'Then we'll look after you.'

Pretty soon the drink makes me not care about getting back to Ma and Aggie when the trains stop. They will be fine. They always are. They don't need me and nor does Evie. Ollie and Johnny come back triumphant having fleeced the West Enders. They eagerly display a wallet containing nearly fifteen pounds. Perce takes it and buys us some rum, which we take turns in sipping around a fire in a metal drum.

Ollie asks: 'What's the worst thing you've seen?'

'A man with his leg blown clean off.' Says Johnny. 'Tooley St after one of the first raids. Lying there with claret pouring out of him. His leg – still with his shoe and sock on mind – was twenty yards away. I swear, as he lies there, he starts crawling toward the leg, as if he might fix it back on.'

'Did he manage it?'

'Course not. He was dead before he got six feet.'

'Six feet under now.' Says Perce.

'Not a leg to stand on.'

'Legless.'

'What you seen then Ollie?'

Ollie puffs on a cigarette.

'I was fire watching over in Pimlico a few weeks back. The raids weren't heavy over there. I had a cushy number, or so I thought. The first load of bombers came in about ten and that sent the Fire crews up West. The flames made the whole sky red. You could feel the heat of it when the wind came down Victoria Street. Anyway, we were knocking off at midnight, change of shift. I reckoned I'd get me money and slip down a shelter somewhere on the quiet. Thing was, there was a second wave. Not heavy bombs but incendiaries. They fell on the Barracks, Lupus Street. Belgravia. I saw them great black birds go over then the fires start up. There wasn't a phone box near by to call anyone but I reckoned they'd know about it soon enough.'

'So far so normal.' Said Johnny, trying it on.

Ollie was unfazed. 'They must have blown the doors off the barracks because you won't believe what I seen next. A horse. This great big black stallion comes charging down Victoria Street – only it's *on fire*. It's neighing and whinnying and its mane's alight and it doesn't have the sense to stop and roll over. It charges on past me, just screaming into the night. Horrible... bloody horrible. I'll never forget it.'

We all fell silent, thinking our thoughts.

'Poor sod... weren't nothing anyone could do...' He spoke haltingly, aware that the story contained more than the shock of pain and death, that there was no joke to be told. No hope to it. He needed for our sakes to make it right. 'It must have... run into the river... no one could have stopped it.'

Perce took a long shot of rum. 'They'd have shot it. Someone would have seen and they would have shot it dead.'

'Yeah.' Said Johnny. 'They'd have put it out of its misery.'

We didn't think about who. The police and ARP wardens don't carry pistols but someone would.

Our dads would.

They would have known what to do.

We have some more dark sticky rum. I am drunk in the heat of this pocket of hell.

'My turn.' Says Perce.

We look at him, expectantly. How is his story going to top the lot?

'We've all been over the bombsites, scavenging, easy pickings. Never know what you're going to find.'

Johnny. 'I saw a soldier doing it with my sister.'

'Not your mum?'

Johnny scowls. Perce has damped him down.

'In the morning you find them, under the rubble, bones crushed, faces blown open by shrapnel. Babies dead, covered in their Mothers blood.'

'You've seen all that?' I ask.

'The worst was in Bow. I knew the street, knew it well. A direct hit and the gas caught. There was this one house, roof off, bedroom open to the world but the parlour and kitchen intact. I went in the back. They never used the shelter, the family. There they were, four of them. Mum, dad, two nippers, sat around the big kitchen table, food gone cold in front of them. They was praying. Saying grace. Dad's even got the bleeding Bible in his hands. If that ain't horrible I don't know what is.'

The flickering fire makes points of light in his eyes.

'You look at all them idiots hiding in churches thinking God's going to save them – they deserve what's coming to them. I cleaned that house out. Made nearly a score. I cleaned them out.'

His teeth are bared. We are silent for a long time.

The rum is nearly gone. I have to get back. I start to make noises about it but Johnny wants me to tell a tale. I could say about Balham or the church or even the man this morning but I don't feel like it.

'Come on, says Johnny, as we head for Stepney Underground, 'What you seen?'

It is out before I have even thought. 'A German.'

Reactions. What? Where?

'In the Underground, in the tunnels. Aldwych. Wearing a gas mask.'

There's a pause then they burst into laughter and start to make jokes about how drunk I am. I'm the Boy who Cried Wolf.

October 22nd

The 6 am reveille wakes everyone. Ma and I pack up our bedding and begin the trudge toward the exits. Aggie rubs her fists in her eyes and takes my hand and I don't mind but as we reach the escalator there is a terrible scream.

I run back in time to see a boy stagger out of the tunnel. He is filthy black with soot and trying to pick his way along either side of the third rail. No one dares jump down for fear of being electrocuted. People are calling out to him to jump up on the platform but he doesn't know where he is.

A tube train blares its horn then all of a sudden bursts into the station and drives straight over him. The boy goes under the train and even though the driver hits the dead man's handle we all know the boy couldn't have stood a chance. Women are screaming and pulling their children away and covering their eyes and the Station staff are rushing full pelt. The driver steps out in shock and collapses. I turn back to reach for Aggie but Ma has already buried her in her skirt. The boy's mother lets out an inhuman wail. It was the boy on the poster.

***

When we reach the surface, Ma bustles Aggie off to Camden but I stay back as the police arrive in their black cars. Several men in big suits rush in and the public is ushered out and the station locked with a big chain and a policeman at the entrance. Mr. Sands is nowhere to be seen. I suppose he is underground helping.

There is a grey eiderdown over the city. I think it wants to stay asleep forever. Ma left me enough money to get breakfast but I cross over the street and wait. The boy's mother is led out, as pale as a ghost, as numb as others I've seen when they've lost everything. They put her in a police car and take her away and after that a black ambulance comes and they bring out what is left of the body. I scuttle back so I am in earshot when two detectives come out.

71

'Well that accounts for one of them.' says one.

'Bloody horrible way to go', replies the second, 'scraped off the track.'

'Think he'd been in there all the time?'

The other draws hard on his ciggie.

'And these others?

'Form a search party?'

'Where we going to start? Six kids lost in different places. The Chief won't spare the manpower, not in all this.'

'Not in this.' Echoes the other.

I am buzzing with excitement.

'We'd best just file the report, leave it to the top brass.'

The other detective stubs out his cigarette. 'We had a rape last week in a shelter.'

'Get away with anything in the blackout.'

'You're telling me.'

They go to their car and speed away. The policeman opens up the entrance and people are allowed to come and go. I want to talk to Mr. Sands so I go down to the booking office to find the clerk. He's a young man with a short haircut and a nasty skin condition that makes his face and neck all red. I speak to him through the glass ticket booth.

'Is Mr. Sands here please?'

'He don't want to talk.'

'Can you say that it's Will?'

'He takes it personal when something happens on his watch.'

'Ask him, please?'

'You want a ticket or not?'

I move away. Sands will have to come out of the staff room sometime, but a blind has been drawn down over the glass panes. It is nearly ten when he finally emerges. He looks exhausted, shrunk in his coat, a turtle in its shell. I follow him as he shuffles toward daylight. My first attempts to talk to him are met with silence.

The cold stiffens our limbs. Kingsway is all cars, buses and bustle.

'Sands – there are other children lost down there, aren't there?'

He glances at me. His expression does not change.

'I heard the policemen talking about it.'

His mouth opens and closes. 'It's a tragedy lad, that's what it is. This bloody war.'

'There are others missing, aren't there?'

He glares at me. 'I've told you not to get involved. Leave it and bugger off.'

With that, old mister Sands runs down the street and jumps on the back of a bus.

When the sirens go, you sometimes see people mad dashing into the Underground, leaping over sandbags, nimble spinsters, fat people puffing like steam engines. I saw a man once come running out of a British Restaurant with a napkin still tucked into his collar. I never saw Sands run before.

Why do grown-ups always get cross when something is true?

Chapter Ten

Ma, Aggie and I went back to St Peters in Walworth, which was freezing and stinky and filled with the filthy bedding of the people sleeping in the crypt. She talked to the church people who told her to register with the Council and that we might get a new place to live.

'Where will it be?' asks Aggie.

'Somewhere else in our borough I suppose.'

There is hardly anywhere left. The rows of terraced houses, pubs and shops are a wasteland. A battle has been fought here but it's one sided. The bus stop stands on its own like a heron in a pond and we get soaked waiting. Ma gives Aggie two pennies to pay with and the conductor twists the tickets out of the machine.

'It's better further South.' Says Ma.

My heart leaps. 'You mean near Auntie Joan?'

'She's down in Lewisham. Our borough ends at South East fifteen.'

'Will wants to see Evie.' Says Aggie.

'I don't!'

'You do.'

'Why would I?'

'Because you want to go with her…Ow. Ma. Will's hurting me.'

'Will. Pick on someone your own size.'

I sit fuming as the bus winds round the bomb craters.

'I suppose you'll be thinking about girls soon.' Says Ma, absently. 'You know what?' She says, brightening. 'We need cheering up. I'm going to make a telephone call.'

October 25th

Apart from all the advice – *'Dig for Victory', 'Join the AFS now', 'We can do it'* – there are posters in the tube stations for theatre shows like 'The Case of the Frightened Lady' at the Paramount Theatre. I have read and re-read all the playbills and the advertisements until I know them off by heart. There is great excitement because a concert party has been arranged in Holborn near where we are sleeping. Ma made the call and Joan and Evie are to join us here tonight.

Ever since she told me I have been as good as gold and she has become more lenient about the curfew. I've been back twice to Goodge Street but the secret door is firmly locked. I'm guessing they are busy at the Tilbury.

We take our places early and watch as the band set up with their shiny instruments. This whole section of the track has been boarded up and tube trains no longer pass through. Aggie has her best little frock on and I've got a clean shirt and on Ma's orders had my shoes cleaned by an old soldier. I'm looking around for Joan and Evie and suddenly here they are. Ma lets out a yelp, as they look so glamorous. Evie is all grown up in a brown tea dress and round-heeled shoes. The women's lips are a dark red colour, which Ma explains is beetroot. Evie smiles broadly for everyone but all I can get out of her is a hello before the swinging music starts up and we turn to watch the band. I stand as close to her as I can.

It's lovely and lilting and transports us away and we are no longer in a hot dark tunnel but at the Palais de Dance. People start moving to the rhythm, becoming couples, arms high, legs swishing, spinning like tops. The younger men in the reserved occupations start to pick off the prettiest girls.

'Spoilt for choice.' Says Ma.

'Foxes in a hen house.' says Joan.

'You watch it, says Ma. Will doesn't need another cousin.'

Evie gets the glad eye from the men. One of them, a soldier, comes across and asks her to dance. She sends him away with his cigarette wilting comically in his mouth. I want to ask her myself but I have no idea how to dance. Anyway, I haven't forgiven her for not being at school that day. Another man approaches and Joan rebuffs him but the dam isn't going to hold. I'll have to do something. I remember my stolen cigarette case. I've put three ciggies inside it, so I offer her one.

'You don't smoke William Lumley.'

'I do now.'

'Go on then.'

'I don't want one. I'm offering it you.'

'No, ta. Where did you get the case?'

'John Lewis.' I say, which is true. Did your friends tell you that I came to see you?'

'Where?'

'At your school.'

'Why was that then?' She says, folding her arms.

They are pale with downy golden hairs. Her fingers are long and tapered, piano playing, dressmaking fingers.

'I was bored.' I say. She never tells me anything directly. She looks me right in the eyes, hers are green and her brow is furrowed.

'So you just turned up *expect*ing that I would see you?'

I am beginning to understand. 'You *were* there, after all.'

'Maybe I was.'

She told her friends to run me a merry dance. What a mug. I don't want to apologise again. I'm always doing that.

'Well I was too. I was there for hours, and I *didn't* get killed by the bomb at Balham, thank you for asking.' I turn away and when I look back she has been whisked off. Like Mother like daughter. I am really cross now.

Auntie Joan is already out on the floor. A soldier with a funny accent approaches Ma for a dance. He says that he is a Canadian.

'I really shouldn't.' says Ma.

'You're damn right.' He says, with a smile like a Movie star. 'But where would we be if we didn't do things that we shouldn't?'

'Well… I can't then.' Said Ma, her eyes falling on Aggie.

'Then how about the princess here?' he tenders.

I can't see anyone who resembles a princess. I see a silly little girl in a party dress beaming with pleasure. I want to be sick.

He's down on his haunches in front of her. 'So your Ma has two wooden legs, huh?'

Aggie shakes her head.

'Tin legs?'

'My legs are perfectly fine thank you', says Ma nosing the air. 'And they will be dancing when my husband comes home from France.'

The Canadian serviceman gets up and bows gallantly. 'May I enquire if the princess would care for a spin?'

Aggie pleads and mewls and gets the nod from Ma. The Canadian lifts her up by the arms and as the band plays a waltz, he lowers her onto his shiny boots and she stays on his toes as he twirls her round and round. There is alcohol being passed around. Evie is a blur, a flash of skirt. Ma puts a hand on my shoulder but I shrug it away. I do not want her to have a good time. I hate this. Just as I think I will go off and run into the tunnel, it gets worse. I spot Perce, Ollie and Johnny seeping into the crowd as if they had been in camouflage. I go straight over.

'Where've you lot been?'

'Out and about.'

'Up the Tilbury.'

'I was looking for you.' I say, hoping to sound important.

'Why?' Perce keeps his eyes on the crowd, looking for mischief.

I need an excuse. Luckily I have a good one.

'I overheard the police. There's several kids gone missing in the tunnels.'

'So what?' Pipes up Johnny.

'I mean properly missing and they aren't going to do anything about it.'

Perce blows smoke in my face. 'What's in it for us? A finder's fee?'

'I've seen this face in a mask, coming out of the tunnels.'

'The Jerry?' Offers Johnny, sneering.

It's hopeless. No one cares. The police will only do something when a battalion of Storm Troopers comes belting out of the tunnels. Perce has his eye on the dancers. Evie is having a whale of a time and she and Auntie Joan are the centre of attention. They ought to be on the stage in a double act.

'That girl – what's her name?'

'Which one?'

'You blind? The one you was talking to earlier.'

'She's my cousin.' If he does anything I will kill him. Dead.

'She of age?'

I frown at him. Perce looks at me as if I am bait.

'How old is she?'

'Fourteen I think.'

'Near as damn it.' He cackles, and starts moving round the edge of the dance area.

I turn to Ollie. 'What does he mean?'

Ollie gurgles. 'You really are just a kid aren't you?'

'How old are you Oliver?'

'Old enough to know better than you.'

My fist balls up but there is nothing I can do. This is not a fight, not yet. If Evie wants to dance with Perce then she will dance with him. He's over there now waiting for his moment but the soldiers are keeping her to themselves. A wave of relief comes over me. I don't think he'll get a look in. Rather a grown-up soldier than Percy the ponce. I wish I could say something to her or do something that she would understand. I wish I was older and knew what to do. She doesn't even see me. I'm here Evie Wilde, right here, I want to shout but there is a big knot in my throat. The instruments sway and the music floats. Perce closes in, reaching out to say something to her, to make his introduction. I move instinctively, stepping through the dancers toward them but before I can get there I feel a grip on my arm and I'm pulled back into the crowd. At first I think its Ma, but as I turn to yell out at her for being such a meddling old… I see that the hand belongs to Mr. Sands.

'I think you need a spot of fresh air lad.'

Before I know it we are heading up the escalator to the booking Hall. There's only a few sleeping up here tonight, what with the excitement. Mr. Sands undoes the concertina metal gates and out we go into the night. There has been a light rain and the street is shiny. Kingsway is deserted and the scudding night clouds are grey and stodgy like mutton stew. He sniffs the air as we stroll towards Somerset House.

'No bloody Jerries tonight. A blessed relief.'

'Is it over?'

'Far from it. The last war took four years. This one's barely out of nappies.'

'Did you fight in the Great War?'

'Tank Corps. Excused boots for this one, thank the Lord in his infinite.'

The windows in the tall buildings are blinded by crisscross tape and blackout. Sandbags at their feet tie them to the ground. A light breeze hurries the leaves home. I prey that Evie has not responded to Perce's advances.

Sands stops.

'I want to apologise about running off the other day. Not a pleasant sight, first thing. Sorry Sonny Jim.'

'Do you know anything about the missing children?'

He nods carefully. 'It's not normal, eighty thousand people sleeping underground. They do as they please or go AWOL. It's a godsend for some.'

'You're *sure* it's not Germans down there?'

He snorts. 'Let me show you something.'

We come round the Strand to Waterloo Bridge. In the distance, searchlights are playing across the sky, lighting up the clouds and barrage balloons. Parts of the East End are still aglow from last night, but the rain has put most of it out. I look down at the water, rippling bible black and silver, dividing round the pillars.

'This is what will do for Jerry.' Says Sands.

'Water?'

'The channel, out beyond the Estuary. Might be only twenty miles across, but the last lot who made it across was eight centuries ago.'

'The Normans. We learned that at School.'

'Work hard lad. Get yourself some education.'

'My school was bombed out.'

'In any case – don't go becoming cannon fodder.'

'What's that?'

He produces his pipe and thumbs strands out of a pouch into the bowl. 'You join up as a Squaddie and they'll give you six weeks basic training and have you on the front line. However, if you learn a trade, like map reading, doctoring or something then you can be of use elsewhere.'

'But I want to fight.'

He lit a match and the bowl breathed fire. I hear his chest rattle. He shakes the match into the river. 'We all want to fight Son. The question is of survival.'

'What d'you mean?'

'In the Great War we lost thousands because the generals in their infinite bloody wisdom decided that sheer numbers was the way to overrun the German trenches. I saw boys mown down, gassed, dying screaming on the wire – some was begging to be shot by their own men – and all because some old Etonian wants to try out some half-baked battle plan.'

He drew deep. Before the wind whipped away the smoke I got a whiff of its sweet odour, much nicer than the cheap cigarettes Perce smokes, better even than Dad's Craven A's. We turn away from Southwark and head back up the road.

'Them spivs you're hanging out with. You want to watch them. Up to no good.'

It is strangely still, as if there were no one left in London at all. I hear the music, wafting up through a manhole, the band underground. Sands hears it too, a soft mournful back and forth melody that makes me think of an island far from anywhere in the middle of a crystal clear sea.

'You thinking about the girl?'

'Evie, my cousin.'

'You'll have a job with that one. She's popular. Bide your time.'

As the music swells up though the grate I get a tightness in my throat again. I hate to think of her down there surrounded by admirers, showing off to them, not even knowing that I exist. 'I can't even dance.' I say.

Sands cocks his ear to the grate as another tune starts up. 'I know this one. Come on, I'll show you.' He starts to move, dancing on his own, jerky at first like a puppet, but as the tune floats up and swells out in the night air he grows in confidence.

'This one's a slow Rumba. When you begin… the beguine.' He sings softly.

He raises one arm, puts the other by his hip and swivels round on his heels, stepping back and forth. I join in, imitating his moves, the space between us containing our invisible partners, mine, of course, being Evie. His, I don't know.

'That's it lad, let your feet take the rhythm of it.'

Round and round we go, spinning in the street, buoyed up by the music and for a moment free of care. I laugh at how silly we must look but Sands keeps his pipe firmly clenched in his teeth even though it has gone out.

When the song ends, the heavy lump inside me is smaller.

Chapter Eleven

October 27ᵗʰ

Ma has gone to see the people at the Council about a new home so I am in charge of getting food with Aggie. This means queuing at the grocer's with Ma's ration book. There is no more white bread. They have brought in a thing called the National Loaf, which is brown and salty and unpleasant and no one likes it. By the time we get there we are fifty or sixty people back. Because we are children no one talks to us, but I pick up the news. Mr. Morrison, the Home Securities Minster is going to introduce bunk beds for sleeping on the tubes and platforms. They are metal mesh and will allow people to get a proper night's sleep. In order to make it fair, there will be a ticket system. A penny-halfpenny each, first come, first served and no booking ahead. We'll see.

Aggie witters away, asking questions to which I have no answer for, so I have made up a series of things to say to her like. 'Ask Dad when he gets back from the war', or 'Because Mr. Churchill says so' or 'Because it is'.

'Let's play Happy Families.' She says.

'We play that all the time!' I have a dog-eared pack of cards. Some of them are missing just like in most real families.

'What's this – a mother's meeting?'

I look round. It's Perce and Ollie.

'Mind if we join you.' says Perce – but it's not a question and they shoulder their way in. This causes a commotion.

'You can't come in.' says Aggie.

Ollie says. 'Your brother saved us a place.'

I hesitate. People are glaring.

'No he didn't.' says Aggie, indignant.

Perce prods my shoulder. 'We're your mates, aren't we?'

'Course you are but…'

I smell his breath. It's rank. 'But what?'

A redoubtable woman appears. She wears a headscarf and has a florid face.

'You can't push in. We've been here for hours. Be off with you.'

'He was keeping our places.' Ollie says.

An old man pipes up. 'No barging in – who d'you think you are?'

Perce is tight-mouthed, gimlet-eyed. 'Tell them Will.'

I shake my head. 'You'll have to go to the back. It's the rules.'

'Whose rules?'

The red-faced woman stands her ground. 'British rules. Without them 'Itler would be all over us. Where's your parents?'

'We're war orphans.' Sneers Ollie.

'Orphans can queue the same as anyone.'

Perce leans in over my shoulder and hisses. 'We was only having a bit of fun. I could've got you whatever you want, off the ration, had you been nice, had you been polite. Like your cousin.'

I tense up. Is he telling the truth? Did he see her after the dance?

'We got work to do. Be at the den. Nine o' clock.'

Perce steps out and gives a low bow to the crowd. Some of them jeer and some blow raspberries as the pair saunter off, heads held high. Aggie squeezes my hand.

'Good lad, stick up for yourself.' Says the formidable woman. 'Bit of pluck.'

'We're all in it together.' Calls out an old man and people start agreeing and the queue moves forward with everyone in a better mood until they get inside the shop where there is next to nothing. No sugar, no cereal and no fruit.

There is a letter from Dad. It has been kept at the sorting office in Walworth. Ma picked it up when she went to see the council. I wanted her to open it immediately but she told us something as special as this could keep. Apparently the council can't re-house us yet as there isn't anywhere that has been declared safe in the municipal borough of Southwark. She is on a list. She cannot give them the telephone number at Swan & Edgar, as she is not allowed to receive or make calls there unless it is a 'dire emergency'. People are being told to 'Make do and mend' so the rich ladies are bringing their clothes to Ma's department. Yesterday she went to work in her slacks from the night before in the canteen and Mr. Bloody Watson said she was improperly dressed and docked her wages.

I hope Dad comes back and punches his lights out.

***

There's no places at Holborn and no sign of Sands so we travel down past Charing Cross to Lambeth North, from where you can see Waterloo through the tunnel. It's crowded and stinky and not full of the friendliest of people. I'll have an extra journey tonight. We eat our tea and Ma opens the letter and reads it out to us. Because of the censors it doesn't say much, except that he's made new friends and they are off somewhere soon with a more temperate climate, which Ma takes to be somewhere hot. She reads the rest to herself and there is a tear in her eye.

'When's he coming home on leave?'

'Doesn't say. Can't say.'

'He'll be back though, soon?'

'I don't know Will. Be thankful he's alive and well. He sends his love and there's a drawing – see?'

She shows Aggie and me his pencil scrawl on thin paper, a funny drawing of him in an outsize boots, hat and a tunic that's far too big. I smell the paper hoping for I don't know what, but it just smells of paper. I read a line, "Tell Will to look after you."

'Will he be home for Christmas?' Aggie asks.

'He says he will, my sweet. Come hell or high water.'

Ma gives a wistful smile and we settle back. I gaze at the tunnel mouth, hoping he might come marching out of the darkness. I lost his coat. Ma produces a cigarette and hunts for a light.

'Why did you start the smoking Ma?'

'Oh, I don't know. It's something to do.'

'Are they good for you?'

'People say so. For the chest.'

'You don't have a bad chest.'

She lights up and does not blow the smoke any better.

'You have to breathe it in.'

'Will, do be quiet.'

'Was it one of those soldiers who started you? The Canadian?'

'It was the women at the canteen.'

'Are you cross?'

'Course not.' she says, but she says it clipped like the women in the films.

People ought to say what they mean. She puts out the cigarette halfway through. I know a few old men round here who would collect that stub, unravel it and use the tobacco a second time. We watch Aggie playing with her doll, making up her stories.

Ma asks. 'Did you ever think he might be having a high old time?'

'Dad? But he's fighting?'

'I bet he's got a desk job. Born lucky, your dad. This papers' quality.'

She flutters it a moment and then slides the sheaves back in the envelope.

'What about the stamps?'

'Two four penny's. I can't read the post mark.'

I pore over it. It might be Durham or Dunkirk. I don't like the idea that Dad isn't fighting but as Sands says – if he's not then he won't be cannon fodder. It's horrid down here, people with their sweaty feet and stinky bedding. I get up to put on my coat.

'Where are you off to?'

'I said I would see some friends up West.'

'Don't you want to stay with your sister and me?'

I think for a moment. 'I promised them.'

'Those nasty boys from this morning?' asks Aggie.

'Yes.'

Ma sprouts a puzzled expression. I have to jump in quick.

'They're all right. I'll be back before lights out.'

'What are you doing?'

The lie comes easy. 'Playing cards.'

Ma's eyes go hard but she doesn't have the energy for another interrogation. The fight has gone out of her, despite the letter or maybe because of it. Instead, she reaches out a hand for me to take, which I do.

'Just be careful Will, and come back safe.'

The way that she says it makes me feel worse for suggesting going. After all, we are going to get into trouble. I walk along the platform edge toward the tunnel mouth. It looms dark, the arch over my head. I put a foot over the edge, hanging my shoe in space, wondering if what's in there is looking for fresh victims.

A tube comes in and stops at Waterloo. The floodgates have been closed and I cannot get under the river. I will have to go on foot. I come out in the busy terminal and look for the footpath to take me over the Charing Cross Bridge. It's pouring with rain, teeming down. The footbridge is closed so there is no way over.

Why am I risking everything for this? They can do without me. They won't be out in this anyway. I've all day to find them tomorrow. I will go back to Ma. It's time we had a family evening. It's time to celebrate. We heard from Dad. I have a couple of shillings in my pockets and with it I buy some hot fish wrapped in newspaper and take it back down.

***

Ma is in the middle of a huddle of mothers. There is a Station Marshal with her. Seeing me, Ma wails.

'She's gone missing. How could you? How could you not be here?'

She slaps me on the arm, hard, and then again and I don't say anything because there isn't anything I can say except sorry, and that becomes nothing after a time, doing about as much good as praying. The Marshal assures her that Aggie cannot have gone far, not out of the station. A policeman arrives. Black uniform, steel helmet like the ARP. Pencil, notebook. I hear bombs overhead, thudding on Kennington, Southwark and Bermondsey, the giant is angry tonight. Ma spills out the story.

'She was playing in the tot's area. I never had my eyes off her for more than five minutes. She's a good girl. Never leaves my side.'

83

I don't know why she has to talk about Aggie's character but it's true that Ag is a Mummy's girl. I treat her like my gas mask, extra weight, unwanted on journey. There are times when she says funny things and she doesn't have a bad bone in her body but she is a pain. The policeman is fat and old with whiskers and an air of having heard it all before. He establishes that she is Agatha Deidre Lumley, aged eight. Floral dress, beige socks and brown cross strap sandals. Brown hair, brown eyes and a blue coat and carrying a doll with one eye missing. That's not her. Those are facts or numbers like you get from the Ministry of Food and Shelter. He kneels down to me and I hear his knees crack. He needs more milk, the backbone of young Britain.

'Where were you when this happened lad?'

'Outside.'

'During a raid?'

'You have to send a search party into the tunnels.'

'All in good time. Does she usually go wandering off on her own?'

'Never. There's something in the tunnels.'

'Could she be with friends elsewhere?'

I shake my head.

'Play mates?'

'I don't know her playmates.'

'You don't know very much lad.'

I want to badger him about the missing children but he's already turning back to Ma.

'Can't do much now. Tomorrow, as soon as they open up, I suggest you and the boy go stand by the entrance, see if she doesn't come out by then.'

'What about the tunnels?' I say, more loudly.

'Be a good lad, look after your Ma. Things'll look better in the morning.'

He throws me a stern look that says not to ask again and tells Ma that if Aggie does not appear then she is to report to West Central Police Station. The policeman and Marshal go off, assuring others that all will be well.

Things will not be better in the morning because London is full of dead and dying and soon there will be nothing left of us.

***

It is after midnight and Ma is all in. She can't keep her eyes open. As soon as her breathing slows I creep toward the tunnel past the Elsan toilet. There is a gas rattle on the wall so I borrow it. The tunnel is an open mouth. Aggie would not have followed anyone in. She would not have gone willingly.

I have only a box of matches I took from the boys in the den. In the dark gulley between the tracks the tube mice are scrambling round, hunting for food. They dart in and out, finding impossible holes, searching out bits of bread or fruit peel or nosing the cigarette butts. That's it!

Aggie would have befriended them, named them, tried to get one to come close and play. There is a strong earthy odour mixed with cinder and soot. I light a match but see nothing in front of me but silver shining rails. As the station recedes, the tracks sling low into a dip, the gentle curve straight to Waterloo. There is just enough light to see by. I hear the snoring of the masses behind me.

Then.

A faint cry.

A female cry, more like a yelp. Someone being held against their will.

I surge forward between the rails. I am only a few yards in when out of nowhere a shape looms, a pointed, clawed thing slashes at me. There is pain as it finds my flesh. I feel a thunder of what might be wings, its rage. I fall away – almost into the arms of another – this one in a long cloak and a huge rubber gas mask, the ventilator swinging wildly, a writhing tentacle. Without thinking I raise the gas rattle, twirling it above my head and let out a terrific rat-a-tat-tat that echoes off the ancient tunnel walls.

It goes off like an AA gun.

Daka daka daka.

I rattle it until I have no energy left and it slows to a gentle ticking. I hear angry noises from back on the platform, sleepers awakening. I've scared them off, whatever they are. I gasp for breath, trying to slow my inhalations as we were taught on gas mask drill. I need to silence the drumming in my ears so I can hear Aggie again. Waterloo is up ahead but after that the steel floodgates will shut off the tunnel. They cannot get far up that way. If they're not to be discovered they must come back towards me. If I keep going I... I can't do this alone. They'll lash out again, whatever they are, man or beast, flesh or fowl. I light match after match, revealing a series of dark arches set into the tunnel walls. There's room in there to avoid passing trains. They can't hide in there. They will have to come out at Waterloo. I have to go forwards, flush them out. I pace up the rise and come round the curve and get another terrific shock.

There are three of them spread out across the line.

They are tall, hooded creatures. Two are wearing gasmasks; one has an impossibly long pointed beak. They glide toward me. I do not need to be told twice. I turn tail and bolt back the way I came, skipping, jumping over the tracks. The amber light of Lambeth North looms large as I head for safety. I leap back onto the platform and collapse in a wet sweat. I can feel them, their hands, their claws, whatever on my ankles. I kick back as hard as I can until I pull myself free. I scramble to my feet and bolt along the platform. I rush to Ma and sink down, wrapping my bedding around me, shuddering. I look at the tunnel mouth. Black nothingness. The energy drains out of me. This is all one awful waking nightmare.

***

Next morning outside the Station entrance, Ma's face is a mask of concern. Her eyes dart across the children's faces like a radar of hope. It is a cold grey day and spats of rain daub the pavement until it is proper wet and the eddying leaves go damp. Smuts are blowing about from last night's fires and getting in our eyes. The crowd thins and Ma decides we will go to the police, so we take the bus.

The Thames is sluggish and swollen, with a few small boats fighting the wind. West Central Police Station is a square white building behind Charing Cross. The entrance hall smells of polish and the Desk Sergeant takes our names and tells us to wait on a long padded bench. Policemen come and go, some on duty, others going home. A couple of mad people are released from the cells, wide-eyed and lost. Ma sits rigid, not seeing any of it. There is a big white clock with black hands that says seven forty-seven.

'Ma – aren't you going to be late for work?'

She barely nods.

'Won't you be in trouble with Mr. Watson?'

'Doubtless.'

'Why don't I stay? I can tell them all we know.'

'I have to give the information.'

'But you told the policeman last night. I've got plenty of time.'

'They need an adult.'

'You said I had to be the adult now.'

She looks at me and I see the worry of her years: about me when I first rode my bike and fell off it, about Aggie when she upturned a pan of boiling water on the stove. When she speaks I notice a little downturn to her mouth. Ma was always smiling before the war, even when we lost Gran. Even pretending on the day Dad went off to war.

'You're all I have Will.'

'I know.'

'You've got to tell them everything you know.'

'I will. You bet.'

She hugs me and I sink into the warm smell of her, the soap, or maybe perfume from her work. She produces a compact and puts her face back on.

'You tell 'em where I work and give them the number at Swan & Edgar. Explain we were sleeping at Lambeth North but usually it's at Holborn Kingsway where we're to get a berth.' She kisses me on the cheek. 'Bless you love. Come tell me all later.'

She hurries off through the double doors and I'm glad I made her feel better.

After half an hour Ma's name is called and I go to the desk. A suited man leads me through several sets of glass doors until we get to a bare room. There are tiles halfway up, then a green coloured line and the rest of the walls and ceiling are grey. There is a table and two chairs, both of which scrape when he asks me to sit. He has a file, which he reads, in no hurry. He gets out a pen, unscrews it and makes a few marks here and there before looking up. He has a pudding face, neither kind nor cruel. I thought detectives were supposed to be deadly handsome but he's not. He's too old to fight, I can tell that.

'So what's to be done?' He asks, flatly.

'You need to make a proper search. It's not just my sister gone.'

A pause. 'How so?'

'For the things that are taking the kiddies.'

He raises an eyebrow. We're playing a game where he says as little as he can. I don't care if he wins so I speak out, with my face burning.

'I overheard two policemen. I know there are several kids who have gone and I've seen who's taking them. I got attacked by them in Lambeth North last night. There's three, maybe more.'

'Three what?'

'Things. Beasts. One's got a gas mask, the other a great long beak.'

'In the tube tunnels?'

'Yes.' I say, loudly.

He looks at me without blinking.

'Have you been caught in a bomb blast, or near one?'

'Not lately.'

'So you have?'

'I missed Balham just. My house was bombed but that a long time ago.'

He writes something in the folder. 'What are you writing?'

'It's not easy for anyone, son, living through this. Here today, gone the next. I expect you've seen plenty of distasteful sights in the last month or so?'

'So what? You have to *do* something.'

He weighs his words, leaning forward on his elbows. 'I'm not denying there are missing children. There are, however, a great deal more missing adults, those who we don't find in bits every time 'Itler pays us a night time visit. Our resources are stretching to breaking. We'll keep an eye out for Agatha but let's not hear any more ghost stories, eh?'

'They're real. They attacked me last night in the tunnel.'

'In pitch darkness?'

I feel it all draining away.

'They're calling it shock, son. Shell shock. Apparently you can be several yards away from a bomb blast but the effects are in your mind. You start seeing and hearing things, behaving oddly. We're getting all sorts in here and in the hospitals.'

'But it's true.'

'To you, yes. I suggest you and your Ma find some friends or relatives outside of London and get a few nights good kip, God knows we could all do with it.'

'No. I'll tell. I'll tell people about the missing kids and the things in the tunnels.'

He releases a metallic squeak from the chair leg.

'We don't want a panic. There's a lot of shelterers down there and if you spook them, where are they going to go? We'll have a riot on our hands. Can't have that. We're all on the same side.'

'Doesn't look much like it.'

He sighs through his nostrils. 'If you bring about dissent we'll have to take you in.'

'But I haven't done anything.'

'I know you're young, William, but causing civil unrest in time of war is a very serious charge. Do you understand me?'

I thought of the people who clamoured to be let in at the East End Underground Stations a few weeks ago who only wanted to protect their families. About Stoke Newington when a hundred and ninety-seven people died when a cement shelter collapsed. It was never reported but we heard about it at the Tilbury.

'Do you understand?'

I nod once.

'Then let's hear no more about beasts in the tunnels and let us do our job, ok.'

I understand, but that does not mean I will do what he says.

***

Wandering out, I cross Trafalgar Square and head for the Dilly, I have one thought. I've got to enlist the gang; Holborn is the place to start. The West End stations are closer together so it'll be easy to move between them. We'll need to cover the Northern line from Goodge Street down to Waterloo, the Piccadilly from here to Russell Square and the Central from Holborn to Oxford Circus. We'll go tonight when the electricity is off.

First I need some kip so I go to the 6/- Newsreel cinema in Lower Regent Street. Inside there are a few people dotted about. They've all had the same idea, sheltering from the cold or bombs or from life. I take a seat near the front and wrap up warm. The Pathé News is met with no reaction. We are making great inroads in France and our Commonwealth allies are pouring in from all around the world to help. Here at home we are bearing up and showing great Blitz spirit. There is a short film of people being given tea and buns at Knightsbridge station. The cinema is a cloud of blue smoke. I loll my head back to look at the twinkling lights on the ceiling.

I'll find Aggie.

I'll beat the bloody Jerries.

I will.

I am Will.

William.

When I look down again there is a man in uniform standing by the curtain at the exit. He beckons to me and I realise that it is Dad. I almost jump out of my seat but something seems wrong. I can't see his face properly. I can't move: my body is too heavy. He doesn't speak and I still hear the newsreel voice, repeating the same story from before. Dad's gesture becomes more insistent. He pulls back the curtain but instead of the exit door there is the black arch of the tube tunnel. Out of it slithers a huge fat slimy worm, glistening with horrible juices. It has no face, just a smooth rounded off stump with two long blind slits for eyes. It swells and grows and fills the tunnel, swaying from side to side as it moves out toward me. I scream but there is no sound. I try to turn my head to warn the others but I cannot move my neck. As the black worm emerges, it shrinks, smaller and smaller, more like a snake now as it twists under the seats. It goes under the first row and the second and the backs of the seats rise and buck as it forces them up, like soil off its back. The head of it sticks up, two seats in front of me and hovers there, trying to get the smell of me. It changes slowly into the sharp ebony beak of a crow. Its pincer jaws snap open like scissors, or like Mr. Punch with his wooden slapsticks. The beak stretches wider and wider still and in my head I scream and scream and suddenly I'm awake. I look round at the other people in the auditorium, sleeping, cursing, spitting.

We are all having a bad dream.

Chapter Twelve

October 28th

Action Stations. I meet up with Ma at Swan & Edgar to tell her that the police have assured us they will be on red alert, number one priority. We get fish and chips for tea and Ma manages to secure a bunk bed and is feeling brighter after talking to her workmates. She has decided to go to work on the refreshment tube so she can put the word out herself and have the best chance of finding Aggie. This fits right in with my plan.

I am charged with looking after the bunk but once she's gone I make friends with the woman in the next berth, explaining that I have to go do war work and can she keep our places? She agrees and I head off.

The secret door at Goodge Street is unlocked. I find the light switch and make my way along the workman's corridor, down the curving steps, along the wet passage by the breezeblocks behind the trains and right up to the den. No time to waste. Low candlelight spills out of the workroom and I hear voices inside. Perce, Ollie and Johnny are playing cards. I go straight into my speech.

'My sister's been taken. She's in the tunnels.'

'Jerries again is it?' Offers Perce.

'There are lots of kiddies gone missing. One's been killed.'

Ollie. 'Killed how?'

'A tube train hit him.'

Johnny claps his hands together.

Perce. 'What d'you expect us to do about it?'

'Help me find her. We can search the tunnels, the Northern Line, the Dilly and—'

Ollie breaks in. 'what – *all* the tunnels?

'In the West End. She's—'

Perce. 'And when d'you want us to do that?'

'Once the current is turned off.'

'What about the Rozzers? Why ain't they gone looking?'

'Too busy. They don't want people to panic.'

Perce leans into the light so his face is lit from under. 'Where was you last night?'

'The train stopped at Waterloo.'

'I said we needed you.'

'I couldn't get over the bridge. I was stuck down South.'

Ollie. 'Why didn't you go over another bridge?'

'It was closed off.'

Johnny makes a noise like I'm a big baby. Ollie joins in and soon they are both mocking me and I realise I sound like a weakling. I want to punch them hard – as Dad says, knock some sense into them. Perce holds up a hand for silence.

'What's in it for us? Is there a ransom?'

I shake my head.

'If it's the brat you was hanging around with in the queue the other day, you looked more like you wanted to be rid of her.'

I feel my face get hot. Dad says to use your loaf and people will listen to reason.

'What if it was one of your sisters?'

'I don't have no sister.' Sneers Johnny.

I look helplessly from one to the other. Ollie and Johnny are waiting on Perce, who has a fixed expression I cannot fathom. I never know what he's thinking, which must be what makes him the leader, that and being older and bigger.

'Are you going to help?' I try, for the last time.

Silence, except for a train rumbling past in the distance.

'Then you're all cowards!'

Feathers ruffled, Johnny clambers to his feet but Perce waves him down.

'Enough of that.' He says.

'What else would you call yourselves then?'

'I am not a bloody coward.' Yells Johnny, lurching towards me.

He swings his fist but I turn away and he only gets a glancing blow on my chest and falls back, stumbling over the loot. I crash my fist down on his back and I feel more pain than I ought. I remember. I still have the livid scar from the candle, the initiation. As Johnny comes at me again I hold up my palm like a Red Indian, so they can all see.

'I did this for you. You said I was one of you. You've got a duty to help me out.'

Johnny freezes. I have played my trump card. They look to Perce, the keeper of opinion and instruction, lawgiver and kingmaker. In a flash his expression changes. With a wolf like smile he rubs his hands together.

'Will, old son, you are spot on. We was only ribbing you, see where you stood. Course we'll find the girl.'

***

We congregate at Aldwych with a plan to walk up the boarded up tunnel to Kingsway Holborn and then split into pairs. We start picking our way among the sleeping bodies on the escalators calling out her name. This only serves to rouse the sleepers who grumble and fuss, which in turn annoys Johnny, who will not be told.

'We're looking for a girl, right.' He announces, belligerently.

'Do it quietly then.'

'And when you found one,' says an old cockney. 'Find one for me.'

We are in a foot tunnel heading towards the platform when I hear a faint cry, short and sudden. I stop to listen. A girls' cry. The children are being kept at the eastbound end and that's too far for an echo. I put my ear to the grimy tile. I think I can hear my name, faint and growing fainter coming from behind the wall.

'I hear her!' I call out.

We hunt for a hidden entrance like the one at the den, clambering over tree trunk legs and humps and lumps of blankets and bodies, not caring if we disturb people or not. They moan and roll out of the way, disturbed and disgruntled. Ollie uses a metal torch to drum the wall to see where it might be hollow, drawing more complaints from the shelterers. Perce, our overseer, brings us to attention.

'We're making a spectacle. She's in the tunnel. Let's get in there.'

***

At Kingsway the trail grows cold. I'm bristling with excitement to have heard something so soon. She's somewhere near. The chase is on. Perce pairs me with Johnny to patrol the Piccadilly Line to Covent Garden and to rendezvous with him and Ollie at Leicester Square. He gives me a torch but as soon as Johnny is in the dark, he demands it. I refuse but he keeps on.

'My eyes ain't all that good. Give us it.'

I carry on. He climbs over the third rail and tries to grab it off me, making the light splash about on the brick roof. 'Get off.' I hiss.

'Then gimme the torch.'

Johnny barges into me and it goes flying, clanging off the rail. It goes out. He scrambles for it, never afraid of getting dirty. I hear his sour voice.

'It's broke in two. Can't find one of the batteries.'

'Let's just keep going.'

'In pitch black?'

'We'll be at the next station soon.'

'There's nothing in here. Let's go back.'

The thrill of the hunt has drained out of him. He's no longer interested now that there's no one to show off to. A silent tunnel offers nothing for him to attack or bully. 'We're to meet the others at Leicester Square.' I say.

'I'm going back.'

'You scared?'

'Course not. This is stupid. I don't care about your sister.'

'You agreed to it.'

'So what?'

We fall silent, walking in tandem but I become aware he's hanging back and soon he stops dead.

'Are you coming or what?'

Nothing. He plays this sullen game to get what he wants and I'm not going to let him. I take a few steps back and locate the torch pieces. Fumbling round, I'm able to fish out the batteries and put it together again. I flash it on and all I can make out is the back of him bobbing away back toward the station, no doubt to make up some lie about me. Well, he can says what he likes. This is more important.

I listen for any sound. I feel that presence again, close, a sixth sense. A foreboding like when the bombs fall and the air compresses. Out of the blackness something reaches for me. I bend at the knees, drop down, falling back over the live rail, between the tracks. I lay still. My eyes are growing accustomed to the dark and I do not like what I see. That big grey gas mask, hovering above me, the asthmatic wheeze of its respirator and above, bat like wings unfurling, stretching out impossibly wide to encircle and swallow me. I grip the long barrel of the metal torch and with all my strength, hurl it at the demon. It hits one of its glass eye pieces, which cracks and splinters. A bestial howl. I hit it. I hurt it! I got it. I roll away and leap to my feet but it has gone. Where? How can it disappear into a solid brick tunnel? I hunt for the torch, get it working again and find that the feeble light it produces penetrates only a few feet. It won't last. The thing has gone, like a magic trick. I slap the walls looking for some kind of secret passage. There must be something. They must have a way of getting around down here. It can't spirit Aggie right through London brick. The torch flickers out. Damn and blast. I shake it. Nothing.

Wait.

Under my feet there is a glimmer of pale light, under the rails. It flickers an instant, moves along and then goes out. I shake the torch and it gives out enough light to make out a manhole. That's the answer. It is like a crossword; if you don't go across you go down. I shine the torch down into the dark and it swallows the light. All I can see is a metal ladder on one side, an inspection shaft. I start to climb down.

If it ran then maybe it is as scared as I am.

I go hand over hand, rung after rung. Clang, clang, go my shoes.

The ladder ends.

The void.

I swing a leg, reach with my toes, nothing.

I try the torch again – sweeping it beneath me. There is ground below, about three or four feet. I jump down onto a railway sleeper and fall awkwardly, turning my ankle over, a sharp pain, which I massage until it softens. I put my weight on my foot. It's just about ok. The rails here are closer together. A railway under the railway, tunnels beneath tunnels. The arch of it is smaller too. Any train running down here could not possibly carry passengers. I can only just stand upright at the highest point. Which way did the thing go?

I walk, using the torch sparingly to conserve batteries.

After a minute I hear a low rumble. The noise grows and behind me in the distance I make out twin stars. Headlights. A bloody train moving toward me! To my horror I realise that it will fill the whole tunnel and there will be no space and I will be crushed against the wall. Without thinking I dart as fast as I can back to the shaft where I came down, praying that I will have enough time. My ankle is agony but I don't care. I run full pelt right at the train. It's madness but it is my only choice. The torch picks out the hole above.

I leap for the ladder.

I miss.

The train is fifty yards away. Forty yards. Fear sluices through my body. I crouch on my heels, cram the torch in my deep coat pocket and spring upwards. Twenty yards.

I get my fingers on and grab the lowest rung. I swing up.

Ten yards. I scrabble hand over hand, two rungs, three, one leg up, now both.

The train thunders past below.

I glimpse its roof, covered in metal ridges as it clacks away along the rails. When I am able to breathe again I release my grip and drop down after it. I flash the torch on the rear of the train. There is a dirty brown crest: The Royal Mail. This must be how they get around, using the under-tunnels, clambering in and out of the inspection shafts.

There won't be another along soon. I start to walk, stepping gingerly on my bad ankle, following the curve of the tunnel. It's so quiet here. In the tube tunnels you always hear the muted snoring of people back on the platforms and if it's close to the surface the stamping of the angry giant. Sometimes the all-clear penetrates, but here it's silent as snow.

This is Old London; the place that Sands warned me was full of ghosts.

Here, the blackness bubbles and boils in my mind and out of it a dim glow forms, pencilling in a line of brickwork and a row of low arches beside the tracks. The fourth one along reveals a short tunnel, which leads off at ninety degrees from the rail track. I duck down and go through, entering a short antechamber. The torch reveals a higher vaulted roof, maybe eight feet, and below me the ground is dry dirt. Other low tunnels lead off in several directions, each one only four or five feet in height. A maze. There is a metallic taste to the air. I hear water, a series of rhythmic drips. I choose one of the passages, ducking down as I scurry along. The drips become a flow and then a torrent.

I keep going until I come across a big circular grid on the wall. Behind it, water rushes down, through and away below. It stinks, foul and rotten – the sewers. There must be a river running beneath my feet. I carry on past. The tunnel kinks and I am sure that it is getting smaller and damper. Just when I think it will shrink down to nothing there is a low arch and I have to drop to my hands and knees to go through to another chamber.

I turn off the torch. My heart is thudding. There is some light up ahead. I follow the flicker and find myself in a high arched space, maybe forty feet square. A huge cavern illuminated by paraffin lights and in the middle, three rows of old wooden school desks piled high with schoolbooks. I recognise the history one, the geography one, and the logarithm tables. The Shakespeare. There is a row of pegs on the long wall opposite and on them a row of child's gas masks hang beside their cardboard boxes. At one end of the room is a blackboard, one of the movable one's on castors. There is writing on it. It looks German. It doesn't make sense. Is this a training place? If there are desks then where are the children? The desks are old, pitted and cut by a thousand compasses, the inkwells as dark as the dead eyes of the beast that tried to get me. What's a classroom doing down here, so far beneath the surface? Is it a relic from a previous age? From the Victorians? I hear a muffled sound. Over on a low bench I glimpse what looks like a doll in a child's orange coverall rubber gas mask.

It is Aggie.

Aggie is in the mask with her hands tied. I unbuckle it and her head lolls. Her hair and face are wet and hot and damp. I pick at the ropes and in moments I have her freed. She's pale and scared. I take her hand.

'Let's get you out, ok?'

She nods feebly. I carry her back through the schoolroom to the tiny passage. It is hard work to get her through and I have to almost drag her along. We get to the grate and the gully where the water rushes past. The smell is so awful that it revives her like smelling salts. She cries out.

'My doll – I must have my Jemima.'

'Aggie, for God's sake, we have to get away from here.'

Her face crumples up and her lower lip starts to tremble and I am annoyed that I bothered to come all this way for her and all she can think of is her bloody stupid dolly. But if she cries out we are both sunk.

'Wait here, ok?'

I rush back and scan the classroom for her doll. I start opening up the desks, letting the wooden lids clatter back down until at the end of the row I find the stupid thing. I hear a sound. I freeze. I have disturbed the things. There are feet on cobbles and a rustle that sounds like a heavy bird fluttering in a cage. I don't wait to see what it is. I bolt back, almost yelping as my ankle gives out more pain. I drop down into the low tunnel, crawling on my hands and knees until I get to Aggie.

I scoop her up and charge back to the room and then we head for the tunnel where the Mail train is. She clings to her doll and to me. I hop, skip and jump along the rails and all of the pain from my foot is forgotten. It seems an age before we find the chute above us. I am not even sure it is the same one. I lift her up onto my shoulders and get her to hunt about for the rung. She finds it and I coax her to climb up, hand over hand, as fast as she can. Once she is safely up I crouch and leap, grabbing the lowest rung and hauling myself up into the shaft.

There is a rush of I don't know what – it sounds like wings – and feet thundering past. I don't know how many. They disappear off as we crouch in silence.

I push Aggie to scramble up; up toward the top, whispering urgently to her that we will be all right and that there will be light and safety up there, but I do not really know this at all and I pray that it won't be the street level or that London is on fire.

'It's closed.'

'What?'

'It's shut. I can't open it.'

We have got to get out.

'Aggie, go down under me and hold on.'

Carefully, we rearrange ourselves as she clambers down past me. When I get right to the top I first try the manhole myself and when it will not give I put my back to it. One-two-three-heave. Nothing. I brace and try again. Two-three-heave. This time there's the tiniest of movements, a bit of give. A third time the heavy iron cover lifts and I am able to move it aside, sliding it off my back. I push it aside with my fingers and put my head up above the ground.

Above, it is just as dark and there are the rails above me, but there is something on top of them. I get the torch and flash it around. It is solid, like a coffin. I knock on it and realise that it is wooden board. I knock again and from the other side there comes a response. We crouch into a ball, holding one another. I knock again.

Rat-a-tat-tat.

I hear two knocks in response.

Tat tat.

I recognise this as a friendly answer. There is a scuffling above us as the board is pried upwards and moved away. There is light from paraffin lights and shapes. People.

'What the blooming heck you two doing down there?'

It is an old man, flanked by a couple of cross-armed women.

'Gas board?" I offer.

'Come on, out of there you two.'

As we are pulled up I realise we are back at Holborn Kingsway on the Aldwych branch line, the one that was boarded over – barely a few hundred yards from where we're sleeping. I can't stop it. I begin to laugh. A giggle that sucks Aggie in and soon we are both convulsed in laughter. We are black from soot, filthy dirty. The shelterers are amazed at two kids climbing out of the bowels of the earth but I don't want to answer their questions. I explain that we have to go and find my Ma and that Aggie was the child who was missing in action the previous day.

Aggie hugs me and on tiptoes gives me a kiss.

'Euurgh', I say.

She beams. 'Let's go and wake Ma.'

***

Her face is a picture; going from drowsy to wide-awake and leaking tears in a moment. She scoops Aggie up in her arms and waltzes her round by the bunk bed laughing. She grabs me and pulls me into a hug and I allow her to, even though there are people watching. She is not at all interested at all in how Aggie came to be back here with me, just happy that we are safe and sound not blown to bits by bombs.

After a while she puts on her serious face and using one of her magic hankies she dabs at Aggie, checking her for damage. Satisfied, she gets us some hot tea and a couple of slices of bread and soon Ag is cuddling her doll and she is as right as rain. I think I'll never sleep again. I'm alive with my heroic act and aching to figure out what was going down underneath us – the meaning of the schoolroom, the location of the hidden lair. I have learned so much more now about how they get around. I need Sands to maybe get me a map of the underground Postal Railway, the access points and everything so that we can trap them, whoever, whatever they are.

I'm still turning it all over in my mind when I fall fast asleep.

***

Ma is taking both of us to the British café in Chancery Lane for breakfast. Special treat. As we rise up the escalator, people sink down to go to work in bowler hats and suits. Up by the booking office Sands is sleepily trawling the ticket stubs.

'Turned up then has she? Told you they don't go far.'

I nod and smile but it isn't until we are up top that it comes to me. I never told him about Aggie going missing. I turn to Ma.

'Can I go and talk to Mr. Sands?'

She's ok about it. She would be fine about me going off to become a Spitfire pilot after saving Aggie's life. I trot back, unsure of what to say. Sands is in the little office behind the glass-paneled door. I knock. Another man opens it, tall and gangling with his hair shaven at the back. He carries a copy of *The Daily Worker*.

'What can I do you for, Sonny Jim?'

'Can I speak to Mr. Sands please?'

'Archie?'

He's bent over a small primus, on top of which is a blackened kettle. He beckons me inside. 'You're a bit of a mess this morning.'

'Can I ask you something?'

He offers me a stool. I remain standing.

'How did you know about my sister?'

'We do talk, the Station masters and Shelter Marshal's.'

I press on. 'Then you'll know that there's half a dozen children gone missing.'

'That's the rumour.'

'It's not a rumour.'

He raises his eyebrows and moves the kettle, which is coming to the boil. 'Bert, you mind clipping tickets for a bit while I speak to the lad?'

Bert rolls up his newspaper and clips me round the head with it on his way out.

'Kids.' He says.

Sands is more welcoming. 'Sit yourself down and tell me what you know.'

I tell him about my adventure while he fiddles with the pot and strainer and fetches blue-and-white-banded cups and his secret supply of sugar lumps. He grips the bottle of milk to see if it's cold and fresh. I tell him about getting the gang to explore the tunnels. The tea brews and he pours it out. I drink the hot sweet liquid as fast as I can even though it burns my tongue. When I tell him about the train with the crest, he perks up.

'That'll be the Post Office Underground. They've got their own line that takes the mail from Paddington to Clerkenwell and Whitechapel. It runs right under here, goes on under the viaduct down to the sorting office at Mount Pleasant.'

'Can you get me a map?'

'Probably, why?'

'They're using it to get around. I found this place, a sort of classroom. Aggie was being kept there.'

'A what?'

'I'm sure it's the Jerries.'

'Did you see any?'

'I saw one dressed in a long coat and a gas mask.'

'You been reading too many Penny Dreadful's.'

'What would they be doing in the sewers and tunnels Sands?'

He sips his tea. 'Don't ask me.'

'There was another one. It looked like big crow with a huge beak. It bit me on the arm.'

Sands sits thinking as steam from the kettle gently evaporates in the air. I hope he is going to come up with some kind of brilliant solution but I am shocked and surprised by what he says next.

'Will, I don't want you telling no one about this. For starters the tunnels aren't safe. For second, we've enough trouble what with Adolph chucking all he's got at us. We've got to keep up morale.'

The party line.

'But Aggie was captured and there are other children down there.'

'Did you see any?'

'No, but—'

'—Or hear 'em, make any contact – any faces or names?'

I open my mouth but nothing comes out. He scratches the white stubble that has sprouted on his chin overnight.

'Will, we're all scared. There's no shame in admitting it.'

'What's that go to do with what I saw.'

He chooses his words. 'We've had one poor kiddie hit by a train and your sister found after a day. You're the only one what's seen whatever it is. I see the Law calling that 'overactive imagination.''

'But it's true.'

'From a boy who likes his comic books.'

'But they know, the police.'

'And I'll fill them in later about what you've told me. Leave it to me.'

'You promise?'

He looks at me in a way that Dad sometimes does. Did. A way that says 'don't question a grown-up.' *Do* adults always know everything? I used to think they did and I trusted my dad completely until, well, until he sent me and Aggie away.

'Finish your tea.'

It tastes so sweet that normally I would have wiped my finger around inside the cup but I don't feel like it today. Sands stands and takes it from me. There is a little white porcelain sink in the corner and he makes a nest for them there.

'I don't want you going in the tunnels again. That's got to be a promise.'

'But the things I saw…?'

The cups clatter. 'I don't care what you think you saw. If I hear you been nosing round in there again, you and your Ma might find it difficult getting a bunk.'

My heart sinks. I cover my face. I don't even look up when he places a big old leathery hand on my shoulder and softens his tone.

'I'm sorry Lad. I've got responsibilities to half the population of London it seems like. You leave this to me and I'll see it gets sorted. The police have got a lot more to go on now. You found your sister safe. You're the hero of the hour. Enjoy it.'

Next thing I know I am fumbling the brass doorknob open and running up the stairs. I have one thought in my mind. Proof. I am going to get proof.

It's a proper London fog outside, what they call a pea-souper. Broken facades of the buildings loom out of the gloom like a stage set. There is no colour anywhere at all. There is the usual stink of burnt wood and ash and cordite but here and there you catch a cooking smell – mutton – drifting on the air. People are wrapped in coats with the collars held up. Ma will be fussing about scarves and gloves. If the fog stays all day, the bombers won't be able to find their targets tonight.

I find the British cafeteria. Outside, strips of ARP brown tape on the big window spell out the words. "Carry On – Don't Panic". Inside it is steamy hot and buzzing with news of those who bought it in the last raid. Oxford Street was hit bad again and there has been bombing to the West in Fulham and Chelsea. Some are worried it will spread further but others are convinced the more likely targets are munitions dumps in the north, the Arsenal and railway depots around Finchley. About time North London got some.

Aggie has put her finger on the window and the moisture has run down the glass in rivulets. They've had half a sausage each and there is a whole one for me along with toast. My conquering hero, says Ma, ruffling my hair. I eat as she chats away. I'm glad we are all back in the fold again and I relish the food. I forgot how incredibly hungry I was. I slowly realise Aggie is not saying anything, as though she has been given a telling off. I tune in to what Ma is saying—

'I've had enough of bombs every night and not knowing if you two will be alive or dead in the morning. She adds in her "that's final" voice. 'So I've made up my mind.'

'To do what Ma?'

'I'm sending you both away.'

Chapter Thirteen

I have my objections. 'Away where?'

'To the countryside.'

'We were evacuated before and we hated it. You fetched us back.'

Ma sighs. 'It won't be Wales this time. Somewhere closer.'

'What if they're horrid people again?'

'I'll come visit. Make sure they're acceptable.'

I stuff sausage in my mouth. 'I don't see what use we'd be to anyone.'

'They're telling us all to turn every bit of land to good use. All hands to the pump.'

'They won't want the two of us.'

Ma lights a cigarette. 'We'll have to see what turns up.'

'I can be useful here, helping the war effort.'

She rubs her eyes. 'How's that Will?'

'The Boy Scout fire-watching troupes, the boys on bicycles.'

'We don't have a bicycle.'

'They'll lend me one.'

'You're under age for fire watching.'

I'm losing this argument. 'I'd be no use to any farmer.'

'I'm not saying you have to go on a farm.'

'I don't want to anyway.'

'You'll be safe out of London.'

''Itler's not getting me out of where I live.'

'You live in a filthy tube tunnel and I've had enough. It's not forever. You're going and that's that.'

I won't go to some smelly farm. It's cold and dark and you have to get up before dawn and work all day until you're so tired that you can't stand. It stinks of shit and everywhere is muddy and there are no streets or people for miles. You can't even understand what the people are saying and they make you go to church.

I prefer the bombs and the ghosts.

November 4th

It's stopped. Fifty-seven nights of bombing and last night there were no sirens. Everyone was all hunched up as if waiting for a smack, like the calm before a storm when the birds go quiet and animals hide. People started to give each other puzzled looks. Is it a malfunction? A trick to fool the Jerries? To fool us?

We did what we always do – queue up and get down to the shelter. You can't trust anyone so we all waited. After a quarter of an hour, a thrill of anticipation spread among the shelterers. What if it is over? That'd be Christmas come early. Maybe the Jerries have run out of bombers, or bombs, or the Air Force turned them back at the channel or the AA guns have blasted them all out of the sky? If they've given up then that means Ma cannot send me away.

We sat and waited for reports to filter through.

Some of the older wardens and fire fighters have been saying that 'Itler has done us all a favour by clearing the slums. Bet they're regretting that traitor talk now. There's always suspicion down here, of anyone sounding foreign, or acting different or having things that aren't British like the Balkan Sobranie cigarettes. We're Londoners here. We *are* London. The Ministry of Information has people asking questions, officially, but we don't like talking to them because it's like telling tales at school. Some of them *are* teachers I think. I wonder what happened to Mr. Bennett? The map of London is being changed every day. We're all changing too, always with an eye out for loose talk, making sure we're near a shelter, checking our bedding and possessions because you never know who's about.

I wonder where the gang is tonight? Nicking what they can, while they can, I bet.

What would they do if life began again tomorrow?

What would I do?

I would find my dad. My dad would make all this right again and we'd go and flush out whatever those things are in the tunnels.

Seven thirty and word comes down. No bombs tonight. The Coastal Watch has rung through to confirm it. The Shelter Marshals say we can stay if we want to, but it's safe up top. About a third of people leave for the pubs, but most of us remain down below. What's there to do but walk the streets in the blackout? They have put in electrically heated boilers at each station for heating the tea urns and warming the baby's bottles. There is milk for the children at a penny and a half a mug. At Lambeth they've introduced numbered tickets, so you can stray from your bunk, but that's no good to me as I'm baby-sitting Aggie and she'll blow the whistle if I go off again. Ma has been sleeping on the refreshment train on an inflatable mattress.

Tonight she finishes early and joins us.

'Is it all over?' I ask.

'Careless talk costs lives.' She says, with a wink. That's on the posters now.

'But is it?'

'We've just to enjoy what we've got. She cuddles Aggie. 'I've found you a nice family in Kent.'

I brighten. 'Does that mean I don't have to go?'

'We'll see.' Says Ma, producing apple turnovers, jam rolls and a meat pie.

I eat, hoping to have won my freedom. I haven't seen Sands.

November 6th

The bombers are back. Worse still the clocks have gone back an hour, robbing us of daylight. A northeasterly wind freezes my face to stone. By five o' clock the sky is a rich deep blue and people are grim as they tramp down to claim their bunks. The newspapers, more slender each day, tell us that morale is high and we are beating back the Jerries but last night a woman would not stop wailing. She was holding her baby in a blanket and rocking him from side to side. A copper was called in to calm her racket. It didn't do any good. Her face was red from howling. I wanted her to shut up and you could see others wanted it too by the way they leaned away from her and gathered up their faces like a bag of washing. The copper put his hand on her shoulder and this only increased her cries. He took her by the crook of her elbow but she shook him off and sank into herself to protect the child. You'll smother it, called out one of the mothers. Take it off her, urged another. A couple of busybodies went up to help. 'She's been like this for hours. She's not capable, not a fit mother.' I thought of Auntie Joan and the trouble she has. I wonder if Evie's had it rough at school? Has her school been bombed? The copper and the women approached with a united front and it was all 'now then, this won't do, let's have a bit of calm', but she wouldn't be touched and in the tussle the blanket unravelled and we saw it for a second before she grabbed the little blue thing and wrapped it up again. It didn't move. Shortly after that they had her removed. Not a good night.

***

'I'm going to have big sisters.' Says Aggie.

I frown at Ma.

'She means the Land girls. They'll be working where she's staying.'

Ma has been given an hour off work to go and see Aggie off at Charing Cross. We have a voucher for her ticket and she's got a big cardboard tag to identify her as if she was a parcel. She is to be met at Ashford. She will have to count the stops because all the names have been painted out. Ma has done her best to make Aggie look smart, which is a chore. Aggie holds our hands, skipping between us and trying to swing in the air. I have to carry her case. The station concourse is full of busy soldiers with kitbags, Canadians and Poles, men in khaki and great big boots and greatcoats, *in transit* to their next posting or going about their war work. I wonder if Dad passed though here?

'You've nothing for the journey.' blurts out Ma.

She leaves us at the barrier and dashes out to Lyon's Corner House. Aggie tugs at my sleeve. 'Are you going to be OK?'

'Of course.'

'Don't get hit on the head by a bomb.'

'I'll try not to.'

'Will you see Evie again?'

'I don't know.' I say, frostily.

'You like her.'

'Do I?' I watch the soldiers coming and going, wanting to be one of them, to go off and fight 'Itler on his own turf. Some boys lie and sign up early so they can fight at fourteen. That's only a year and a bit away.

'She likes you.'

'No she doesn't. She never even looked at me at the dance.'

Aggie scrunches up her face and pulls a mean look.

'Do you want to know how to get a girl to like you?'

I let out a long sigh. 'Oh do tell me *please*, eight year old woman-of-the-world.'

'Pretend that you don't.'

'What?'

'Pretend you don't like her very much when you really do. Like you do with me.'

No Aggie. I don't like you all that much because you are a pain and you're selfish and you hang around me all the time. You are there when I least want it and it will be great when you are not around because I'll be free and I won't miss you or your endless questions one little bit.

'Shut up Aggie.'

'You shut up.'

We blow raspberries at one another and that makes things better. Ma hurries back as they are sounding the big whistle to warn us that the train is about to pull out.

We rush along the platform and Ma speaks urgently to the guard who wrenches open one of the heavy wooden doors, exposing its shiny brass hinges. He takes her suitcase and puts it in the string rack and Ma kisses Aggie all over and promises her to write. The guard shuts Aggie in and slides the window down by the two catches on either side. She holds out her doll and waves its hand at us.

Its red little mouth is almost rubbed away now and the white shellac cheeks are cracked, showing the stuffing underneath. The big locomotive starts to move and wheels scream as it pulls out of the covered part of the station. We trot alongside as the windows flash by and wave like mad until the guards van, all blacked out at the back, disappears, exposing the rails and the rusty old red iron sleepers. Ma stands watching as the train curls away over the river and then magic's a tissue from her bag and does her face. She turns and offers a smile.

'I've a treat for you.'

It's tea and a bun at Lyon's Corner house in the Strand. The nippie is a pretty girl, a bit older than Evie with her hair up in her cap and a smart white pinny. I try out Aggie's plan by ignoring her and she ignores me right back. Evie ignored me even when I wasn't interested in her, so how am I going to pretend not to be interested in her *and* be interested in her at the same time? Why does it always have to be the girls in charge? Maybe it's because we men are too busy with the war.

'I'd like you to come on the refreshment canteen now there's just you and me.'

'To keep an eye on me?' I ask, through a mouthful of dough.

'You wanted to help with the war effort. Well, now you are.'

November 10th

People talk about luck as if it were a friend who turns up when you least expect it. I was lucky on the horses, lucky to get that bunk space, lucky not to get blown apart by a shell. He's a funny sort of friend though because if he doesn't show up we hate him like a drunken uncle: Curse my rotten luck, we say.

Luck came to visit me tonight at Bethnal Green. I was out helping Ma when I saw a couple of white flashes go off down by the platform exit. I hurried over. It was a tall man in a baggy suit with a scarf. He had a big Rollieflex camera and a flash bulb and a square leather case for his rolls of film. He was just putting in another bulb.

'What are you doing mister?'

'Photographing the shelterers. For the Ministry of Information.'

The women are making the best of themselves and daubing at the children. He chivvies everyone along, making jokes and causing a general stir and making them feel special. He places the healthy looking kiddies near the front and begs some buns off me so that the people look well fed and happy – a tea party. He shoots off a couple of photos and the bulbs crackle.

'Will it be in the papers?'

'Once the Ministry has examined them, yes. I hope so.'

'Have you been to lots of places so far?'

'Spitalfields. A crypt. I hope to cover much ground. I need to get to Piccadilly. To capture the general spirit.'

It comes to me. 'I've an idea. Why don't you join us on the refreshment train and we can do Holborn, Kingsway and the whole West End.'

'That would be most useful. He offers a hand. 'Bill Brandt.'

His hand encircles mine, wrapping it up like last night's fish and chip supper.

'William Lumley.' I'll be Bill too, one day.

Off we go on the refreshment train with our special passenger. He has to stoop in the small space. All the time my brain is bubbling with my new plan. Once we reach Aldwych, I ask him—

'Will you show me how to take a picture?'

He agrees. The people are content with pies and buns and the canteen service is boosting morale. We set up his equipment on the platform edge.

'You look through the viewfinder and press this button. Hold the camera as still as you can for as long as you can. I will operate the flash.'

He hands me the camera and I look through at the tiny image. He nods and I click as he flashes. I make sure I get the tunnel in.

'Wind on the film and take one more'. He says. Take a couple.'

I do so. 'Now what?'

'Now I develop it in my darkroom.'

'Where's that?'

'In my kitchen.'

'Can I come and watch?'

'You're very keen.'

'I look at Picture Post and Weekly Illustrated whenever I can.'

This is a bit of a lie. I have seen the magazines at the bigger stations. I even had a look through some of the big black and white grainy photographs but I've no money for that sort of thing. I look at him, imploring. He thinks for a moment and then produces a small white card from his inside jacket pocket. It is an expensive suit.

'Friday two o' clock. Belsize Park. I'll be developing then. My wife will let you in.'

I take it as carefully as if it were a ten-pound note, glancing at the posh North London address. He packs his equipment into the leather case, clipping the catches. The silver flash fan darts away like a fish going underwater. Around us his subjects return to knitting, playing cards or nibbling at their rations. He shakes my hand and marches off to take the next tube. I slide his card into my top pocket.

He is a man who takes pictures of the tunnels.

***

Working on the canteen I come across the gang at Baker St. I'm still annoyed about Johnny turning tail so I pretend not to see, but Ma has me carrying a tray along the platform to the shelterers so it's unavoidable. They clock me in my long white apron. Perce and Ollie slink toward me as I give out buns and pies. My tray is on a cord looped around my neck: beneath it I have a fat leather purse around my waist for change, like the one Dad wears in East Lane market.

'You find your sister then?' Asks Perce, right out.

I nod curtly. Johnny appears out of nowhere and grabs at my tray.

'Give us a bun.'

I grab his wrist in mid air, 'I'd rather give you a white feather for running off.'

'I never did.'

'You weren't there when I got chased.'

'Chased by what?'

'Exactly. You weren't there to bloody well see it.'

He uses his other hand to reach round me and grab the bun.

'Put that back.'

'Make me.'

'They're tuppence each.'

'We helped you out the other night,' warns Perce.

I raise my voice 'I can't do favours. These have all got to be paid for.'

Perce looks as if the idea of paying for anything is completely foreign to him.

'You've changed your tune.'

'I'm just working.'

'Working is for mugs.'

'I'm a mug then.'

'This is volunteering, isn't it?'

I give a single nod.

'Then you're a bigger mug if you're not on a wage.'

I say nothing. Perce gives me that stare, close but also a thousand miles away.

'We may need you soon, stick around.'

Ollie adds. 'We'll come for you when we need you.'

'What about when I needed *you*?'

Ollie. 'We searched the West End tunnels, came up with nothing.'

I glare at Johnny. 'So it was only him running away then.'

Johnny bares his teeth and tries another grab. I spin the tray away and one of the buns falls to the ground. He reaches for it but I kick it over the edge under the refreshment train. The mice and rats will eat well tonight.

'You can have that one.' I say.

Johnny fumes as I back into the carriage. They melt away and we move on. The train rattles, the ladies chat and the air is warm with dough and pastry. It's womb-like, soft, the best place to be. Ma taps me on the shoulder.

'Your friends – where are they from?'

'The East End.'

'Bombed out as well, eh? What about their families?'

'We don't talk about our families.'

'You mean you don't tell them about *moi*?'

She says it in such a funny way with an accent and a hand fluttering on her chest that I have to laugh. Ma smiles and leans in, conspiratorially.

'I've been in touch with your Auntie. We're all going dancing again on Saturday.'

My heart starts to thud against my ribcage. 'Where?'

'Wherever we can get in: Cocoanut Grove, the Astoria or the Café de Paris.'

'But none of those places will let me in.'

'Just you wait. I've got plans.'

Sometimes Ma is the best woman in the world.

Chapter Fourteen

November 15th

The Jerries have turned their attention to Coventry and Liverpool, which are getting the brunt of it. No one wants to be ungracious but it's good not to be the ones getting it every night. We still hold our breath every time the Minnies go off, and they do, as regular as ever. There's a new problem in the underground. Mosquitoes. People are itching and swatting them away all the time. I'm counting the days 'til Saturday and planning what I will say to Evie on the night. Actually it's more about what I won't say to her because I am going to try Aggie's trick. I'm going to pretend to be bored with her. I won't ask her if she's doing war work or if she is thinking of being an auxiliary nurse as many of the girls are nowadays. I won't complement her dress or shoes or whatever she uses on her mouth to make it look bigger. Her hair can go to hell. She'll probably have that stupid berry on anyway, tilted to one side with her hair all wavy. I'm going to go off and talk to someone else, anyone else so long as it's a girl: a prettier one than Evie if that's possible. Doesn't matter who she is, she just needs to stand there long enough for Evie to see and for her to think 'Will's so grown up now. Why didn't I take my chance before?' I'll let her find me smoking on a balcony, looking down on the dance floor as if I owned the place and she'll ask me what's wrong? I'll say 'nothing' because that's what girls say when they mean something and they want the other person to guess what it is.

On Friday morning there is a slab of blue sky behind the jagged saw teeth of London. The churches stay proud, St Paul's' the greatest. I meet Ma at Swan & Edgar, going in through the rear entrance and keeping an eye out for horrible Mr. Watson. She is surrounded by other women, peddling their machines furiously, cutting long swathes of cloth on benches or sewing acres of material. I am fussed and cooed over and Ma shows me the dress she has made for the dance in green organza. She puts it on and swirls around in it.

'It's too short' I say.

'It's the fashion.' Says Ma.

'It swirls around too much. Your legs are showing.'

'Isn't he a prude.' Says one lady.

'He's just looking after his Mum.' Says another.

'Jolly good thing too.' Says a third.

I'm terrified Ma is going to get angry but she ruffles my hair and says 'Good for you Will. You do like it though, don't you?'

'Sort of.'

'Then I hope you'll like your present.'

She has made a suit for me in black wool. It is very smart and although the legs are too long she says she can take them up and stands me on a box and starts pinning them up around me.

'The sleeves too?'

'Ok Little Lord Fauntleroy.' She says through a mouthful of pins.

Evie is going to be so impressed. Now I see why Ma said that she could get me in. With a proper suit on I'll look fifteen, sixteen, old enough anyway.

'Ma, what if the doorman asks my age?'

'Mumble at him – you're good at that. I'll do the rest.'

She produces a crisp white shirt, which to my surprise is one of mine that she has had cleaned. There is a laundry here, as well as a service started up in the Underground. Together with a tie and a bit of spit and polish on my shoes I will be smarter than for Church at Christmas. The women say I will cut 'quite a dash'.

***

I take the Northern line through Camden Town and Chalk Farm to Belsize Park. The stations are well kept and people's bedding is neatly stored against the tunnel walls. It's less grubby too, unlike Lambeth North or the Elephant, which smell awful. Up top, few of the shops have been hit. They are neat with canopies and people milling about, not all ash covered or higgledy-piggledy like in East Lane or down in Camberwell. I check the address on the card. Once I am away from the parade of shops there are long rows of houses stretching off into the distance. They have front gardens with gates and shrubs and even little lawns, all 'shipshape and Bristol fashion'.

Some of the bigger Victorian buildings have been made into flats. Mr. Brandt lives in one with a wide flight of stone steps and a shiny black door. The glass panels have no brown tape on them and the ground floor and basement bay windows are shuttered. Maybe people have boarded up and left. There is a row of bells on the left and his name is written on one. I push it and wait, watching a postman passing by on his bike, women pushing prams, a couple of ARP wardens cadging a smoke. This is another London. I ring the bell again and a distorted female voice answers.

'Who is this please?'

'My name's Will. Mr. Brandt said I could come in and watch him develop his films.'

There is a long pause. I think she's gone away to ask him. 'Third floor please.'

The door clicks and I enter a hallway with checkerboard tiles. Leading upwards at the end is a staircase with brass fittings and a smooth oak handrail, which ordinarily I would have loved to slide all the way down. Mrs. Brandt is at the top, a slender redhead in a light brown dress, which stops at her knees.

'He's in his dark room. You will have to wait.'

She leads me into a reception room where I sit on a posh chair. I don't think she is used to young people because she doesn't seem to know what to do with me. She offers lemonade, which I accept but keeps on asking if I want things when I don't. Eventually she gives up and starts to knit. Women are knitting for Britain at the moment, jumpers, socks and tank tops, anything to keep busy. The needles clatter as she nervously fingers the wool. A slim line of red light glows under the kitchen door. There is loud coughing and throat clearing coming from inside. After several minutes the light goes out and Bill opens the door, wiping his hands on a towel.

'Sorry. I couldn't let you in whilst I was in the middle of it.'

I go to shake his hand but he declines.

'Best not. I have a touch of influenza, I think.'

I follow him in. There is a hulk of an enlarger with corrugated sides like bellows and shallow plastic trays filled with sharp smelling chemicals. Developer and stop, he says. He uses tongs to remove wet photographs from the bath and pegs them up on a clothesline stretched across the room. The pictures are of shelterers, an old woman huddled against the cold, people bedding down, propped up on cases, shoes off. Their horrid old feet don't seem so stinky in the pictures.

'Stepney last night. A fair effort. The ministry wants only the best. No children crying, no hungry open mouths.'

'Why's that?"

'Propaganda.'

I've heard about Lord Haw-Haw on the radio and German pamphlets being dropped from planes. 'You mean we do that too?'

'Fifth Columnists also read Newspapers.'

'What does that mean?'

'It would be logical to assume there are *some* spies among us, yes? '

'I suppose so...'

He goes about his business, tidying up. 'If the government were to allow the press to reveal exactly how many have been killed or injured or how the Luftwaffe has reduced much of our city to ruins then it would only help the German cause. Information is kept from the public to avoid panic and revolt.'

'But that means lies.'

'Yes of course.'

There is always mistrust in the shelters, especially strangers or the foreigners at Oxford Circus with their barking guttural voices, but this? 'You mean everyone's lying?'

He coughs into a hankie. 'A network of deception, yes – we're all part of it.'

'I don't want to be part of it.'

'Too late.'

'I want to fight the Germans.'

A smile blooms. 'That's what we need. The idealism of youth to win it for us.'

I frown. 'So you don't show the people as they are?'

'The choice of print is down to what the editor or Ministry considers suitable.'

'But you must have got lots of *other* pictures then?'

He puts the hankie away in his pocket. 'I'll show you.'

He goes into his study and returns with a box of photographs, opening it to reveal strips of negatives placed inside thin translucent paper.

'This is a contact sheet. A print of all the shots in each film. From this I can see which are most likely to work. Here.'

There are twenty or so small pictures.

'Do you have the ones we took at Aldwych and Holborn?'

He hunts through. 'Ah yes, Monday's shoot. Some good, some not so good.'

'What about the ones I did?'

He passes over the gossamer sheet and I hold it to the light. I look desperately to see if I can see anything in the tunnel shots. He lays out the final photographs and taps one.

'I couldn't use yours. You're shorter than me so you took the shot from a different angle. The result is shadow – you see the black areas?'

There is a pool of shadow on the arched wall, also darkness on their faces, in their eyes and below their noses, making them seem grim or starving. He indicates one of his own pictures. The faces are bright and clear and moon like.

'See the difference? My mistake not to lower the flash.'

'Could I see some of the others?'

'By all means.'

We go to his study. Piles of brown cardboard boxes of prints fill the room from floor to ceiling. There are cameras on the windowsill and other dusty photographic equipment lying everywhere. He brings three boxes of photographs, each containing a hundred or so eight by tens.

'I don't print so many now. The paper is too expensive.'

I sit on the floor to go through the pages. Mr. Brandt has other things to do so I take my time looking, not at the shelterers, but at the tunnels behind. Suddenly I let out a gasp. Aldwych. A reject shot. A group of people huddled on the platform not looking at the camera. A boy of about my age is standing too near the tunnel for comfort. Behind him is a faint shape, an outline where the flash has lit the eyepiece of the gas mask. There's part of an arm too, plainly reaching out to pull the boy into the blackness. I call Mr. Brandt over.

'See this. It's someone in the tunnel wearing a mask.'

'Could be a tube signal, these round shapes here.'

'But it's too high, and the arm.'

'Let's look at the negative.'

He brushes some papers off his desk to reveal a light box. Plugging it in, he slides the strip of negatives in place and uses a small glass eyepiece to closely examine them.

'Could have been a double image.' He says, squinting.

'What's that?'

'I may have put two negatives in the machine.' He stands, coughs again. 'Or the paper may have been partially exposed. Let's make another print.'

I want to jump from foot to foot with excitement. In the darkroom he puts on the red light, slides the negative between two plates in the enlarger, turning the dials this way and that so the image comes into sharp focus. He increases the size, focusing on the top left to get in the tunnel and part of the arch and platform. I can see the mask, even the broken eyepiece where I hit it.

'I can't go any closer or we'll lose the image. Hand me paper. Hold it by the edges.'

I open up a sealed box of photographic paper and ever so carefully hand one over. He places it under the light, exposes it for several seconds and then puts the paper into the developer, then stop and fix. I watch as an image begins to appear, deep black and grainy grey. The mask is clear but there's no outline of the person except his arm.

'What is he doing in there?' Asks Mr. Brandt.

'Could I have a copy?' I ask.

'Sure. I'll make another.'

He repeats the procedure, talking of spirit images that were popular in Victorian and Edwardian times, of fakes and fakery and the Cottingley Fairies. I wonder why he hasn't connected this with the disappeared children but then I get it. He's only been in the Underground for a week. Spitalfields and Stepney. He won't have seen the missing children posters. Bill coughs harshly and births the second print in chemicals.

'You're an observant boy William.'

'So what do you think it is?'

'It is a man in a mask.'

'He and others are kidnapping children.'

'You knew this when you came to me?'

'Yes Sir.'

'And what do you expect me to do?'

The temperature in the tiny kitchen has grown cooler.

'I... I don't know. I wanted to get proof.'

'And now?'

'Could you... could you maybe get it published so people can be warned?'

He hangs the wet prints on the clothesline, seals up the photographic paper and turns the normal light on. He stands in front of the door, barring my way out. His voice has that the low growl of a cornered dog.

'This would be dismissed as a ghost, an anomaly. The Press is not going to put it in people's minds that there is some threat Underground, not with the bombers raining down on us from the sky. Do you wish to know the real number of people Underground?' He allows a short pause. 'Over one hundred and fifty thousand shelterers and that is only an estimate. Who would scare them further? You?'

'I just needed evidence.'

'And you took advantage of my good nature to get it.'

I'm getting upset and I don't know what to say to him. It's all out of control. His face contorts in anger.

'How dare you! If I were to raise the balloon on this then it is *I* who would be held to blame, me whose reputation would be on the line.'

'I'm sorry for asking you.'

'I cannot do anything with this. It's bad enough the restrictions they put on me...'

A massive cough attacks his chest, twisting his torso this way and that, throwing him about like a man lost at sea. He falls forwards and grips the side of the sink so hard that his knuckles turn white. He bucks and spits a ball of foul red brown phlegm into the sink. He runs the tap and sucks water into his mouth. I see my only chance. I slip the second print off the clothesline, under my coat, back away and throw open the door. Light floods in and he flings out an arm helplessly as he lets loose another hacking cough. I glimpse his wife, rising from her seat at the commotion, her mouth making an O of surprise. There is a pile of *Illustrated News* by the door. I take one and slip the picture inside. I flip the latch and scramble down the stairs, down and round and out of the main door and down the street as fast as my legs will carry me.

***

At Aldwych I run up and down the passages hunting out Sands. I eventually find him with an ARP man heading up the escalator to the office.

'Sands? Can I show you something?'

'In a moment lad.'

The talk of Elsan toilets and chemical ablutions goes on forever. The other man finally goes and he offers a wink. He doesn't invite me in today.

'Now then Sonny Jim – where's the fire?'

'I found the thing in the tunnels.'

He remains impassive. I pull out the photo and hand it to him. He puts on a tiny pair of half glasses and examines it closely, his mouth hanging slightly open.

'You see that shape in the dark.'

'Gas mask. Maybe one of the shelterers left it hanging there'

'A train would have knocked it out of the way.'

'Someone mucking around.'

'It attacked me. It's the thing, the beast or whatever.'

He removes his glasses, puts them away and rolls up the photograph. 'I'll give it straight to the police. Well done.'

'Can I come with you?'

'I don't see the need. You've told the story – it's the picture that's the proof.'

He puts his hand on the brass doorknob.

'You will take it as soon as possible – won't you?'

'I've said so haven't I?'

'When will you go?'

He opens the booking office door. 'After my shift – unless you'd like me to rush over there now during the air raid?'

He pulls the door to behind him. Through the glass I see him drop the photograph on top of a pile of old newspapers.

***

Next morning, as we traipse past on our way to the ablutions, I see that the photograph has gone and so has Sands. Out in the street it is the usual chaos. Cold, smell of embers, fires burning. Holborn is one of the hardest hit places after the East End.

'Looking forward to it?' Asks Ma.

She sees the confusion on my face.

'Had you forgotten?'

'What? Is Dad coming home on leave?'

Ma forces a smile.

'No love. Tonight's Saturday. It's the dance.'

Chapter Fifteen

At the Café de Paris the doormen barely give me a second glance as Ma and I walk in. It is dead posh. There are anterooms filled with glamorous people, girls in lipstick, and silk, soldiers in dress uniform, men in smart dinner suits checking their hats, everybody smoking. We go through plush scarlet curtains into the main room and find ourselves on a long curved balcony with a balustrade and a staircase curving down to the dance floor. The dance band is all lit up in the middle and the band is playing 'Oh you beautiful doll'. There are golden tables with red tablecloths and little shaded lights on them. There are all sorts here, even black soldiers in uniform. They won't get stick here I think, unlike in the shelters where if you're any kind of foreign they don't want to know. Outside it is bitterly cold and everyone is rushing about doing war work; ARP wardens keeping tabs on all and sundry in the Raids, the Heavy Rescue Squads, the Stretcher Parties, the Firemen, Ambulance people and Mortuary vans, busy all night every night and here we are inside, happy as Larry in this warm soft mouth of a place. Tonight, I don't care about the thing, about the beast in the tunnels, because I have done my bit in saving Aggie and giving over the photo to Sands. It's the grown-ups time now.

Auntie Joan is here. She looks like a Hollywood star with her hair in a wave over one eye and a skirt too short above the knee. She waves to Ma and we come down to join her. I look about for Evie, remembering my plan. Ma and Joan start chatting nineteen to the dozen and order drinks and I am given a Coca-Cola. The two women put up no resistance when asked for a spin by a couple of airmen. Dressed in my nice suit and shirt and tie I sit and try to look as suave as Ronald Coleman. I take out a cigarette and hold it in my fingers. She must be here somewhere. I crane round the dancers to see if she is already being courted but she is not to be seen. I will ask Joan about Evie when she comes back. With all that dancing she'll soon be thirsty. Drinks are brought for them in cocktail glasses. I look up the staircase and now I see Evie descending. She smiles and it is like sunshine bursting out of cloud and instantly all my plans to be rude are forgotten. She has her hair done the same way as her mother, except its reddish-brown. She wears a green skirt that swirls soft round her legs and the men throw glances her way as she floats across the floor straight over to me. She drops her clutch bag on the table as I stand to greet her.

'Get you Clark Gable.'

'I thought you were supporting the Free French?'

'Even Communists get the night off.'

'Nice of you to spend it here.'

'Charmed I'm sure.'

'I would ask you to dance but my left leg was shot off in the Great War.'

'I'm terribly sorry.'

'I have another. We could hop.'

She laughs. Her lips are bright red.

I gesture elaborately for her to sit down and she does so. I haven't the chance to offer her a drink before a waiter comes over to deliver a glass of champagne. She smiles and thanks the donor, an Army man in dress uniform who waves from the shadows. She raises her glass but to my relief she doesn't ask him over and to my delight she instead leans in to talk to me. I'm glad she's not noticed I am drinking Coca-Cola. If she asks I'll say there's whisky in it.

'I hear you were quite the hero when it came to rescuing your sister?'

'Little pest. Someone had to go and find her.'

'I'm surprised it didn't make the *Times*.'

'Ma didn't want to make a fuss.'

'What happened? Where was she?'

I explain about hearing Ag through the station tunnel walls and going in, missing the parts about the gang – I don't want her knowing about that – and saying about the strange underground classroom with the German handwriting in it.

'Who d'you think is down there?'

'I keep trying to tell people it's the Jerries but no one will listen.'

'Bloody hell.' Says Evie.

I take my advantage. 'I even got a photograph of a man hiding in a mask.'

Her mouth opens wide. I want to press myself on her and kiss all the lipstick away. I want to hug her tight and be alone with her, but not here. This is light and glamour and everything shines. This is what we shall remember in years to come when the war is over.

'What photograph?'

I explain about Bill Brandt and she punches me on the arm.

'You silly boy.'

'Why?'

'You should have taken it to the Press yourself.'

'The *South London Press*?'

'Fleet Street. There's bound to be a journalist there who'll do a story. Now you've given away the only bit of proof you had.'

'Sands has it.'

'Can you trust him?'

'Why shouldn't I?'

'What's he going to say? Some kid gave me a photograph of a man hidden in the tunnel. He's going to feel a bit stupid isn't he?'

'He'll go to the detectives.'

She looks at me like she did at Blackheath, as if I am really dim.

I'm no Richard Hannay. I should have gone to the detectives. I can't possibly go back to Mr. Brandt and ask for another photograph, not after stealing the first. Worse still, Evie has realised all this in a second. She's cleverer than me and that's not good. I've got to go to Sands and get the photo back. Evie sees I'm cross and rests her hand on mine.

'Enough detective work.' She sips her champagne and offers it to me. 'Better than Coca-Cola.'

'Whisky and Cola.'

'Really?'

'It's a bit light on the scotch.'

'How light?'

'Very. Watered down I'd say.'

We share the champagne and the light and bubbles and swing music takes us away from everything. There can't be war where there is champagne. It's the first time I have felt like this since I can't remember when. I'm sick of stinky people and having no clean clothes and mosquitoes and nits and rats and chemical toilets and bombs. This is how life should be all the time. And the moment I think this, the tall stupid handsome man in the uniform comes to ask Evie to dance. I throw her a look but she is already halfway up off the chair.

'Don't mind, do you chum.' Says the airman.

He is only a corporal. I have no chance to object as he whisks her onto the dance floor. I grab her champagne flute and want to strangle it. Instead I swallow the bubbles until I almost choke. The women are all up dancing together and I am alone and empty. So this is what women do? Why didn't Dad tell me? The band continues to play all the tunes. *Kiss Me Goodnight Sgt. Major; When the Lights Go On Again; Shine On Harvest Moon; Slow Boat to China; Sentimental Journey...* I hate them all as the men swing Evie round. She hardly touches the floor. Ma, glowing with pleasure, comes over to down her drink.

'Look at you Billy Grump. Come on, have a dance with your old Ma.'

'No ta.'

'You want to sit here all night, moping?'

'That is the plan.'

I'm tipsy and don't care what I say.

'Well that's up to you because we're all having such a wonderful time.'

'You shouldn't be dancing with men.'

'William you are such a prude.'

'Is this what Dad would want?'

Her face darkens. 'Dad would want us to be happy and when he comes back at Christmas we'll all be together.'

'If he comes back.'

She pretends not to hear and drinks Auntie Joan's drink too.

I press on. 'He could be dead in a ditch, shot up by Germans.'

'That's a horrid thing to say.'

'I'm sorry.' But it's true, I am thinking. Anything could have happened.

'Your father is fine.'

'You don't know that. You don't know that.'

I glare up at her, defiant.

'I see so much of him in you.'

I want to answer but I can't because then, the roof falls in.

**

The bomb was a direct hit on top of the building. 300 kilograms of metal and explosive smashing through the roof, the top three floors and exploding outwards, showering Haymarket with rubble, bricks and glass. The first floor staircase collapsed and it was the impact of that which caved the roof in. The noise was incredible and a great shower of bricks and metal struts and supports rained down, killing 12 people.

I grabbed Ma and pulled us under the balcony as some of the pillars gave way. Those on the dance floor bore the brunt. There was total silence but I began to realize that I couldn't hear as my ears were ringing so badly. Chaos. People with bloodied heads and torsos, some with arms or legs crushed, one or two with limbs missing. White shirts bled bright red; dresses ribboned, silk and crimson. Shoes abandoned everywhere. The smell was incredible. Cordite, brick dust and blood. No one was moving, too shocked. I looked desperately for Evie's lime green dress. Please don't let her die. Please. Don't let her die don't let her die don't let her die. Ma is curled up out cold but I think unharmed. I have saved the family. We are lucky. We are the lucky ones. Where is Evie? She was dancing. Others are starting to climb, crawl and clamber out from their hiding places looking for survivors. I join them, working on impulse, adrenalin they call it. A couple of soldiers are trying to pry free a body from under the rubble.

My heart stops as I spot a strip of green silk under a stanchion. I bend down to touch it. I start to pull at it and when I meet resistance I see that it is the tie for her waist. She must be close. I stand up to scan the room and as I do I see her leaning against a pillar. Her arms are sprinkled in red where she has been hit by shattered glass; she is barefoot, her dress is in tatters but she is still a vision of purity in all this carnage. She's trying to pull something from the pile. It seems to be a mannequin's arm but as I step closer I see it is her mother's. Her mouth is opening and closing, but no sound comes. I am underwater. I step up to her and as I touch her on the shoulder she shrinks away. I wonder why and touch my own face. It is wet with blood. I feel no pain and I realise it must belong to someone else. I use my sleeve to wipe it away and immediately bend to the task of trying to free Auntie Joan. Even as I try to pull at the wreckage I see that it will be fruitless. She's under a great mass of concrete. There is no movement in her. Evie holds on for as long as she can, screaming in perfect silence then folding into me, her hot tears wetting my neck. I am pricked by them too as we hold fast to one another. We are statues of pain.

People start to arrive. My hearing returns – muffled at first, the sound of my heartbeat crashing in my ears – but then real sounds from outside and above. The Heavy Rescue squad with their picks and shovels trying to dig down to us. I fear an unexploded bomb but what difference would it make in all this? Soon they will all be here, the ARP, the doctors and Ambulance men, the mortuary crew. I pull Evie over to where Ma is curled up under a table. We huddle together in shock.

But now, crawling over the piles of brick is not what I expect – a rescue team – but two men, no, boys. Perce and Ollie. At first I am delighted that they have sought me out but as they go about their gruesome work I realise this is not at all why they are here. They have no thought for me. Like rats, they crawl among the dead and dying, systematically going through their pockets, sifting jewellery, lifting wallets and picking out purses. I am the only one to see this: the injured are too dazed or in too much pain. I am too shocked to say or do anything and it is only when Ollie approaches Auntie Joan's limp lifeless body that I find my voice. My legs move as if through water or heavy treacle. In the cloud of brick dust I wave my arms.

'Bugger off. Bloody well bugger off. Leave us be. Leave us alone.'

My hand finds a glass ashtray and I hurl it at him. Ollie ducks out of the way and it smashes against a pillar. He glares at me. Perce calls out to him. He is disguised by a scarf wound round his face but his lank frame is enough to tell, the long trousered legs, the big lapelled coat. He stands amid broken tables and bodies, affronted to have been interrupted in his dirty work. I reach down again and lob a half brick. Ollie yelps. I shout god knows what bad language with no thought of Ma or Evie as my hands seek out what they can – a chair leg, a broken lamp – to bombard them. Perce is defiant until I'm close enough with a brick raised ready to strike. Murder in my eyes. I hurl it and hit a pillar and there is a rain of brick dust and a fall of masonry. Perce and Ollie turn tail and they are away. Good bloody riddance to bad rubbish.

The First Aid party arrives, SP in white on their tin helmets, tending to the minor injured. To the bodies they attach big luggage labels, writing in indelible pencil. As there are so many, a doctor uses bright red lipstick to put an X on their foreheads to indicate internal injury, or a T for 'tourniquet applied'. We, the walking wounded, are led out to a shelter where we are given hot sweet tea.

We don't feel any better.

December 3rd

It is a few days since Auntie Joan died and Evie has been in our care. There has been little talk amongst us except for Ma establishing priorities and practicalities. She made a telephone call to the Home for Unwed Mothers and was told by Mrs. Halstrom that the regulations do not permit Evie to remain there without a legal Guardian. She tried to put herself forward for that position but it wouldn't wash.

Ma is her next of kin but there will be forms to be signed and endless offices to wait in if they have not been bombed or relocated. Mrs. Halstrom said that Evie might collect her things at any time. They will be kept there but not in Auntie Joan's room as it has already been reallocated, so Evie can't go home. She is silent most of the time and has been sleeping any chance she can get. We have the regular berth bunk at Aldwych and we've shared out the blankets. Ma is feeding us with what she can get from the refreshment train. I tried to hold Evie last night when she awoke from a nightmare but it produced instant tears.

'Don't be *nice*, Will', she said. 'I can't take any kindness at the moment'.

I watch over her, watching her sleep, glad when she is at peace. Ma has lent her some clothes for the funeral, a sensible shirt and a blouse and has got her washed and cleaned up.

Today we are on a double-decker. Our destination is the Lambeth Cemetery and Crematorium at Blackshaw Road off Garrett Lane in Tooting. The last leaves are off the trees and the branches are black scribbles on a flat sky. Even though there is a war on, funerals take place as usual, just many more of them. The ambulance man at the Palais told us that as we had identified the body it had to be claimed at the morgue. The local council arranged the cremation. No one knows how many have died so far. The mortuary worker was far too cheery for his job and spoke to me while Ma was doing the necessary paperwork. He said there are many who are blown to bits. Sometimes they have to assemble chunks and humps of flesh to approximate a human body.

The crows screech in the air as we walk towards the tall brick building, our sorry procession of three. There is a cremation before us so we stand waiting outside, me in my dancing suit, Ma and Evie in black.

'Didn't think we'd have to queue here as well.' I say.

'Don't be rude William.' Says Ma, sniffing the air.

The mourner's file out, their faces collapsed in resignation. They board a black car, which backs away, exhaust billowing.

Inside, we perch on a hard pew in the cold chapel. There should be more of us. There should be all the friends Auntie Joan had, but there was no way of letting anyone know. Mrs. Halstrom promised to put up a notice at the home but it produced no results. I imagine the other mothers were too busy working or queuing up and anyway death is as regular as the milk or paper delivery before the war.

Before.

I don't have any memory of what things were like before hell rained on us, before walls collapsed and food was stopped and the world was flooded in shrapnel and glass and the stink of blood and sewage. There should be more to remember her here, something to light this awful antechamber. There ought to be some way to show all the light and love and laughter she created because Auntie Joan was always ready for fun. She had a real spirit of mischief. People said she was no better than she ought to be and she had to live with being ostracized and spoken about in a bad way but it wasn't fair because Evie whispered to me last night that her dad had run off to sea and was killed in the South Seas.

The Vicar is old and bald and as soon as he starts to speak I get cross because he doesn't put meaning into the words. It is like when teachers read by rote. He makes reference to the war effort and those who fall and nobly gave their lives but Joan didn't bloody well choose to give her life; she was just having some fun before the bloody Jerries bombed it dead. We have to read out from the book of Common Prayer: the words of men in committee who want to make sure the right thing is said – like the spies in the Ministry of Information asking how we are coping so they can report it how they want. Like the newspapers that are only printing Mr. Brandt's pictures of people bearing up and coping and showing Blitz spirit.

Well, maybe London *can't* take much more of this.

Evie holds it in while the coffin is up on the altar, but when it slides into the oven she breaks down, which causes Ma to lose height. Wet tears run down my cheeks and my throat closes and I cannot breathe. Great heaving sobs curl my mouth into a grimace and Ma puts her arm around me, pulling me into her. Evie folds into us and we are three people in a chilly church against the world.

Chapter Sixteen

December 6th

Ma has taken on Evie to help her with the mobile refreshments. She used her wages to get her an olive green frock and badge and is saving up for the tweed overcoat and proper uniform. They each have a red armband with TR on it. Evie has perked up as women do with new clothes and she even got an old man to shine her shoes. We are ticketed, so we can leave our stuff under the beds but Ma does not trust everyone round us and I have been charged with looking after the bunks until they return.

Sands has gone to Tottenham Court Road for a meeting. I go there on the Central line and I am climbing the human scarp face of sleeping people on the escalator when I hear a shout ring out from down below. Perce and Ollie are at the bottom, standing there in greatcoats. They beckon me to come down. I don't like the idea of joining them so I continue to pick my way between the bodies. They start after me, moving fast, unconcerned about waking or annoying the shelterers. I speed up but it's like climbing the muddy banks of the Thames and soon they are alongside me.

'What's the hurry?' Perce calls.

'Got to see someone.'

'There's a raid on – you can't get out.' Ollie says.

'A friend in the ticket office.' I say, so it sounds official, but not the law.

'Can't it wait?'

'Not really.'

Perce. 'We just wanted a word.'

'What about?' I try to sound innocent.

'Stop and we'll tell you.'

I'm at the top of the escalator so I have little choice. Ollie breathes down my neck. Perce circles, eyes gleaming, his face twitching in thought.

'Johnny's been taken.'

'You sure?'

'Couple of nights ago, wheezes Ollie. 'We were down dipping in the Dilly. One moment he's there, next gone. You know about it, don't you?'

'What d'you mean?'

Perce. 'You found your skin didn't you?'

Rhyming slang. My sister. I nod.

'We'll need you with us for the search party.'

We go down in single file, me between them. Have they forgotten about the Café de Paris? About me throwing anything I could at them? So much happens every day that there isn't time to think. The only way you can survive is to not look back.

We bundle onto a tube train. Perce lights up a Star cigarette even though we are in a non-smoking carriage. His hair has grown long, falling over his eyes. He brushes it away and inhales deeply. He has a new watch; I'm guessing it's lifted.

'Where did you find your sis?'

'There's another railway line under this one, for the mail train.'

Ollie. 'Is that how they get about?'

I don't like the way he says it, as if I were responsible for the disappearing children.

'There's catacombs down there, old passages. You could get lost forever.'

Perce studies me. 'Not now we have a guide. A scout.'

There's a dull thump from above and the tube lurches to a halt. Air raid in progress. The train shakes, heavy bombardment tonight. Perce and Ollie take little notice.

'I've a plan.' grins Perce.

Suddenly, the train begins to rock violently from side to side. It isn't a bomb. We fall from one side to the other and try to regain our balance. There is a metallic scraping and a series of rapid blows on the sides of the carriage. I grab the blackout paper on the window and rip away a corner. What I see outside makes me shriek: a long black beak pecking at the side. One glistening soot black eye. A dead eye. A hole in a skull. Perce and Ollie start trying to lever open the doors but are unable to pull the hard rubber apart more than a few inches. Ollie gets a foot in the gap but the beak pecks at him and with a yelp he pulls it back. The doors shudder shut, snapping off the end of it.

As fast as it began, the tremor stops.

All is silent save for the ack-ack guns firing above. Two razor shaped black bones lay on the wood slatted floor. Despite the horror of it, an odd kind of relief flows through me. I'm not dreaming. I'm not mad.

'What the hell was that?'

'Bloody loads of them.'

Perce produces a flick knife and uses the point to hold one piece up.

'Might be poison-tipped.'

'This ain't the Germans.'

'Christ knows then.'

'Like a giant bird. A dinosaur.'

'What's it doing rattling our cage?'

'Maybe it's a warning?' offers Ollie.

Perce looks evil when he smiles. 'Good. I like a challenge.'

The tube begins to move. When we get off at Warren Street there are scratches and pecked holes all over the body of the carriage.

'Looks like a shotgun blast.' Says Perce.

'Shrapnel.'

'How many of them buggers are there?' Asks Ollie.

'A lot more than before.' I say darkly.

'Well, we've got more and all', says Perce.

***

What happens next is like a military operation. From the den at Goodge St, Perce dispatches messengers, bringing back a dozen boys to congregate there. Weapons are chosen from whatever is available. Metal poles, wooden clubs and bits of timber. Perce has his flick knife. He's to lead one half of the gang from the Western District Post Office at Rathbone Place near Tottenham Court Road. It's one of the main Post offices on the route and he knows how to get down into the tunnels from there.

Ollie and I and some other lads – a raggle-taggle bunch of thieves from the Tilbury Shelter – are to head for Farringdon Station to try to find a way in under the Mount Pleasant Sorting Office at the other end of the Post Office underground railway. We start at lights out. Perce's plan is a pincer movement – to trap the monsters in between us.

As we are waiting for the last tube to go, one of our number notices movement up at the end of the platform. A whisper goes around that it is a couple 'doing it'. This is not uncommon and there's always a chance to edge up for a closer look. We can see shoes poking out from under the blanket they have drawn about them. He's grunting away. The woman is keeping hush so we don't know if she's enjoying it or not but the man's exertions draw sniggers from the younger boys. One of them throws a boiled sweet at the lumpy couple. They don't notice. Another follows and the man slaps his neck as if it were a mosquito bite. I get the idea to throw one of my marbles. I am about to do so when Ollie wrenches it off me and hurls it hard. The man, unshaven and sweaty red in the face, turns and growls at us.

'Piss off you little bleeders.'

'Go on stick it in her.' Shouts a thuggish lad from Beckton. His parents died in the Tate and Lyle fire.

The man hisses angrily. 'I'm gonna kill the lot of you once I'm done.'

'Hurry up then.' Calls out Ollie. He loves being in charge.

The woman has had enough and pulls away from him. Frustrated, the man gets up with his trousers round his ankles and his underpants half on. We take flight, shrieking and screaming and tumbling over bodies in our way. The general population makes remarks and the man has to pause to do up his trousers but by then we're hidden round the corners ready for hide and seek. We beam at one another, holding in the laughter until we can take it no more. We explode in snorts and snot and a tube comes in so we rush on. It pulls away, just giving us time to peel away some of the netting and make rude signs at him before we are safely away.

'You see the *size* of it?'

'*That's* the monster in the tube.'

'You'd need a rake to kill that thing.'

'He should get a public warning.'

'What for?'

'Assault and battery.'

'With a deadly weapon.'

'No wonder she was quiet. He's probably killed her with it.'

Every time we run out of funny things some other bright spark else has something worse or more cruel to say until we get to our stop. It has gone ten thirty by the station clock. Ollie gathers us together.

'Right. As soon as the currents off, we're in.'

The lights go down and they have prayers. There's the odd vicar down here now or someone to say something over the Tannoy. Some have brought gramophones, others have radios that work nearer the surface for the BBC nine o' clock News or Lord Haw Haw. His information is better. As soon as we can, we troop off the end of the platform. Ollie stays at my side as we get in good and deep.

'Lights on.' He orders.

They have torches with stolen batteries and a hurricane lamp.

'How far?' He asks me.

'I'd say it's a good mile to Holborn. The way down to the lower tunnel could be anywhere.'

Ollie adopts the voice of a Sergeant Major. 'March on then, chaps.'

With light splashing on the sides of the tunnel we spread out either side of the third rail and skulk along companionably. There's nothing to see, the blackness ahead breeding no monsters, nor even any images in my mind. It's dry and warm enough. On occasion a ciggie is lit up and handed round, its red ember circling like a spark. The lack of excitement or danger produces grumbles – that is until we hear the sound of another train go past underneath us.

'The mail train.' I say.

'How do we get down to it?'

'There'll be a manhole in the tunnel floor.'

We shine our torches without luck, only black soot and muck and rats.

'Better not be a wild goose chase.' Says Ollie.

Others echo the sentiment. We've been in the tunnels for over an hour with no reward and their patience is slender. 'We will find him.' I say.

'How d'you know?' asks Ollie, with that hint of provocation that's always there in his voice. 'For sure?'

I shut up but the damage has been done, as Ollie uses this to bait me.

'You think you're it 'cause you rescued your sister. You don't care if Johnny buys it down here, do yer? And what about what happened at the Palais?'

My heart sinks. I knew he'd not forgotten. He's the type to hold on to anything and now he has me trapped with the platoon. Worse, they're what's called the 'hard lads' of West Ham, Beckton and Poplar. There's not a lot to say as he goes on and gives his version of the story.

'So this bomb goes off near the Dilly and we see an opportunity what with all the poshoes round there. Them that have bought it ain't going to miss what they can't take with them. Perce and me get inside and go about our business, when what do we find – Lord Bloody William Lumley Esquire here in his flash whistle.' He's stoked up his anger now, boiling with it. 'You give us a right treat, didn't you? Heaving bloody bricks at us! Perce nearly lost an eye and me...'

Ollie tears open his shirt and has one of the others shine a torch to reveal a livid purple bruise on his chest. It's all the colours of the rainbow.

'He's done that?'

'It's out of order.'

'Traitor.'

'I lost my Auntie in that bomb.' I say.

Ollie comes back fast. 'So why have a go at us?'

'I just wanted you *away* from her.'

'She was dead.'

'I wish you were bloody dead.'

'You tried to kill me. Want to try again, big man?'

Dad would have hesitated. Dad would have known he was in an impossible position, surrounded, betrayed and about to get into a fight he could not win. Dad would have said something to defuse the situation, carry all that anger away like they do with the UXBs to Hackney Marshes. Dad would not have launched himself at Ollie in the way I did, trying to get my hands round his thick throat and putting in a kick to his fat thigh, only to be pulled off and thrown back. The boys set about me then on Ollie's orders. He yelled about my always having been a sneak and never to be trusted. The blows rained down and because they had weapons they made use of them and when I tried to crawl away they pulled me out and beat my legs and kicked my ribs and torso and punched me in the face and that was it.

***

My eyes are so swollen I can hardly open them but opening them is no better because it is pitch black. I have no way of knowing what time it is or how long I have been out. I am slumped over the rail, its hard metal biting into the parts of my body that are not stinging with pain. It's everywhere, a dull ache in the ribs, a knot in the stomach and my mouth wretched and foul. I was sick at one point and I still stink of it. My legs are badly bruised and sending urgent distress messages. I could die here. I can't imagine how hard it is going to be to get up or to walk to the next station. I cannot crawl along in the muck with the rats. It's too late.

I am wrong.

It is not late, not late at all. There is a clicking noise and I can taste metal in my bloodied mouth. Something makes me leap back to the side of the tunnel, back against the crumbling mortar. Worse, I hear a sound that floods my heart with fear. A regular rattling, accompanied by two slits of light on either side of the tunnel as the tube charges toward me.

It is not late, but early.

All my pain is forgotten as I desperately look for a way out. There is no room beside the rails. The suicide pit only runs along the length of the station platforms, not in the tunnels. The only thing I can do is to crush myself against the tunnel wall as flat as I can and pray there's enough room. It is coming closer, thirty yards, twenty – ten and all of a sudden it is upon me, the wind rush, the rattle, the deadly beat on the rails. I hold hard against the breeze as the carriages thunder past an inch in front of my face.

The train passes. I fall to my haunches and start to weep.

I stop.

I am not alone.

Two elongated beaks loom toward me.

This time the blackness is total.

Chapter Seventeen

A high-walled cell deep in the catacombs beneath old London. In the door there is a hatch with three short metal bars imbedded in it. Candlelight from outside illuminates thousands of scratches on the walls. They are hand-carved; names and phrases and drawings of what might be old rooftops, buildings or boats. The cell – *my* cell – is seven paces long and three wide. The bars are so high up I can't peer through. The floor is damp earth and straw and underneath it solid brick. I tried scrabbling at it with my hands but that's as far as I got. I can't imagine tunnelling out. Going down would only be to Hell. There is a bucket for ablutions in the corner. Before I used it I thought to upturn it and stand on it to peer through the bars. All I could make out was a brick passageway. At the end it opened out to a wide space but it was so full of shadows I could not guess at its dimensions. Food was left while I slept; bread, bully beef and cold Blitz broth. I devoured it immediately. I have no idea how long I've been here. I have no sense of time. A constant low rumbling tells me I must be near an Underground, maybe under one of the lines.

The night I was taken, I was half dragged, half carried along a series of small brick tunnels, some of them no wider than my shoulders. There was a gulley at the bottom with a stream of water. Light came from an oil lamp, sloshing at impossible angles. Later, I saw a vaulted ceiling and cobbled floors. I smelled wetness, the stink of shit and my throat rose with vomit. The sewers. I blacked out.

My injuries have subsided but there is still a lot of pain from the livid bruises on my legs and upper body. I may have broken a rib because it is awfully sore. My right eye has closed up and feels weepy. I ate the food, I am guessing, around five hours ago because my stomach is yearning for more. Why I am being kept I don't know. Aggie never had enough time to find out either. I'm comforted in the knowledge that they don't want me dead because they wouldn't have made these provisions. This means they want something from me. Wait and see, Ma used to say when we were hungry, not thinking of fish and chips or meat pies but of steamed pudding or roly-poly. Dreaming about food is not good and makes my tummy growl all the more. Time is rubber. I could have been thinking for minutes or hours or even days.

I pace. Both legs hurt and it's a shuffle and a hop from end to end of the cell. I count eight laps before I tire. Bedding down on the platform at night there was always something to do, a game of cards, a book to read, a board game or an ENSA entertainment party – a band or a singalong. People got along. I remember the first nights with Ma and Aggie in the Public Shelter and St Peters. The awful screaming of those mad women who were all convinced we were to die at any moment. Those of a 'nervous disposition' were right in their element. All their fears proved true.

Ruddy 'Itler. Strange thing, though. We didn't all go mad. You'd have thought the population would have lost their minds but we never did. Once we were down in the Elephant tube, it calmed down. People got on with it, no choice. "If your name's on a bomb then that's your lot," they said with a shrug – and by the second week a wink. Worse to think about injury: Jerry didn't get me in the streets or at the Café De Paris – maybe I was luckier than I thought. Lucky? Not now.

I hear footsteps.

Nowhere to hide as the rusty iron bolt scrapes back and the door swings open. In they come, the raven-heads. My face is strapped into a gas mask and I get that horrid smell of rubber, the respirator farting in and out. My hands are held behind my back and I am frog-marched out. The eyepieces mist over with my breath. Blood pumps in my ears. I stumble along, twisting my head to try to see either side of me but all I make out are my captors, hooded, beaked.

I am forced to my knees, too scared to rise even when hands grapple with me to remove the mask. I gulp stale air as I try to get my bearings. I am led to the cavern where I found Aggie. Oil lamps cast vast shadows around vaulted brick arches. A school blackboard has been positioned in front of me. There is writing on it in chalk. *Was ist dein plan?* It says in neat script. I slowly turn my head. Behind me are several of the hooded creatures. There must be ten, twelve of them in the first rank, others behind. They stand, waiting for someone, something.

I daren't get up.

From behind I hear footsteps and a low asthmatic wheezing. The raven-heads stand stiffly to attention. A chill shadow passes over us and a man enters in a cape, no a *gown*, and gas mask with its long trailing connector. He carries a long thin switch. He raises an arm (was this the hand that plucked the children from the stations?) and smacks the board with it. He indicates the words. What am I supposed to do? Say them? He smacks the board again and the mask looms in my face. I can barely look. One eye is opaque glass, the other a deep hole where I splintered it: nestling in the socket is a single bloodshot impassive eye. I hear wheezing stifled breath.

The baleful eye gloats.

After what seems an age he moves away behind me. The mask tumbles to the floor and even as it does, I know I must not look.

'*Was hast du im tunnel getan? Wer hat dich auf den schienen gelassen? Bist du Deutsch? Was ist dein plan fur London?*'

I've no idea what this means. I will give only my name and my address and a fat lot of good it will do they since they bombed it flat. He repeats the sentences over and over again and when I think it is all to confuse me, he speaks in English.

'Are you German?'

'No.' I say straightaway.

'You are German.'

'I'm bloody not.'

'You are German and you will tell me everything. *Sprich mit mir Deutsch.*'

'I'm not a Jerry.'

Suddenly he has gone. I am taken back to my cell and the door is bolted.

I was right, but I take no pleasure in it.

The Jerries have formed a unit down here.

Maybe because I saw them, they took Aggie as bait? Now what? They must be planning an invasion. Sands said they couldn't just parachute in and climb down the sewers. Maybe they're landing in the country then coming in disguised as Londoners? Forming a platoon? How many do they need to overthrow London? A thousand? Where's their armoury? Another thought hits me. Mr. Churchill. Good old Winnie is fighting the war in the cabinet rooms and using a bunker at Down Street Underground station. The station is closed for the duration but if you are down here in the labyrinth it might be accessible. If they could get to Winnie, it would be all over. They only need one fighting Unit – one platoon of Stormtroopers to bring down the whole of Britain. It makes my blood go cold.

I pace round my cell, thinking of escape. I need my strength. Can't run in this condition. I need a diversion or an ally. I need so many things. One hope is Ma and Evie. Ma will kick up a fuss and no mistake. On the first night she'll think I'm playing truant but when I haven't returned on the second she'll go to the police.

I hear a noise, which at first I think is rushing water but then I realise is feet, stamping in unison, marching. An order is barked out. They turn, marking time, square bashing. More orders then they march off. After a while I realise that I can tell the time by them. The raven-heads drill every few hours, which by my reckoning is once in the morning, then lunch then early evening but I could be wrong, it could as easily be three times during the night. There is a purpose here. In the dark there is nothing for my mind to do but go round and round and sleep creeps up on me again. The rats have come into my cell so I use the bucket to try to crush them. I kill one and it puts the others off.

Every day, between the morning and lunchtime drill, they come for me with the same routine. I am taken to the interrogation room where the head Jerry demands I speak German to him. The other ranks stand impassively by as he hits the words on the board. I won't say them. He has a persistent cough, like Bill Brandt. It can't be good for anyone down here, for so long with no light and no fresh air. When we were banned from sleeping on the tube platforms the reason given was that we would never want to come up again, and that we would start living like cavemen. A few nights of the stink and the heat and the mosquitoes soon put paid to *that* idea.

Each time I give nothing I am dragged back to the cell and my rations are reduced. Blitz broth, stale bread. No bully Beef. I count up the meals I have had in here and reckon I have been here for four days and five nights. The bread is stale. Where are they getting their food? It is the same bread as we get in the WVS or Salvation Army refreshment canteens. It is not the national loaf from outside.

Dad always said to look at a situation in a different light. Look at the question and ask it another way. Always look for the information you are getting that people *don't* tell you. They have a food source, but it's only what they can scavenge, which means someone has to go out above ground. If they go out and communicate then their English must be good enough to pass, which means… that they understand me. Next time I am taken out of the cell and forced to kneel in the schoolroom, I am ready.

'*Bist du Deutsch? Was ist dein plan fur London?*

'You speak English, so why don't you?'

This produces an unexpected reaction. He comes into view. The gas mask is off. I see that he is wearing scuffed brogues, flannel trousers, a white shirt long gone to grime and a tie hung around a scrawny neck. He is a young man in his late Twenties with a drawn face, small, pursed lips, pallid cheeks, a weak chin and eyes that burn in deep holes. The whites are veined with blood. His hair, already beginning to recede, is a wiry maze, a wild halo round his head. He sniffs me like an animal. His fingers take my chin, moving it this way and that. The nails are broken, dirty and long as talons, his shirt cuffs frayed and rimmed in grime. He doesn't look like a German, not like the drawings in the comics, square-jawed and brutish. He's scrawny and emaciated and when his hand grips there is a tremor from nerves.

'Would you tell me your name?' His accent is perfect. You'd never guess.

'William Lumley.'

'And who is the Minister for Home Security?'

'Morrison.'

'Which bus would you take for Peckham Rye?'

'The number twelve.'

He turns to the others. 'See how well trained they are.' There are murmurs of agreement. He continues. 'These things may of course be researched. The Number twelve is a major bus route. Where does it stop William?'

'South Croydon.'

He nods. 'Now something more specific. What are pips?'

'Sweets.' I say. 'We buy 'em from the jar.'

'You are most convincing.'

'That's because I'm *English* and bloody proud of it.'

'Of course you are.'

'But it's true.'

He seems amused, but in the way that Perce is amused, for his own reasons.

'I'm sure you could sing 'Oranges and Lemons' and tell us where to get cheese and bacon but these are facts you could have been told and we require more. Take him back for now.'

Again I am manhandled away. More what, I wonder? I don't know anything except for the layout of the tubes and they know that already. Why was he testing my knowledge of English? It's them who are the Germans. It doesn't make sense. Why wear a gas mask down here and what are all those horrible crow beaks the others are wearing? Best thing is to remain silent. As we reach my cell, one of the raven-headed captors punches me in the ribs and blurts out—

'Always thought you was a spy.'

I recognise the voice.

Johnny.

***

Back in my cell I try to understand. Has he joined them? He was taken, I guess, around ten days ago? More? It's so hard to tell time. Is he with the Germans or just pretending? Or… or… are they even Germans at all? I need to make proper contact, but he never liked me before and certainly doesn't now.

Was him speaking to me a mistake?

The only contact I have with my captors is at the interrogation, feeding time and Latrines. At mealtime the door is pushed open enough to slide the food through then immediately shut again. The empty bowl and plate are collected later. I devise a plan. I put the ablution bucket right over in the corner. They have not given me a cloth to put over it but as I'm eating so little there isn't much in there. What there is, I pad down with straw and then fill it with earth from the cell floor to make it heavy. I figure my chance will come when Johnny is on Latrine duty – but how to tell which one he is? Can I risk calling out his name?

***

133

The solution arrives when I least expect it. They come in pairs, one standing guard at the door as the other comes in for the bucket. I recognize Johnny's slight limp, as he brushes past me. He picks up the bucket, grunting with the extra weight. I shoulder him and he topples over. Grabbing the bucket, I twist round and hurl the contents at the guard by the door. The lad yells out and I slam the door behind us, locking Johnny and me into the cell. He gets straight on me, punching me here and there but I kick his legs out from underneath him and when he's down I rip the mask off him and get my hands around his throat.

'What's going on Johnny?'

'You tell me. You're the bloody Nazi.'

'That's a lie.'

He rounds a punch at me, but I am stronger than him and soon have him back on the ground. Others are trying to push the door in so I get Johnny up against the door. Each time they kick it, it hits him, jamming it still further.

'Are they Jerries? In the masks?'

'Course not. We got to take London back.'

'From who?'

'The foreigners. He's shown us. You hear them at Oxford Street and the Dilly – its crawling with Nazi's.'

I am taken aback. My indecision gives him time to make a space so that one of the others can wedge a foot in the door. The raven-heads burst in and the blows rain down as Johnny shouts about Nazi pigs.

***

I've never been so scared or miserable, not when the bombs came or when we lost our home or even when I saw people blown to pieces and the Rescue parties putting the bits in a dustpan. I wasn't even this scared when Dad had me sent away. I've no one left. I crawl up into the tiniest ball I can and cry myself to sleep.

***

Later, food comes but the interrogation stops and the raven-heads make me carry my bucket to the door and step back before collecting it. I stop looking for ways out. I still hear the occasional bombing up top, as if the giant has lost interest in us. A rat gets in and crawls over me as I doze and it is all I can do to shush it away. I slip into a waking dream where I see Dad's army helmet at the bars or imagine Ma and Aggie coming to get me. In one glorious moment Evie appears in the cell in a green and burgundy dress and kneels down to kiss me as she did in the cupboard under the stairs. I wake thirsty and aching.

***

134

Sometimes there is movement outside. From having seen Johnny and then hearing the pitch of their laughter I realise that they are not men. They are boys, young men like me not old enough to fight. These must be the taken ones, the missing children.

There is wailing in the night. I figure there must be others, here in the cells. I try tapping in Morse code on the boarded walls but the old gaol is so solid that it would take an army to be heard. I am sunk under tons of London clay. I am buried History.

***

This time they come for me with masks off. As I suspected, they are boys with grimy faces like me. Their eyes do not meet mine. I am marched through to the classroom but the man in the gas mask is not there. They lead me under an arch through a series of brick cellars and caverns. I see camp beds, their sleeping quarters I guess. We reach a small end space that might have been the back of a wine cellar. It has been made into a sort of study. There are piles of hardback books and an old-fashioned desk with a candle at each corner. The wax has dripped down the legs making small white molehills on the brick floor. There is a clothes rail of shirts and jackets. The gas mask hangs flaccid, a dead black rubber thing. Maps and diagrams are pinned up. There is a plan of the Underground lines with pins in it and a crudely drawn map of the Post Office Railway. There is a camp bed and a chair with a soft cushion, something from a posh house. A lot of the big houses are empty because their owners fled to the country when the bombing started. It is all topsy-turvy, this little room down here in the depths. The air is stale and fetid and everything is dank. How could anyone live in all this? The man enters, coughing harshly. He wears a tattered black professor's gown and beckons me to sit.

'Had enough of solitary?'

He looks at me to gauge my reaction. His accent is flat, not posh but not one of us. He perches on the desk, his gown billowing, almost catching the candle flame.

'Your mother is a seamstress, currently serving in the refreshment canteens. Your sister Agatha has been sent away.'

A bout of coughing racks his frame. I reckon it's tuberculosis. There's all sorts down here – lice, malaria, cholera. His eyes sparkle. There is something intense about him.

'You're English, aren't you?' I ask.

'Indeed.'

'Why did you keep speaking German?'

'All the new boys must be thoroughly checked.'

'For what?'

He scratches the back of his head. 'Loyalty.'

I decide to be bold. 'You do know there aren't any Nazi's out there.'

He smiles to himself like an old soldier who's seen it all before. 'Have you not heard them speaking their native tongue out there on the platforms?'

'You mean the Jews from Poland and Hungary. The Refugees?'

'NO. That is what they *want* you to believe!

He bangs his palm on the desk, upsetting one of the candles. He coughs again and spittle flecks round his mouth.

'They're fantastically organised. Many are Fifth Columnists. They are amassing, gathering strength whilst the Luftwaffe bombs the rest into submission. Once morale hits the lowest ebb they will rise. Our small band is all that remains, protected, safe.'

He scratches his head again and when his hand comes down I see fresh blood on it.

'Was that why you kept speaking German – to see if I was a Jerry?'

'Head of the class.'

'But if you know about my Ma and Aggie then it's obvious we're English.'

He gives me a conspiratorial look. 'The others must be convinced. Had to see you interrogated. Our strength lies in total commitment.'

I don't know what to say. Who is he, the beast in the Underground? Now we are face to face I realize that he is just a man, and an injured one at that. I gaze at his red hand. He wipes it on his gown. Maybe I ought to fight back.

'Why do *you* speak German so well?'

'I taught languages.'

'Why don't those others think *you're* a Jerry?'

He crashes a fist on the desk. 'Because I've *shown* them the Germans. They're all around us, up top, in the air, down here, everywhere.'

He goes to the map, pointing out the stations where he believes the Germans are gaining ground. I do not pay full attention because as he turns away I see that the back of his head is a nasty suppurating wound. A patch of hair is missing and underneath some jagged bone is visible. The wound is livid, all dried blood and scabs.

'Why do you all wear masks?'

'Fear. A face behind a mask is anonymous, *unheimlich*, as the Germans would say. We need to scare off the curious.'

'But why ravens? Those horrid beaks?'

'Serendipity. The plague doctors used to operate right here during the Black Death. These physicians – many were not real doctors – would try to cure the plague victims by wearing a long oil-coat and this beaked mask to keep out the infected air. The mask was soaked in camphor, lilac or salts to protect them. I discovered a cache of them down here.' He is warming to his history lesson. 'You worked out where you were being kept, I imagine?'

'I don't know.'

'It is a lost part of the old Fleet prison. It was destroyed, but we are in an older part, the dungeons, the *oubliettes*.'

'Who are you? What do you want with me?

'I have a task for you.'

'I'll go straight to the police.'

He steeples his hands, bony index fingers resting on his upper lip. 'And you think they will listen to you?'

He's right. They never did before. 'How long have I been here?'

'It is the third week in December. Above us the Hun has turned their attention to the provinces: Liverpool, Glasgow, Southampton, Bristol – the shipping ports.'

Three weeks since my capture. It is almost Christmas. A wave of sadness comes over me as I think of Dad, fighting in the desert heat. The man holds me with his mad eyes as he scratches his itch once more. How deep is that wound? If he keeps up it will never heal. Maybe this is what is driving his madness? Maybe it's why he wears the mask – to keep the others from seeing his weakness?

'We need fresh supplies. You will be taken to the end of the platform at Holborn where you will bring back the rations.'

'Why don't you send one of your boys?'

'It is your test.'

'And if I refuse to help?'

'The others won't take well to a traitorous act.'

I think of Johnny. Brute force and ignorance. He would smash me to smithereens. When I'm out, I can go to Sands. He'll know what to do.

'I don't have a choice, do I?'

'You must do your duty William.'

He holds out a bony hand for me to shake. It is paper dry and the nails are splintered. His grip bites into my wrist. His face changes to a grimace.

'Do not defy me, William.'

I bite my lip against the pain. I could try to explain that he is putting the children at great risk, keeping them here but I know he will not understand. He will go on taking them until he is stopped. As soon as I am out I can act. As his sunken eyes search mine I see only a broken man, maybe wronged. He releases my hand.

'It is time.'

'Now?'

'The boys are hungry.'

I get a sudden rush of excitement. Not only am I to be freed, but right away. I'll see Ma again and Evie too. He rises, his gown unfurling and swirling around us.

'All you will need to do is pick up the supplies. There will be someone to meet you.'

One of his boys. I'll knock him out, call out for help, anything. They won't risk coming out after me in their masks, not all of them.

'And we'll be watching. I have faith in you William.'

He fixes his mask back onto his face and calls for the guard.

***

I am led along cramped passageways, passing the wet stink of the sewers, under archways and up into the higher tunnels. The air is different, earthy and sooty. A couple of raven heads hold up the rear. We clamber up and soon we are in the pitch black of the tube tunnel. They glide along without hesitation, knowing the way, leading me toward a half crescent of yellow light. My eyes are greedy for it and I surge forward, excited as the prospect of freedom. I hear music, drifting hollowly toward me in the distance. I know the tune. *Begin the Beguine*. The man's fingers jab into my shoulder and he wheezes through the ventilator.

'From here you go alone. Your contact will be there.'

'How will I know him?'

'He will know you.'

I make my way along the rails, preparing for a fight, balling up my fists and tensing my muscles. Once I'm past his contact I will raise the alarm. The arch of the tunnel looms above me, and now I emerge, feeling as though I have been disgorged from the mouth of that terrible blindworm. I clamber up onto the platform. First comes the smell, damp clothes like a wet dog, the rich, nostril curling aroma of feet, hot breath, farts and the stale smoke of a thousand Player's No 6 and Craven A's.

There are people at the other end gathered in clumps around the conjoining tunnels and exits. A concert is being held on the other platform. There is a mad energy in my legs. I prepare to sprint. I risk a look back. The masked man and his raven troops have melted away. The tunnel is carbon black, dead as ever. For a second I wonder if this wasn't all some awful dream. No. I must act and act now.

I dash forward toward the noise and light and laughter, rushing into the throng. 'Please help me. I was taken. I need a policeman. A Shelter Marshal. I garble breathlessly to any grown-up but they are engrossed in the fun, the respite of the ENSA chorus. After so many days and nights bombing they want a quiet Christmas. There are a couple of comics at the mike and laughter drowns out my pleas. I search for Ma or Evie. No luck. Here, says one woman. Shelter Marshals, they're over there. I fight my way to where the crowd thins. Look for tin hats. There is a Christmas tree at the end of the platform. Paper chains have been hung along it. I keep expecting the beaks of the ravens to peck at me, to pull me back.

I run straight into the portly figure of Mr. Sands. I cannot hide my delight.

'Sands. I've got to talk to you. They took me.'

'Yes lad. I know.'

Chapter Eighteen

December 19th

We are sitting in the warm booking office. Everyone else is downstairs enjoying the concert. Whispers of a tune drift lightly up the wooden escalator. Sands has locked us in. He is tired and baggy looking, busying himself making tea, warming the pot, straining the weak leaves, milk in first, contraband sugar lumps, one each. He hands me a mug and as I drink.

'Here's what you're thinking Sonny Jim. Run for it, tell the coppers and make them understand about these boys living in the tunnels. About right?'

'Yes sir.'

'Bit formal Will?'

I shrug because I have been betrayed.

'Who's going to believe you, and at Christmas? They're telling enlisted men not to come back to London unless they live within ten miles of Charing Cross.'

'Someone will.'

'It's a mad story, I'll grant you that, never said it wasn't, but you're going to help us whether you want to or not, Savvy?'

'Why should I?'

'We need to keep 'em all as healthy as we can down there until something proper can be done about it.'

I frown. 'What do you mean?'

He sips his tea. 'That's for me to know. Now here's what you're to do. I'm going to put you back with your Ma and we're going to put together a believable story. I reckon we ought to think about scapegoating that gang you was hanging about with before.'

'Perce?'

'That Spiv, yeah. He's not done you too many favours.'

I still have the bruises on my arms and legs, even after all my time below.

'You can give a description to your Ma and the coppers. They've got it coming anyway. She is presently residing in Regents Park.' He puts on a high-class voice.

'A better class of shelterers *don't you know*.'

'Why's she there?'

'The canteen delivery stops there. I need you back working on it so you can half inch as much food as possible. Want some toast?'

I nod dumbly – my stomach is more mercenary than me.

'I thought I was to pick up one parcel of food.'

'At first, yes.'

Half the truth – it's what every grown-up tells you, so you're never thinking about all the other plans they've got for you. I've got to ask more questions, like Dad said. Sands uses a toasting fork and the one bar heater to cook the bread. Even though it's dry it tastes like heaven. I demolish two rounds.

'Why are you protecting that man down there?'

'Because he's sick. Have you seen him without the mask?'

'The head wound?'

'Shrapnel. He got hit fleeing a bomb blast. That's what sent him down there.'

'How do you know all this? Why don't you go in and get him out?'

'I'm too old to go risk wandering about in there. And as you know, the officers of the law haven't the manpower.'

'But he's been taking the children. He's convinced we're all German out here because he's heard the refugees in the West End. He thinks he's saving them or something. We have to *do* something.'

Sands closes his eyes and his face shuts down as if I had turned off a light switch. Twin tears run from his eyes and he makes no attempt to wipe them away. I've never seen a grown-up upset like this before. I look away in shame.

His voice, when it comes, is reedy and exhausted, drained of hope.

'When he wouldn't come out, I started leaving rations. He'd come as far as the edge of the tunnel and I'd give him what I could. Some nights he'd turn up, other nights nothing. When the kiddies started going missing I had an idea he was behind it. I just couldn't figure out what was going on in his head.'

'So you know him?'

His head, hanging low, rises briefly. 'I do.'

'He's a teacher of some sort isn't he?'

A grunt. 'He was, before the war. He needs help. Will you help me Will?'

'Why?'

He looks up at me, startled.

'Why *should* I help you when all you've done is lied? You knew about this from the start. You kept the picture, warned me off, protected this monster—'

His face is a crumpled paper bag. 'Then do it for the other children. Down in there they might catch scabies, cholera, all sorts.'

'All the more reason to go to the police and get them pulled out of there.'

'If this becomes a manhunt we'll have members of the public tagging along. A lynch mob.'

'*Why* are you protecting him?'

'Will – wait 'til Christmas. If there's a let up in the bombings we can get hold of enough ARP and police to get in there and save them all.'

My head feels like the sky above London, black and full of smoke and death and bombs. 'Why?' I ask.

He sinks into his uniform like a turtle. 'Wouldn't your dad do anything to protect your family?'

'Of course.'

'Even if it seemed wrong at first?'

'My dad would never do anything like that.'

Sands reaches into his tunic, pulling out his wallet. Out of it he takes a small, creased photograph, which he hands to me without another word. I examine the face, a young man in his twenties wearing a tweed jacket and gown, a mortarboard damping down his thatch of hair, a proud man, full of promise and the hope of achievements to come. It is the man in the tunnel.

'Who is he?'

'You haven't twigged it?'

I look at the deep lines carved in his forehead, the worry etched around his eyes, the jowls and his tarnished teeth.

'I thought you was Tommy smart.'

There is a silence between us that no amount of bombs could break.

Sands drains his cup, sets it down, takes a deep breath and haltingly, tells me the story.

'His name's Victor. His Mother died in childbirth. I raised him. He was a smart boy, gifted, won a scholarship to the Haberdasher's Aske. The first in my family to ever get an education. Trained to become a teacher. He'd always suffered from bad headaches, sensitive lad, got it from his Mum. Days in a darkened room didn't make it easy to hold down the job. The war came along. He was in a reserved occupation so he wasn't to get his papers just yet but the school got shut for the duration. This put him in the Lottery for the call up so he declared himself CO.'

'A conchie?'

A nod. 'Point of principle. I taught him war was no good thing. Said he ought to join the NCC.'

'What's that?'

'Non-combatant Corps. Admin, construction, maintenance. He'd have joined the RAMC, Medical Corps but they stopped taking recruits this year. He was back living with me in Sydenham, got himself into a terrible state. Convinced he'd not pass the tribunal if and when it came to it.'

'What tribunal"

'If you're a conscientious objector you've to be on a special register and stand trial. People think they're cowards, well maybe they are, but it's not easy to stand up for yourself and your beliefs. If you fail you've to register for military service or risk a fine or prison. You wouldn't want to be in a prison right now.'

'Isn't he medically unfit?'

'He joined the Fire Service. One morning after the start of the Blitz proper he never came home. That wasn't so unusual – they work all night as you know, but it took a week to find him in a Medical centre. Got caught out in a raid, shrapnel.'

'The head wound?'

Sands nods. 'He was having nightmares, delusions; convinced children were after him with white feathers. As soon as he was discharged he went underground. A week later I saw him in the mask. If I came too close he'd sink back like a frightened cat. I started leaving food out. Never thought it'd come to this.'

Sands thumbs tobacco into his pipe and sets about lighting it. His fingers tremble.

'What about when he started taking these other boys?'

'I'd no idea until he sent messages that he needed more food.' Sands draws deeply on his pipe, making the bowl glow. 'In his way, he's no less of a patriot then you or I. You understand that son?'

'I think so.'

'So will you help us?'

***

Regent's Park Station Refreshment area is crowded with women blustering about doing their bit, all in green overalls and hairnets, busy as bees. Sands and I have agreed on our story and I am free to wend my way through the sorting, packing, smoke, laughter and chatter. Some of the women recognise me from before and this causes a ripple of surprise that grows to a wave as I approach the back of the carriage where Ma's making sandwiches. She's tired and pale but no more so than the others. Our eyes meet and mine are immediately pricked by tears.

She sags as if she's in the heat and suction of a bomb blast.

The next second she's yelling out my name.

'Will. Oh my boy, my darling boy. My boy is back.'

She barrels forward like a tank and almost crushes the life out of me, kissing me over and over as her face gets wet. Where have you been? My little man. Oh, you little monster. My boy alive, safe and sound. She says it to everyone and a lot of the women have their handkerchiefs out and are dabbing at their eyes and their faces are melting like an incendiary attack caught us all.

'I thought you was dead for sure. Where you been you terror, you little horror.'

'I missed you Mu—' I say, nearly calling her mummy like I did when I was a baby.

'You sit right down – let's have a look at you. You're hurt.'

She finds a quiet corner and lights up a ciggie and investigates my bruises and though most of them aren't so painful anymore there are big livid patches on my side and legs and ribs. She gasps and tries to stop herself crying more and the interrogation begins. This is what Sands said would happen. His instruction is that it is important to say very little. Invent a short truth and keep to it. Don't polish it or you lose yourself like a dog chasing its tail.

'It was this bunch of spivs. They kept hold of me.'

'We'll go straight to the police.'

'They got caught already. That's how I got away. They were thieving and the police came down and caught them with their loot.'

The lie relies on me not seeing Perce in Ma's company. She's got good eyes Ma, even with all the sewing in the dark.

'Where was they keeping you?'

'They've got this den under Goodge St.'

Always have some truth in it. You use that as the stepping-stone.

'Why weren't you caught and all?'

'I ran off when the coppers chased them. I found my way out.'

'What on earth were they keeping you for?'

All this is asked between her wiping my face with her magic hankie or straightening out my dirty clothes and tutting about what will need to be cleaned in the laundry.

'They wanted me to thieve with them before Christmas. I kept saying no.'

'Good boy.'

'They didn't care about the war, just wanted to have what they could.'

She stopped asking then, and I knew she was assessing the story, weighing up the likelihood of whether it was true or it being a yarn. The choice was to come down on my side or what was the alternative? That I'd been bunked down with Winnie Churchill or lying under rubble in a bombsite for a fortnight? Gone Firewatching on a yellow bicycle and not told her about it? Any of these would be saner than what really happened but she'd never guess it. In the end she ruffles my hair and hugs me again.

'I'm so glad to have you back, and for Christmas too. Gives us all hope.'

'What about Dad?' Is he coming home?'

'No news I'm afraid love.'

'But he promised. He promised he'd be home at Christmas?'

Learning about Sands and his son makes me want my dad home even more.

'He can't very well go telling the Army he's popping off for his turkey and pudding. That's desertion. They're doing what they can to get enlisted men back to their families but there's got to be some left fighting the war… and if he's in a hot place. North Africa or Egypt… well…' She leaves it at that.

I stare at the ground.

'It's so good to have you back Will. I thought…'

I know what she thought.

'They're still coming over, blooming Luftwaffe. You get one night off and you're more nervous than before. Makes you wonder what's to come? Whether there'll be a big push to flatten us all… aw, come here.'

She folds me into her and I feel that Ma smell of bread and clothes washed too many times. She rocks me back and forth and I don't mind at all and let her stroke my hair.

'I'm sorry Will.'

'What for?'

'While you was gone I was thinking about all the things I'd have done different. I've been too hard on you.'

I'm sorry too. Sorry I can't tell you the truth and that I am going to have to keep on telling you lies because I made a promise to Mr. Sands and his son because I want to do things for the greater good. I don't want us harmed, any of us, not you or me or Aggie or… suddenly I realise I forgot to ask.

'Where's Evie?'

A smile comes to Ma's lips.

'Out delivering. She'll be pleased as punch to see you. Been going on about you. Torn up, she was. Here, come and have some grub.'

I am given a pie and some warm milk. I'm distracted because my thoughts are going towards Evie. Is her hair still reddish brown and long or will it be all pinned up in her berry or a hairnet? Will she have the beetroot lips? A rosy glow? A skirt that she's made short? But wait. What if she's with someone? What if some Airman has whisked her off at a dance? She had no reason to wait for me and never gave me pause to think it either. She melted a bit after Auntie Joan died but she never really showed she liked me. I feel awfully tired all of a sudden and Ma sits me down while she gets on with her war work. I doze off and next thing I know she's shouting my name.

'William Lumley!'

'Evie. You're a sight for sore eyes. '

And hearts. She looks just as I imagined. She gives me a peck on the cheek and starts gabbing away nineteen to the dozen just like Ma. She wants to know everything and I give her the war story but this being the second time my escape is more derring-do and I punched some of the spivs and outran a copper. This gets big eyes and I see she has painted some black stuff onto her eyelashes. She even tells me I look taller. I am pleased as punch.

'Have you been all right on your own?'

'I've had all these lovely ladies around me. My new family.'

'No more dances then?'

When she shakes her head her hair swings about her shoulders.

'Not yet but we will if Adolf lets us have a Christmas. People are determined to have a good time. Fortnum's has fruit. There's tons of posh women in the West End getting stuff wrapped in brown paper and ribbon.'

'Where've you been sleeping?'

'The canteen train or the berth at Holborn. It's a right party there some nights.'

'Are we going tonight?'

'Once we've finished up. You want to help?'

'Evie? Did you miss me?'

'Don't be silly.'

'But did you?'

'Course.'

'How much?'

She breaks into a grin. 'Oh tons and tons. The war work hardly went on without you. In fact they were thinking of stopping the war so we could look for you.'

'I wish they had.'

'The Luftwaffe wasn't having it. Now, let's get to work.'

She went back to it and got me to help as the next round went out and I felt like just her stupid cousin again.

By the time we got back to Holborn I managed to steal and pocket quite a bit of food. As Ma and Evie went about their ablutions I excused myself to use the chemical toilets at the end of the platform. There, I unloaded the contraband food. There wasn't enough to feed all of them but it is a start. After a few moments there was a scrabbling in the dark tunnel and I saw a pair of eyes down by the track. A grubby pair of arms reached out, snatched the package and scuttled away into the carbon blackness.

Chapter Nineteen

December 23rd

I am working with Ma and Evie on the refreshment canteen and taking what food I can, slipping it into my pockets and stowing it under my bunk. I wait for Ma to drop off, which doesn't take long as she's sleeping like a log these days. Evie's on a different shift and comes back late so I take the contraband to the tunnel. Sometimes a raven head will emerge and snatch the food, other times Victor Sands is standing there in his gas mask. I try to communicate with him but he does not reply. Behind the mask his eyes are wide and staring. I sense his fear but I remember that he has astonishing strength.

Up top, London is much the same – full of holes, rubble and fires. The West End throngs with men in bowler hats and women in woollen coats in Oxford Street. You forget that in the middle of all this there are places that never get troubled by the Jerries; Hounslow, Harrow, Uxbridge, Wembley, Enfield, Barnet, Richmond – all the ends of the Underground tube lines. Jerry has pretty much dropped their load by Fulham, plus the big spotlights and Ack-ack guns and barrage balloons are more effective now. There's a feeling of resilience and anticipation, hopes of a Christmas lay-off. Ma has got her I've-got-you-something-secret smile on and I'm supposed not to look in her bunk. I have of course. It's a toy Spitfire for me to paint. I want it, but I wonder if this isn't a child's toy.

There has been no sign of Perce or Ollie and I'm going to keep well out of sight if I do see them. I suspect they're hunting for rich pickings in the streets and dipping down in the tube around Tottenham Court Road. Maybe they will get caught in the way that a lie can breed the truth, like once when I didn't want to do a Mathematics test so much that I pretended I was ill and then I did catch an awful chill. The Dilly is decorated with banners saying "Merry Christmas 1940". The canteens have got bunting all over them and there are buns for sale. There's to be a Carol service and another ENSA concert on the platform at Aldwych with songs and comedy sketches. The community Christmas tree has been decorated with whatever baubles and decorations people can find.

Someone managed to drum up some glue – rabbit probably – and I was roped into making paper chains out of newspapers. At Swan & Edgar the seamstresses are in great demand for those who can't or won't 'Make do and Mend'. Ma has a stream of women wanting to make the old look new and unable to do it from the magazines.

There wasn't a raid last night.

We cringed and held our breath but it never came. People went to the theatre to enjoy a pantomime or revue; the Lyon's Corner shops were full behind the criss-cross glass and the restaurants too. Evie is busy with Christmas preparations and seems to have made friends with every single person down here so there is no chance to get her to myself. I'm in the bunk underneath her and I gaze at the depression her body makes when she's asleep. After lights out, I gently caress the mattress but she doesn't know. Ma is all in when she gets back. Everyone is all in these days. This makes it easy to get hold of food during the day and evening and I collect quite a haul, so much that I have to do up the milk, buns, cheese and bully beef in brown paper and string, like laundry.

After lights out I go to the end of the platform and place it down. A routine now.

Suddenly, there's a hand on my arm. My heart nearly stops.

'What're you up to Will?'

It's Evie.

'Nothing.' Bad answer. She glances at the package.

'What's that?'

'Clothes.'

'Bit lumpy for clothes.'

Saying no more is probably for the best. I shrug and smile. 'You're back early.'

'We had a rush on. Your Ma and I are trying to find ways of putting together a Christmas meal. People have been saving fruit.'

'I hope it'll be good – Christmas.'

'If you tell me what's in the package?'

'Do you want to see my smelly socks and underwear?'

'You're not washing them back here at eleven at night.'

'No I'm not.' I say, picking it up.

She looks at me with her pretty head cocked to one side. Her eyes narrow above that freckled nose and there is still a trace of whatever she was using on her lips to make herself look presentable. She folds her arms and glares at me, daring me to speak. I do the only thing I can think of. I kiss her right on the lips. She releases a tiny grunt and pushes me gently away but her hands are on the string of the package and they aren't letting go. We're holding it like Mr. and Mrs. Punch fighting over the baby. She gives a tight little smile that says she will get what she wants. Rather than wrestle it off her, I decide to let her have it and come up with another tale for the food. She peels back the paper. Her eyes widen and she gets down on the floor where the platform meets the wall and examines the bounty. Cheese, wheat flakes, bully beef, tins of fruit, sardines. When she looks up at me, there is hurt in her.

'Where did you get all this?'

'Around.'

'Where around?'

'Heavy bombing in Jermyn Street. Half of Fortnum and Mason's stuff was blown out all over the street.'

'You were *looting*?'

'I call it salvage. It would've gone off.'

She raises her voice. 'Will, that food belonged to someone.'

'Don't get high and mighty. They can afford it.'

'Don't make it right. It's still stealing. They're talking about hanging people for looting. They've got soldiers patrolling. What if you'd got caught?'

'I didn't.' I play a straight flush. 'I did it for you and Ma. I was going to hide it away and give it you Christmas Day.'

She rolls her eyes. 'And don't you think your Ma would have asked the same questions as me? You daft? She wouldn't have touched this either, not without knowing where it's from. You learned this from those spivs you hung around with – you still with them? Part of some gang?'

Can I tell her? Would she trust me?

'I'm not part of any gang.' I say. And it is true. I was never part of Perce's people, not properly, and I haven't joined the captured children. I'm on my own as usual.

She stacks the food, putting the tins in neat piles. She stands and looks at me in the way Ma looks at other women who haven't cleaned their front step properly.

'This food can't go back now so I have a better plan. We're going to distribute it to the needy children. It's late so we'll not wake them, just leave a tin or a box tucked in under their bedding or pillow if they have one. Understand?'

That takes the biscuit.

'Is that all right Mister Scrooge?'

'Humbug.' I say.

And this is what we do, silently placing the boxes and tins of supplies in the beds and bunks of the kiddies like Mother and Father Christmas. As I go about my work, I wonder if they are watching me. If they can see that I am doing this against my will? But what greater good could there be than this? Forget them down there. Maybe Evie will be so delighted about this act of charity she will submit to a kiss and a cuddle if Ma is not back. Hang Victor Sands! A night of cuddling Evie Wilde is long overdue and perhaps if I offer enough apologies it might be on the cards.

We thread our way along the platform to the west and the eastbound, in and out. Occasionally I lose sight of her but then she appears to pass me another gift to give away. To hold those arms, stroke the downy hairs. To feel her hot breath on mine, our bodies mashed together on a tiny bunk. She might press me to her again and take my hand. I could lose myself in her. What should I say? How do I get her to my bunk? I look along at the rows of bunks and she's not there. I whisper her name, once, twice, a third time louder. My body floods with dread and I start running towards the darkness in the tunnel, calling out—

'EVIE!' Evie.

I have no torch.

I stand in complete blackness.

There is no sound or movement save the rats.

She has been taken. A reprisal.

***

I fight my way through the sleeping masses up to the booking office to look for Sands but it is locked up. I have to tell an adult but there are no ARP wardens around. I will tell Ma, but by the time I get back to her bunk she is asleep flat out, fully clothed. I cannot bear to wake her. Besides, what can she do that I have not already failed at in this situation? Instead, I remove her worn down shoes, releasing a sigh as each one leaves her heel. I place them by the bed and I lay on my bunk, turning over and over in my mind what to do. I curse myself for all this, for letting it all happen, for not being stronger, for not being Dad.

***

I must have dozed off because next thing I know the early Tannoy is waking people and we're on the move. *Keep Calm and Carry On* says the poster. Ma won't listen to anything because she has to be at work. It is Christmas Eve. We are to meet at dusk. There is to be a candlelit carol service in the Underground at six o' clock. When Ma is a whirl of activity like this I can't stop her. It has been two Christmases now where the grown-ups are more excited about the day than I am.

I have to find Sands. The booking office clerk says that he is not on until two o clock so I wander the foggy streets. There is more traffic today, open trucks and cars and lorries delivering for Christmas. Troops too. Soldiers coming home on leave. I consider going to the police at West End Central and speaking to that copper, but what am I going to say to get them to believe such a crazy story? I move in and out of the shoppers and end up staring in Hamley's window. It should be wonderful; all lit up with a display of wooden planes and tanks and hundreds of lead toy soldiers and I don't want any of it. I want Evie back. If I could get her, I would tell her. I would tell her that I have

149

this lump in my heart that will not go away, that it gets stronger but hurts all the time.

***

Sands is at the bottom of the escalator directing Christmas shoppers.

'I thought it was all going according to plan.' He says.

'Evie caught me with the food package.'

'And you say they've took her?'

'She disappeared. They must think I wasn't doing my bit—'

'What can I do?' He snaps.

'Go in the tunnel and talk to your son.'

'I think she'll be all right. You were all right.'

'She's a girl.'

He is getting cross. 'I know.'

'What will they do with her?'

'Wait.'

The next rush of women shoppers comes down the escalators and he herds them to one side of the brass rail. He has his work face on, chiding the shoppers with his cheeky old grin. Help you Missus, bought up the West End have you? Great, we can all get off home now. Let me guess what's in the box? A hat or 'Itler's head. Yes Madam, we do accept gratuities. As the crowd thins out he tips up his helmet.

'Give me till this evening.'

'What time?'

'After the concert. The peace of it might draw Victor closer in. I sometimes hear him behind the walls. You never know. An English carol service might just convince him that we're not all bloody Jerries, eh?'

***

I can get a torch but I can't go in the tunnels when the lines are live. I ride the tubes between Holborn and Piccadilly, Leicester Square and Russell St, turned around with my knees on the seat, peeling back the blackout paper hoping to glimpse a ghost station, a hiding place, a clue, anything. I walk the tunnels putting my ear against the cool tiles, listening as I did for Aggie. I get odd looks but then, odd isn't irregular anymore when you've seen a woman sitting on a bomb site screaming out for her kiddie, or a man naked in his bathtub blown dead across the street into another building, when you've seen bomb casings twisted like some metal flower off the moon. I never wanted to say about these things before. I couldn't. I didn't want them to become words. I didn't want to make it real. I didn't want to think even when I was in that filthy prison cell, but now?

150

Now it's not just me, it's Evie gone.

I go back to my billet and lay idle on my bunk. The hairs on my neck go up as a voice rings out like the first church bell on a clear Christmas morning. I know the carol. 'Once in Royal David's City' being sung in an angel's voice delivering us from the pain and glass and rubble and mortar dust and blood and fire and bombs. No Jerry could sing like that. Victor must hear it. That voice will carry through into the labyrinth to let them know. To let them all know we are British and we can save all our lost children. The choir joins in and I rise from my bed to watch as the congregation gathers. I start to sing, knowing it from school. I miss Tom and Jim and little Kenneth and Mr. Bennett. I miss sitting in lessons with all my friends.

They dim the overhead lights and people hold candles in reverent silence along the platform. The crowd falls into rank, tallest at the back, kiddies sitting at the front. They have done their best and made a crib out of an old orange crate with straw and a doll for the Jesus. The chaplain stands to one side with his black book. He can speak for God if he wants but for me this is about us Londoners. The carol finishes and many of us have hard lumps in our throats like you get when you breathe in too much smoke from a fire. Ma works her way through the crowd. She's wrapped in her winter warm coat and her cheeks are apple red glowing from the cold. She motions to me to come away and we meet up under a corner arch.

'I've got great news.'

'Is it about Dad?'

Her face twists and she sets her jaw as she produces a letter. Through the thin paper I make out a childish scrawl. There are other sheets too.

'Aggie's people – The Perkins – have invited us for Christmas in the country. What do you think to that, eh?'

My heart starts hammering, my face boiling. 'We can't go away.'

'But we'll see Ag and there'll be plenty of food. It's an open invitation. There's no rationing out there. Think of it, a few days bomb-free, all of us together again.'

'What about Evie.'

'Her too.'

'But she's gone missing. I have to find her.'

Her voice goes stern. 'Will, there's no time for your stories. If she's not here then she doesn't want to be here. She'll have to fend for herself. She has plenty of friends. We have to go.'

'What, *now*?'

'Yes right now. We're catching the last train out of Charing Cross.'

Incendiaries are going off in my head. 'No, Ma, no'

'Right now William.'

'What about Dad?'

'Will, I haven't heard from your father in well over a month. He's not coming back for Christmas and you'll just have to get that through your thick head.'

'You don't care. You just want to see your favourite child.'

She slaps me hard across the cheek. It stings but I won't give her the satisfaction of letting her know how much it hurt. I glare at her.

'I'm not bloody well leaving London.'

She pulls me back to the bunk and starts throwing all her things into her suitcase and when I do nothing to help she throws mine in my case as well. I'll run off and hide. I'll find Evie and rescue everyone and I will be a hero and Dad will come home to see it all and Ma will be very, very sorry.

She thrusts my case at me.

'Pick it up.'

Another carol fills the air. 'Silent night'. The candlelight is pretty but nothing can cover up the stink of the unwashed, the pong of feet or the Elsan toilets.

'I'm not going.'

'You'll do as I say.'

'I'm not a child.'

'Yes you are.'

'I'll run away and you can't stop me.'

'You do it and that's that. You're on your own. For good.'

She glares at me fierce. I fold my arms. She puts down her case and lights up one of her stupid cigarettes.

'Go on Will. Run off and be with those vicious little spivs. Don't think I don't know what's been going on. You never reported them. You were spinning a yarn. I thought you had come back because you'd seen some sense. I was wrong. Go with them and see if I care, but if you do, you ain't coming back to me.'

I don't move. Not yet.

She takes a big lungful of smoke and blows a great plume. I hope it chokes her.

'You aren't going and I'll tell you for why. As long as Dad is away you are the man of the house.'

'You said I was a child.'

'You have a duty to look after your family.'

'Evie is family.'

'Our immediate family.'

'You don't care about her.'

'I do, but she's not here and the best we can do is leave her a note and a telephone number if there is one.'

'She's been kidnapped.'

'Don't start on again with these bloody fantasies Will. You've got one minute to make a decision. You want to be a grown-up, I'll treat you like a grown-up.

You come spend Christmas with your family or stay down here in all the grime and filth with a bunch of thieving little tykes. It's up to you.'

I stare at my scuffed shoes and wrinkled socks as the carol soars around us. Whatever I say she won't listen. Ma never hit me before. Not in my face. Dad put me over his knee when I was little and I got the belt once or twice but he was always the threat and Ma the treat. I don't like it this way round. She's hit me harder than Dad would've done and I don't doubt she'll keep her promise. Thoughts are whizzing round my head but getting me nowhere. I look up. She's belted into her coat with her big brown battered suitcase in one hand.

'What's it to be?'

I feel my face crack open. 'I don't know.'

Without another word she turns and smartly walks off.

I pick up my case and follow her.

***

We jump on a Bakerloo going south. It is a few stops to Charing Cross with the train near deserted, everyone heading home or celebrating. We rise up to the sandbagged front of the Main line station. It is a sharp winter's night. A bomber's moon if they want it, but no siren has sounded, no air raid confirmed. Ma paces over to the ticket office and uses her Christmas wages from a small brown envelope to get our tickets. There are plenty of people bustling round in scarves and coats with gifts under their arms, carol singers here too – everyone defying 'Itler. We go straight to the train, slamming the heavy wooden door. The passenger nearest the window offers Ma a seat and helps her to get the suitcases up onto the string hammock. I get the window. The corridor is crowded with City gents in bowlers with white copies of the evening newspaper. Some have them under their arms, other spread out butterfly style. The air is sweet with pipe smoke. Rat-tat-tat as the doors close like dominoes, shutting out old London.

I could still jump off. Make a run for it.

We clatter over the Thames, all black and silver. There's a fire burning in the docks and the glow of it makes the underneath of a cloud orange. Barrage balloons sway here and there. No searchlights tonight, no warning phoned through. It's calm. Up on the viaduct we pass Waterloo and London Bridge and then it's the long slide past the Old Kent Road down towards St John's and Lewisham, saw-tooth roofs and pepper pot chimneys. Those who are left will be inside tonight, not shivering in the Anderson. The lights in the carriage are kept dim but there is enough to see the reflection of my face in waxy moonlight. My hair is long, my jaw defined. Where is Dad? In the sunshine or dead in some muddy field? Hung out on some barbed wire? Blown to pieces by a shell or gathered around a fire with his mates drinking tea and telling blue jokes? Evie. I hope they feed her. I hope she fights them too. She's strong. Strong enough, I hope.

Hold out for me, Evie. Please hold out.

Chapter Twenty

We alight in the middle of nowhere, a ghost place. The platform is pitch black. The name of the station has been painted out. All the signposts have been removed. There was hardly anyone on the train as we ploughed on into Kent. Ma guessed at it being Tonbridge but this could be France for all I know. We walk through open gate in the picket fence, as the station building is locked. It's much colder than London and I pull my winter socks up as high as they will go. Outside a Jeep is waiting with its engine idling. The door opens and a ruddy-faced man in boots steps out.

'Mrs. Lumley?'

'And son', says Ma. 'Are you Perkins?'

He looks us up and down, as if guessing our weight or worth.

'You best come up in the cab with me. Stick your cases in the back.'

Soon we are bouncing along. There are high frosty hedges on either side and tree branches trail like dead fingers over the lanes. We go up and down between the rolling fields as Ma witters on. Perkins is not a man of words; in fact, he doesn't seem to want to speak to us at all. Maybe it's because we are townies and they are country people. I've heard about this and I start to get a bit scared. We don't even know for sure this is him. Maybe they have kidnapped Aggie and now they want us? We come off the road onto a dirt track and approach a number of low farm buildings. There is a barn and a stable. The only light comes from a square window in the middle of the main farmhouse. It has an old thatched roof. We draw up outside and get out. It's not often I have been in a car and they don't half shake you about. The muddy rutted track is frozen hard. The farmhouse door is cut in half at the middle but Perkins swings open both and the heat and light hits us.

'Surprise!'

And here are Aggie and the farmer's wife and two pretty girls I do not know and Aggie is running full pelt at Ma and she leaps into her arms and suddenly there is crying and laughing and dogs barking and Perkins removes his hat and laughs at the big joke.

155

'I was having you on. I bet you thought I was a right rotter.'

'Well.' Says Ma.

'We were hoping you'd make it. I been there an hour waiting.'

Aggie has colour in her cheeks and looks well fed and has a new dress on.

'This one's been beside herself.' Says the farmer's wife.

Aggie lets go of Ma long enough to clamp herself to me.

'You look different Will. Taller if anything.'

'So do you.'

She tries to hug the life out of me. 'It is so good to see you.'

'I know.' I say, giggling.

Mrs. Perkins has a meal for us even though it is almost midnight. There is a big stove called an Aga, which gives off loads of heat, and a pot bubbling away on top of it. We sit at a long wooden table and are given a bowl of steaming meat casserole. We're introduced to the two girls, Florence and Tilda who are eighteen and are called Land Girls. I'm too shy to talk to them and they dominate the conversation asking Ma all about London news and fashions and it turns out they are from the East End themselves so when they ask about what is left after the bombing I'm able to give a detailed report. Once we've eaten Aggie says she will show me up to our room. Ma and Mrs. Perkins follow us up the steep wooden stairs and Aggie undoes the latch on the door. Inside there are two beds.

'How many of us are kipping in here?' I ask.

'Just you and your sister.' Replies Mrs. Perkins.

'I have a bed... all to myself?'

Ma's eyes are glistening.

'You can get straight in.' Says Mrs. Perkins.

'So long as you get undressed.' Says Ma.

There is a patterned eiderdown; a coverlet and the sheets are bright white. I peel them back, feeling the starched cotton. I kick off my shoes, tear off my pullover and unbutton my shirt as quick as I can. My shorts go next – I don't care if they see me in my underpants. I can't remember what bed felt like, only now as I slide so slowly between the sheets it all comes flooding back and I let out the biggest 'mmmm' you ever heard. I'd like to say I enjoyed it but I fell asleep straightaway.

***

'Shut up.' I'm trying not to open my eyes, which are crusty. There is some animal outside making a lot of noise. Aggie is sleeping in the bed across the room. 'Aggie. Shut it up!' I say again, staying buried under the covers.

'It's the cockerel. You'll have to get used to it.'

I try to stay asleep but other birds twittering soon accompany the hacking sound and now there is thudding downstairs, as people are getting up.

'Ag. Where's the bucket for pee?'

'There's an outhouse. You can break the ice.'

I pull on my short trousers, shoes and a dressing gown. The attic room has sloping walls and cold morning light streams in through a gap in the curtains. I slope downstairs. The kitchen is full of women and dogs, and there is a warm meaty smell that I cannot place. I wander outside. My breath billows in the light, making a cloud. I find the wooden shack, unhook the latch and sure enough, the bowl is iced over. My aim is true and it cracks under my stream. When I come out, I can see where we are properly. There are ploughed up muddy hills, all covered in frost like muslin, and a tumbledown wood and a corrugated iron shed. Pigs snort around in front of a trough and in the other direction there is a stable with a chestnut horse, being groomed by the Land Girls. The fields are boundaried by prickly hedgerows and wild, barren winter trees. The farmhouse walls are heavy red brick and the door a hard shiny oak.

I go back in and wash my hands and Mrs. Perkins gives me a steaming bowl of porridge. It is creamy and full of oats. A far cry from what I'm used to.

'This is the best thing I have ever tasted in my life.'

'You better get washed and dressed right away, young lad.'

I am suddenly afraid. It's going to be like last time. They are going to put us to work all day with the animals or in the fields.

'Why straight away?' I ask, cautious now.

She turns from the pot, holding a big gloopy wooden spoon. Her smile turns into puzzlement. 'It's not Christmas *every* day is it?'

***

Christmas Day passes in a blur. The kitchen smell was a chicken roasting and there was ham too, along with vegetables for boiling, then cooking in the fat. Ma had ironed my dancing suit so I wore it to church. We all walked there over the fields in our Sunday best. The bells didn't ring of course but the church was packed to the rafters. The Parson gave thanks and we prayed for the fallen and for missing loved ones and Ma took my hand and squeezed it hard because she knew I was thinking of Dad. We sang carols and said the Lord's Prayer and afterwards Ma and I were introduced to lots of old fat people who shook my hand as hard as they could. The men drifted off to the pub and I came back with the women and Aggie and I played Ludo. When Mr. Perkins came back it was time for presents and a lot of squealing from the Land girls. I got the wooden plane and marbles from Ma and toffee sweets made by Aggie – you could tell because they were lumpy, but they tasted fine. Mr. Perkins had our best presents though – a penknife for me and for Aggie a doll's house that he had made himself and the girls had furnished. There was so much food, the roast, the glazed ham and sausages and the Land girls made hats out of card. I was allowed some cider and I felt giddy and I flew my plane around and teased Aggie. We gathered round the radio and listened to BBC Radio's Kitchen Front and then the King's speech. Everyone collapsed in a heap and all agreed that although this was our first real war Christmas we hoped there wouldn't have to be another.

In the evening the Land girls took it upon themselves to play kiss-chase and I ran from their smacking lips and puckered mouths and raced under the covers of my bedding and tried unsuccessfully to fight them off. I didn't really mind. If they were fighting 'Itler we could win this war in weeks.

***

Boxing Day was back to work for the Perkins but without Florence and Tilda who, I was told when I awoke, had taken the train to go back to visit their families. I felt bad. I could have gone too. I had forgotten about Evie for the whole of Christmas. I had selfishly enjoyed myself while she is still trapped down there with that man and his Children's Brigade. Before I had a chance to make a plan, Aggie demanded we go exploring. It's something she enjoys out here, safe from the bombs. So after breakfast she found me a pair of Wellington boots and off we went.

She led me to a high point with a view of the valley. The morning mist hung like a hammock. There was a meadow and a long meandering river with willows trailing in the water. Ag took me to a small wooded area in the flood plain, all high frosty grasses and skinny stick like trees. We trod holes in the ice for a bit then she wanted to play hide and seek, darting in and out between tree trunks and appearing out of nowhere. The crackle of her boots gave away her position.

'You wouldn't make much of a spy.' I tell her.

'Good job I don't want to be one then.'

'Oh, you want to be something now, do you?'

'Florence is a mechanic. She knows all about engines.'

'That's men's work.'

'No it isn't. Once all the men are gone she'll have to do it.'

I broke off a branch and threw it, enjoying the thud of it on the hard ground.

'Are you going to join the Army Will?'

'I'm too young.'

'I don't want you to go to war.'

'I'll have to once I'm old enough.'

'I won't let you.'

'It's not up to you.'

She stomped off through icy water, pushing through a prickly hawthorn. I followed but she was moving quickly. She knows her way around here. We came to a clearing surrounded by tall stark trees with thick black trunks and brown dead leaves carpeting the ground. I got out my new knife and tested the blade on my finger and drew a little blood. I then cut into the bark, whittling out a chunk, exposing the white bone of the tree, making young wood from old.

'What's wrong Ag?'

'Dad's gone and no one talks about him and you're next.'

'I'm not gone yet am I?'

'I want you and Ma to stay here on the farm.'

'We're guests... and I have to go back.'

'Why?'

I stop carving. 'They've got Evie.'

She stands there in her winter coat and big rubber boots and I find myself telling her the whole story of my capture and escape and the parts about Mr. Sands and his son and what they tried to get me to do and by the end her eyes are wide as saucers.

'You *have* to go back.'

'I know, but how?'

'Run away to the station. Get a train.'

'Where is it?'

'I don't know – that way.' She pointed vaguely at the angled shafts of sunlight.

'It could be miles, and with no road signs I'll get lost.'

'No you won't. You'll hear the train. Follow it and you'll get to the station.'

'How often do they come?'

'Don't know.'

'Don't know much, do you?'

'I do know what I can do.'

'What?'

'I can make a diversion and get the money for your ticket.'

And that is what she did.

***

It was getting dark when I set off through the woods. I had packed all my stuff and thrown my case out of the window to retrieve later. Aggie's plan had worked out well. She went off and fell accidentally on purpose into the horse trough and Ma and Mrs Perkins rushed out to save her from getting pneumonia. She had given me over three pounds and said not to ask where it came from. I suspect it might have been hidden away by the Land Girls. I had on my winter coat and boots and a scarf and headed back in the direction we came in by car.

There is a lowering sky, gone from blue to sludgy grey. The fields are purple brown. I walk as fast as I can with my suitcase and the rims of my Wellington boots banging against my calves. At least I don't have to carry that gas mask anymore. I clamber over a stile and cross a field, climbing higher. Aggie was right. Shortly after we spoke in the morning we heard a train puffing past and I

159

made a guess that it wasn't more than a mile away. I am making a beeline straight for the tracks and from there I hope to see in which direction the station lies. I figure it can't be more than a couple of miles because the journey to the farm was about fifteen minutes. I hope to get a train by seven 'o clock and be back in London by nine.

I walk as straight as I can but the hedges around the field form a solid crook at one corner and I have to go to the top to find the next stile. There are no easy paths to follow as the field had been turned over and it's all thick muddy ruts. My boots soon pick up great clumps of clay and grow heavier and heavier. I am making progress but the night is against me. With no torch or lamp I have nothing to guide me. The low cloud is starting to make fog. Bad news. I see the black gully of the country lane below but I cannot reach it because the field is up high. I will have to find another gate or some way through the hedgerow. It is needle-sharp with twigs, thorns and brush. I'll get torn to ribbons. The fog has thickened. I struggle to the brow of the hill and over the next all I can see are indistinct hedgerows and trees. Everything is blurred and grey.

I'm lost. The cold is coming in through my clothes. Two choices remain. Press on, hoping to find the road or try and trace my tracks back. Neither is appealing but I choose to go on, trudging through the mud towards the corner of the next field. I make out a shape in the fog, which looks like a person. It might be a scarecrow. No, it's not raggedy enough. Too solid. I drop to my knees. There's nowhere to hide. Whatever it is has two legs but to one side there is something that looks like a gun in the 'at ease' position. Is it Perkins, waiting out here for me? Out shooting rabbits? Not at night. The shape isn't right. Too thin. It isn't moving. It is like it's guarding something but what is there to guard out here? It's too dark and indistinct to make out a face and I'm not even sure if it's looking in my direction. It is in the way of my route, so either I back track and go around it or I'll come face to face with it.

I'm sick and tired of running away.

If it wants me, it can come and get me. I taste the wetness of the fog in my mouth, but there is something else too, something metallic. Cordite: the smell from a bomb or a gun that has been fired. Closer now and the shape takes form and I see it is a man in battle-dress with a tin helmet. As he turns toward me I put together the face from memories.

'Dad!'

'Son.' His voice is parched, husky.

'You ran away?'

'Not likely.'

I go to his arms and although he smells of mud and filth and wet clothes I don't care because he is my dad. He fishes out a stub of a ciggie from behind his ear.

'How did you know I was here?'

'Not much escapes me.' His voice is tremendously weary.

'Are you back for good?'

''Fraid not son.'

'Is it bad, the war?'

'Bloody awful. Been looking after your Ma and Aggie like I told you?'

'Of course.'

'Good lad. Doing your bit.'

I'm happy for the first time in ages. All thoughts of escaping back to London are forgotten. 'Shall we go find Ma at the farm then?'

'Not yet. You should go though.'

'I don't want to – not without you.'

He holds out a box of Bryant and May. 'Spark me up.'

I pry the matches from his hand. It is hard and calloused from digging trenches. I light his cigarette for him and in the orange glow I see that his face is older now. He inhales and exhales slowly and the smoke forms a wraith around him. He looks away across the fields.

'You've done all right so far son. Better than I ever thought you would.'

I whisper my thank you.

'More to do though. You up for it?'

'I think so.'

There's so much I want to say, so much I have been keeping to myself but now with him here I don't know where to begin and, as I think this, he puts his hand on my shoulder and I know that everything is ok. He knows. He understands. The ciggie drops and he treads it out with his army boot.

'We'd best be off.'

'Where to?'

'You're leading son.'

'I don't know which way to go.'

'Trust your instinct.'

I look around. All is swirling mist. The trees loom over us and the hedge is a dark formless mass like a sleeping animal. The evenly spaced ruts are the only sign of human presence. I decide to follow them. Dad shoulders his pack and rifle and shuffles alongside me as we go down, down to the valley below. We walk side-by-side, man and boy. Man and man. I think back to Burgess Park. He has come to get me again. I knew I could rely on him. Sooner than expected I start to make out a tiny speck of light. It is far off but I am sure that it is the Perkins' farm.

'Will you come back to the farmhouse?'

He sighs. 'I can't be letting your Ma see me like this.'

'Please?'

'Tell her I'm thinking of her. Always. And Aggie.'

'You're not going, are you? Dad? Dad?'

He has been swallowed by the gloom. I call out again but he does not answer. I stagger about trying to find him. It's perishing cold and I'm shivering. If I don't get some warmth I will die out here. Dad wouldn't want that. He gave me my marching orders. I have work to do. I increase my pace, hacking through the bushes and clambering through into the next field. I keep my eyes focusing on that light, as I did when I was in the tunnels, looking for a way out. I curse when it twinkles out behind a tree and rejoice when it comes on again. Slowly, it seems, all too slowly, it grows larger and becomes a square.

Chapter Twenty-One

December 29th

I am on the train back to London. I made it back to the farmhouse but caught a chill and the fever lasted two days. During that time I drifted in and out of dreamless sleep, coming awake long enough to eat soup and bread and play a few hands of cards but I hadn't the energy to get up. Mr. Perkins hung my aeroplane above the bed to cheer me up. They had a local doctor come out and touch my head and take my temperature and tap my back and chest and leave horrid medicines in slim bottles. I would not speak to Aggie about Dad. It didn't seem right. Ma did not push me too far about where I had gone but I think she knew what I had been trying to do, which is why she has agreed to let me go back to find Evie. My destiny lies in the carbon black tunnels of the London Underground.

Ma is staying with Aggie on the farm until after New Year. Mr. *bloody* Watson, as she now calls him, being safely fifty miles out of his earshot, can go hang his job, she says. If he can't spare me for a few days without the Great Empire of Swan & Edgar crumbling then he's not made of stern enough stuff. She's washed and laundered all my clothes and packed my suitcase with food and chocolate. They all said their goodbyes at the station. It was a clear day and the long platform seemed to stretch forever into the low winter sun. According to the radio news there has been a respite in the bombing over Christmas.

I watch the countryside flash past and think of what lies ahead.

***

As we pull into Charing Cross I'm shocked at the devastation. The giant has stamped all over it again with its hobnailed boots. I buy a tube ticket and go to the usual spot at Holborn to my old bunk. It is so dark, so small and so smelly after all that clear country air. I do not look for Sands. This is beyond him now. Night comes so early and as the sirens go off people shuffle with orderly resignation down to the shelter. We've had Christmas off and it looks as though it is back to business as usual. 'London can take it' is everywhere on the posters. I don't wait for the first hard heavy thumps. There's nothing Jerry can do to me.

I take the tube to Goodge Street. The noise above is deafening and there are kiddies crying, mothers wailing. I go straight to the stairwell of the emergency stairs and try the door. It's open. Good. I won't need the screwdriver I brought.

I make my way to the lair. I know they will be there. As I come through the familiar dark wet passages I start to hear laughter, a post Christmas celebration. There are more of them now, a squad. A platoon. As I enter I see that Perce is wearing a long Army greatcoat and a military cap and has started to sprout hairs on his chin. Ollie is a little plump general, drinking from a bottle of port. There is a fresh haul lying about them, a hamper full of food and the stuffed head of a fox. Its fur has been tacked up on the wall as a trophy. It looks like they have been house clearing as well as dipping in the tubes and shops. All the rich knobs heading out of town. Easy pickings.

'Hello stranger.' Perce says.

'Come for another dust up?' Asks Ollie.

I ignore him. 'I need your help.'

'Heard that one before.' goes Ollie, as if heckling a music hall comic.

'What do you think about conchies?'

Kill 'em, hang 'em. Put 'em in the Tower is the general response. Perce as ever holds back, judging the mood.

'What's up?' he asks.

'Johnny's joined up with a bunch of them.'

'Explain.' Comes Perce, narrow eyed.

This is a huge risk but I am hoping it is one that will work. Set the cat among the pigeons.

'Where I tried to take you last time. There's this man down there. I know where he is and where he's taken the children. He's a bloody conchie and he's convincing them all not to fight. Johnny's one of them.'

Ollie. 'He's a bloody coward if that's true.'

The rest of the gang growl their disapproval. Perce holds up a hand. It is going yellow on the fingers.

'Why do we take your word on this?'

'They had me for three weeks. I got away.'

'You didn't get the rozzers?'

'I don't talk to the police.'

Almost a smile from Perce.

'I thought that if it came to Johnny you'd want to know first.'

Perce blows smoke, eyeing me. The others are up for it, murmuring about getting hold of weapons. Perce beckons me to approach. He looks at me, head cocked to one side, resigned, as Dad was once when I told him a fib about finding a bicycle. I miss the thing that drops in his hand and suddenly the blade of a razor is at my cheek. I stand stock still, petrified.

'You ain't just larking about are you boy? Cause if you are I've bleeding had it with you. We've had the Jerries down there – and now it's the conchies. If we're to sort this out proper I need to know you're not making a monkey out of me, right?'

I feel the blade draw blood. I dare not try to grip it or push it away for fear of what he might do. He'd do it too; I have no doubt about that. They would cover it up and dump me somewhere, maybe under rubble so it looks as though I bought it in a bomb blast. I know from looking in his eyes that there is no mercy here and maybe there never was. Maybe he never learned it, or what was right from wrong. Maybe he did and made the choice to go the other way. Maybe that story about the people in the blast was *his* family. I glare right back at him.

'Perce, I say evenly. It's the truth.'

A long moment passes.

The razor disappears and he kicks me between the legs. I fall to the floor in agony, cupping myself. Perce steps over me.

'Right you lot. Let's go find ourselves a traitor.'

***

It's bad up top. The Jerries are back in force and there are constant thumps and vibrations from above. The sounds of fire engines percolate through. I lead the gang, whose ranks have swelled, back to the tunnel at Holborn. I had forgotten how dark and complex the tunnels were and despite us all having torches and storm lamps I have to rely on intuition to guess where the manhole covers might be to the lower track. I locate one of the hatches and down we go, each of us climbing then dropping down, landing and rolling, torches slicing through the dark.

We jog along the rails until I find a tributary tunnel and then the first cavern. From there I hear the drip of water somewhere off and we follow the sound until it becomes a rush. We arrive at the junction with the sewers. Perce raises a hand for silence. We hear the sound of feet, running both ahead of us and behind.

'Run, rabbit run.' murmurs Perce.

'They're surrounding us.' I say.

'Let them – at least we'll know where they are. Which way?'

I look around, trying to remember which of the tunnels leads through to Victor's lair. I choose one. 'This way.'

On we go. With each twist and turn the tunnel grows smaller. Filthy water runs along the bottom. We emerge, not into the cavern, but another space altogether. It is a vast old water pumping room where the sewers converge. There are storm lamps set into the high walls so there is enough light to illuminate the huge space. We shine our torches up and around the Victorian brickwork. It must be sixty, seventy feet high, with arches and buttresses and crevices and sluices. It's like a giant underground church, in service of taking away London's effluent. There is even a cast iron plaque with a name, Bazalgette.

The gang has spread out but before we have a chance to make a plan of action there are war cries and the lost children attack. They come pouring out of the tunnels wearing raven's head masks. They too are armed with whatever they have managed to salvage; rods, poles, sticks and bricks. At first the gang is taken aback by these strange black creatures and the attack is brutal, knocking some of the gang to the ground. Perce bellows retaliation and retribution is swift. The lost children are weak from malnutrition, but they know this place and use the shadows to their best advantage. I engage with one of them, ducking below his blow and rolling him over me then pushing him to the ground.

Perce's gang fights dirty, kicking and scratching, but the children are shored up by the belief that they are fighting for their freedom. I can't work out which one is Johnny in the heat of battle, nor can I see Victor Sands. I sense his presence. A general is always going to be watching his troops from some vantage point. Once I get free of a tussle, I pedal back against the wall, scanning the high atrium with the full beam of my torch. Another beak comes sharply at me but I shine the light in his eyes. It's enough to momentarily blind him and I knock the mask off his face with the metal barrel of the torch. He's a small kid, about my age. He looks shocked and terrified and I feel revolted by what I have done.

I slip into the labyrinth. How will I remember the way to the gaol? How to retrace my steps? Chances aren't good to find Evie trapped down here. I call out her name once, twice, a third time. Nothing. My torch judders out. The fight continues behind me but the noise of it fades as I am swallowed in darkness. Can't see, can't hear. I try the torch but it's dead. Total blackness. What's left? I can certainly smell the sewers behind me but what clues can I gather? What would help? I try to concentrate as I slosh though the water. Water doesn't smell, just what's in it. I might get to the old river Fleet but I don't see how that will help. Do the aged bricks of the tunnel roof have different smells? The tunnels are all roughly the same age. What else is there in the air? Paraffin. Of course. The paraffin they use in their lamps to light the lair. There is a faint odour. As concentrate it becomes more pungent. I become surer of the smell, as strong as the rubber in a gas mask. I take two turns and now there is the growing glow of a candle. In a few strides I am in the classroom. There is more writing on the aged blackboard – a plan to repel those they saw as invaders. The remains of Christmas iron rations lie about. A shout, no, a scream.

Evie.

I follow the noise, sprinting as fast as I can until I come to a row of thick oak doors – the gaol cells. Evie lets out another yell and in a moment I am wrenching back the door. She's filthy and cowering on the floor but kicking hard with her stockinged feet at Johnny, whose trousers are round his ankles and who is trying to grab her ankles. I leap headlong, landing blows and extracting yelps from him. He goes down but he's a dirty fighter and my legs are swept from under me. He lands a proper punch on the side of my face. My ears are ringing and I am disorientated. I reach out to block the next blow because I know Johnny will keep coming if he senses weakness. However, it does not come. I swing my arms but there is nothing but air. I clamber to my feet and instead of receiving a big fat punch I see Johnny lying on the floor. Evie stands over him holding the dented ablution bucket.

'You didn't…?' I manage.

'I did.'

'He was always full of it.'

'That bloody hurt.' Moans Johnny, who is down but not out.

'I'm surprised you didn't knock him out cold.' I say.

'It's not the flicks, Will.'

'I still saved you though.'

'You are my hero.'

She says it so flatly that I don't think she means it, until she plants a kiss on my cheek. 'I knew you'd come.'

'I'm sorry it took so long. Christmas got in the way.'

'You went off and had a Christmas?' She pouts.

'It's a long story.'

She frowns at me but she's not really upset. 'What now?'

I look at Johnny, nursing his head and trying to wipe some of the stuff off himself onto the straw. 'He's going to lead us back to the others.'

Evie throws me a look.

'I've brought the dippers gang with me to free the children. Have you been interrogated by Victor?'

'The man in the gas mask? He's barking mad.'

'He was just hit by shrapnel.'

'You can't take us out, groans Johnny. The bloody Germans' are everywhere.'

'You'll see.' I sigh, yanking him up by his collar.

Pushing Johnny in front of us, we pick up a paraffin lamp and follow him back to the big room where the fight was. Perce's gang has won and the lost children are unmasked and huddled together in the centre of the space. They look scared and weary and some are openly weeping. They have also found and captured Victor Sands, who is being held by two of Perce's thugs. They are big East End lads and he looks withered and small between them. He isn't struggling. He is in his gown and his grimy clothes and without his mask I wonder why I was so scared for so long.

Perce paces up and down, playing to the crowd, using his old patter.

'So what we have here, gents, is a conchie what was too scared to fight and so he's preyed on all these young kiddies down here. A coward and a kidnapper.'

Victor Sands looks haunted, his eyes glassy, his cheeks sunken. He has none of the authority he possessed when he was in command of his underworld, sure of his grasp on the truth. His tongue darts out as he tries to lick his parched lips. His head wound has opened up again and I can see glistening blood there.

'So what do we do with him?' asks Perce of the mob.

'Drown him' shouts Ollie. 'Drown him in the bloody sewers.'

The others add more suggestions, schoolboy stuff, each idea more ludicrous than the last. I thrust Johnny forwards. Ollie sees him and does not know how to respond to his former friend and ally, now a turncoat. Perce sees Evie and me.

'Who's the skirt?'

'My cousin. They took her as well.'

Perce looks at her, tall in his long army greatcoat. He doesn't remember the girl he tried to chat up at the dance. I am glad of that but I reckon girls are not all that important to him, except as a trophy, if at all. He's looking for another excuse, more ammunition, as if he needed it for this hasty courtroom. Johnny is gazing incredulously at Ollie and Perce and the others. It is a slow dawn in his mind.

'You ain't been invaded then? London's still London?'

'What's left of it.' says Ollie.

The booming bombs can still be heard above even though we are eighty feet below the surface. Johnny's eyes go to Sands, the beast, the man in the mask. The leader.

'So all the time you had us, and trained us – it was a lie.'

His ferocious gaze is a torch of truth and Sands cannot look him in the face.

'I thought… I didn't know. I didn't know.' He is sad, broken.

Quick as anything Perce pulls out his razor and presses it to the man's neck. 'I say we end this here.'

'Wait. If you kill him, we're all murderers.' Someone is yelling. I am surprised to find that it is me. 'It doesn't have to come to this.'

'What else we going to do?'

'Turn him over to the police, the military. It's not our right.'

'What did he care about rights when he had all this lot trapped down here for months? Why you defending him anyway?'

I want to say, fair trial, fair play.

Perce presses the blade closer. Victor Sands is paralysed with fear.

Johnny growls. 'Let me do it.'

I have no doubt he would. He has been betrayed and in Johnny's mind all that matters is getting his honour back. He moves toward Perce, who drops the blade down into his hand and presents it to his former lieutenant. That is Perce all over. With animal cunning he will get his justice but avoid any of the consequences. If Johnny kills him, he'll be the one to hang. Much as I can't stand Johnny, he is not my enemy. All this time I never ever knew who I was fighting. I fought the mask people in the tunnels and the authorities when they would not listen. I fought Ma, who only cared too much, and myself for my own weakness. I start forwards but before I can get to Perce or Johnny an older voice booms out.

'Stop this. He'll have a fair trial.'

It is Sand's senior, out of breath and red in the face. 'The boy deserves fair hearing.'

Perce is amused. 'And who are you, mate?'

'Albert Sands, Station Master and Marshal at Holborn. His father.'

A shock wave goes through the boys. This is primal now, father and son.

Sands talks with absolute authority. 'True, he took these lads, but no one came to harm. He deserves a court of law or military tribunal – not this.'

Sands steps forward and Perce swings the open blade in warning.

'You stop there old son. Up top it's all mitigating circumstances, insanity pleas, reserved occupations. Maybe a nice quiet war for him in the Scrubs. This is our world down here. He stands trial by us, not them up top.'

The bombs above punctuate the silence. Sands' father looks round at the boys, the dippers and the taken. After a long moment, he answers, proudly.

'Then I'll speak for him.'

This hits home with us boys, those who have fathers gone to war, those who maybe had no father in the first place. Those who would want our dads to speak for us.

Perce gives a slight nod. He lowers the blade. 'I'll decide the punishment. You make your case.'

There is a collective release of breath. We have naturally fallen back in a circle around Victor Sands and his guards, with Perce to his right, almost a court and jury.

Mr. Sands goes to him now, this bundle of rags and confusion. Victor visibly wilts and as he does so, Sands kisses him gently on the forehead. No one says a word as some unspoken communication passes between them. I sneak a look at Evie. She is equal parts terrified and fascinated. Mr. Sands clears his throat.

'My son's crime was to be afraid. Afraid of war and death and dying and who ain't? I know I am.'

Perce: 'What about kidnapping these boys and the girl – that ain't cowardice.'

'He did it out of wanting to save them.'

A voice at the back. 'What, is he Jesus now?'

'He has shell-shock.'

Ollie: 'Didn't stop him taking the kiddies.'

Johnny: 'Interrogations, no food, telling us lies. Months, some of us been down here.'

Sands gives his son a sad glance. 'He got it wrong. He's ill.'

Perce: 'Why didn't he go to war? He's of conscription age.'

'He's CO.'

Perce takes a step up to Victor and comes face to face. 'I want to hear *him* say it.'

It is Victor's turn to muster his strength. 'I am a conscientious objector.'

Sands: 'Before you start on, that means he made a tough choice. Those who wait for conscription are just standing in line.'

Perce. 'If you're fit to fight then you serve your country.'

Would Perce go willingly? I don't see him as cannon fodder on the Front Line, more wangling some cushy desk job. He's got his fake ID cards and ration books stashed away I bet. He's having a good war and not about to jeopardise that. Why did I ever want to be part of his gang?

Sands. 'He's not fit to fight. Look at the wound.'

Ollie. 'He's a stinking lousy coward.'

Victor. 'I wanted to save the boys.'

Perce. 'By forming your own Army?'

Mr. Sands. 'He wanted to be a patriot… in his way.'

Johnny. 'Bloody coward – you wanted us to fight for you.'

Ollie. 'Bloody coward – you hid away down here in all the shit.'

Perce. 'Bloody coward, running away. Run, rabbit, run.'

Mr. Sands leaps at Perce and tries to wrestle him to the ground. Perce is younger and stronger and gets the blade out and slashes it across his hand. Sands thumps down like a sandbag.

Victor pulls himself free of his captors and tries to help his father. The rest of the gang move towards him and I move too, throwing down the paraffin lamp between them and the Sands. The glass shatters and a stream of flame spreads outwards. I follow up by leaping on Johnny's back and pulling him away. Victor, with a kind of mad strength, lashes out at Ollie and his keepers and, spinning around, somehow avoids Perce, who has the razor out, waving it wildly. Mr. Sands, with blood pouring from his hand, makes a fist with the other and drives through Perce's defence, landing one on him. Taken aback, Perce reels and then shouts.

'Do them both.'

Victor's gown suddenly unfolds and inflates like a pair of giant bat wings. Underneath is his gas mask. He grabs the long ventilator pipe and swings it round, catching his assailants and hefting one off his feet. I get to Ollie before he can land a blow and suddenly, up top, another bomb, a 500kg at least, hits the ground and the hurricane lights flicker wildly. The ground shakes and in the next moment Victor is gone, clambering up the metal rungs of a ladder up the wall and disappearing into a circular shaft at the top. We give chase, climbing up behind him, feet clanging on the metal rungs. I am desperate, animal, not thinking except to call out to Evie to look after Mr. Sands as I grab a torch and follow Perce and the others.

***

Clattering feet in the shaft, then sloshing through water. It is angled slightly upwards, perhaps a run off. It is warmer here too, with a hot breeze blowing toward us. Johnny is in the lead, bellowing curses, the turncoat turned. I follow him with Perce and Ollie a few feet behind. Johnny yelps and flashes his torch. There is mass movement up ahead and what looks like a writhing brown carpet rolls toward us in a tide. Shrieking, screeching, gnashing teeth, glistening black bodies. The disease carriers. Rats – hundreds of them scramble over our feet. There is nowhere to hide, no way of getting up the sides of the slick shaft, so we kick and jump and plough on, crushing them under our shoes. The living river rises and floods and then as quickly as it came, sinks once more. I fear for Evie and the others, as when the vermin come to the lip of the shaft they will pour out into the big sewer treatment room, a rain of rats and pestilence. Hopefully she or Sands will think to take them another way. Sands can help. We have to press on.

A vertical shaft of old brick. On Johnny's urgent call we ascend once more. It is a short climb before we push open a large rusted door and now we are in a long sewer, brick arched, stinking. Here the water is *boiling*. It hisses and roils and stinks of excrement. Our faces are wet with steam. I do not want to breathe in but I cannot avoid it and the disgusting sensation is so bad that I vomit. We all vomit until our stomachs are empty and Ollie slips and falls into the water, screaming like a baby as he is horrendously scalded. He jumps out and collapses on the curb of the path on the other side, nursing his burns, gritting his teeth, screaming and bawling, his face piggy red. A big burnt baby. And that is it for Ollie.

Johnny's beam doesn't linger on his former friend and instead goes to the path through the steam. A shape, twenty feet ahead, moving swiftly: Victor, with his gown billowing behind him. He knows each and every twist and turn of these tunnels. Perce yells out and we go after him. The long tunnel curves round, slowly at first but then abruptly. As we edge around, an actual mist rolls toward us, rising from the water. We plunge into the steam and Johnny stops dead. My torch beam cannot penetrate more than a couple of feet. We cross beams like the searchlights on the London skyline. As above, so below.

'Wait, listen.' I say.

A roaring from above, which could be more water. Are we below the Thames? It doesn't seem right. No. I hear feet on rungs. Johnny lifts the torch beam up. Another exit. He goes up again and as we go, bellowing and shouting, I see

171

Victor's feet as he pushes open a manhole cover. A bright rose pink circle replaces the darkness. It grows large like a full moon. It shades from pink to orange to the yellow of dawn as we rise and come out and find that we are in daylight.

No, it is not the day.

The night has become day. The heat is immense. It is as though we had crawled right into a furnace. I can barely touch the hot iron of the manhole cover. The City of London is a living hell on Earth. Around us there are fifty-foot sheets of flame swallowing those buildings that remain. There is almost a solid wall of fire on all sides. The streets are alight from end to end. Embers rain down upon us like incendiaries. There is a high wind, which lifts great bushels of sparks, which dance and spit in all directions. Burnt out fire appliances litter the street, their rubber tires and flaccid hoses melted to the ground, their carcasses abandoned for the fire to pick over. Bits of wood smoulder in the road. Masonry and debris are everywhere. Even the bricks have wisps of flame around them. The heat is scorching and I have to shield my eyes to sneak a look upwards. Above the gutted buildings stands the lone squat cathedral of St Paul's, surrounded by flame. If that goes, London is lost. From the Guildhall to Ludgate Circus, Holborn to Farringdon, it's all going up. Fleet Street, Smithfield, Liverpool Street. London Wall – the whole bloody lot. The night is on fire.

The heat fells the three of us. As our hair fries and our skin puckers and blisters we cover our heads and half crawl, half stumble along. Victor Sands is a short way ahead, clambering over chunks of masonry and using them as stepping-stones. Johnny goes for him, scuttling like a crab up over the rubble and grabbing a hold of his flapping gown. He pulls him over onto his back and I see Sand's terrified face. The noise is terrible, a deafening roar of destruction. He's got him trapped under bricks and the wooden sash of a window. Broken glass lies all around, reflecting the flame, intensifying the heat.

Johnny stands with a raised stick about to lay into him but, as he swipes down, Sands frees a foot and kicks Johnny in the stomach. Johnny goes back and falls onto the scorching pavement. Perce yells to him to move. Johnny gets to his feet but he never sees the great black burning mass as the whole side of a building comes right down on top of him. He is enveloped by it and we are blown backwards by a ball of heat. I feel my eyebrows and hair singe away. My trouser leg catches fire and I have to beat it out. I feel as though my eyes are melting and my insides are bubbling and boiling. When I finally look up, Perce is silhouetted against a hundred foot sheet of orange and rose flame, his greatcoat flowing, his razor arm raised, poised to strike, Victor Sands is prone beneath him, a halo of embers and sparks all around us. I get to him first, holding his arm up high and pressing my body against him.

'Don't kill him Perce.'

'He's a bloody traitor.'

'He's misguided, mad, but he thought he was defending us.'

'Johnny's dead 'cause of him.'

'Johnny's dead cause of Johnny.'

Perce lays into me with his other fist, a sharp blow with his knuckles under my ribcage, pushing out all my breath. I breathe in burning air and I have to let go. I lose my footing and see him go for Victor once more. Sands is trying to crawl away. Perce slashes at the gown with the razor, turning it to tatters and cutting into the flesh of his shoulder. Victor cries out, a high keening wail.

I leap forward as he strikes again. Victor manages to block it but he has no strength left. The next slice will be fatal. I have to get in between them. I grab the nearest object to hand. It is the brass nozzle of a discarded fire hose that has come away from the rubber. It's boiling hot but I hurl it at Perce and it strikes him with a satisfying smack. He drops the razor and comes for me. There is a huge crack as another building comes down and then another rain of incendiaries. That can only mean one thing – another wave of bombers is on its way. I have no time to avoid the body blow as Perce barrels into me. We roll over on flaming wooden cobbles and agonising pain shoots through my body. Perce is vicious and relentless and pummels his fists into me, spitting curses. I manage to deliver a punch to his kidneys and he falls away.

'Had enough of you.' He shouts, as he rises. 'You die and no one will be any the wiser.'

Flame glints off the razor where it lies nestled in bricks and burning rubble. We both go for it at the same time. He gets to it first but I am on him again and battering him with all my might. I know it is a losing battle against his greater strength. I back off. I remember what Dad said: a time to fight and a time to flee. Pick your battles, Son. The heat is searing and I feel my skin blistering. I have to get away. Perce keeps coming, razor aloft like the scythe of the grim reaper. I back peddle, coming around the rubble where Victor Sands had lain before. There is no sign of him. Perce's face is mad, merciless, twisted in the heat with rage. This boy man murderer has found his true vocation. I was wrong. He would do well in war. He looms large, so huge and powerful and like the fire, an absolute force of destruction. I shield myself, ready for the blow, the slash, the cut, knowing my blood will boil as it gushes out and escapes. And then it comes, our deliverance. The blast. A huge bomb is dropped like a dead bird from the sky.

I do not see or hear or feel the impact.

Instead I fall once more to darkness.

Chapter Twenty-Two

January 1941

They called it the Second Great Fire of London. When the six o' clock Minnie sounded in the city, three hundred incendiaries a minute began to fall in the area around St Paul's. By seven o' clock there were fifty-four fires. By nine a hundred and twenty tons of high explosive had been dropped. The five fire stations, Cannon Street, Redcross Street, Bishopsgate, Whitefriars and Carmelite St couldn't contain the fires. The Thames was low and the firemen couldn't get their suction pumps through the mud to the water in midstream. The buildings came down, blocking the narrow streets and a strong west wind whipped up the flames. Twenty-eight bombs fell around St. Paul's, the last one at eleven forty. The all-clear went at midnight.

The fires burned for two days and a hundred and sixty people died. Five hundred were injured. There was a photographer on the roof of the Daily Mirror building near Holborn Circus who managed to capture the dome of St Paul's in the middle of all that smoke and fire. They put it in the papers as a symbol of resistance.

***

There's bright sunlight through the window and birdsong coming from outside. I'm in a bed, a crisp sheeted hospital bed, in a ward. There's a bright red blanket. My arm and left leg are bandaged and there is gauze on my face, which feels blistered and burned. My throat really hurts. There are others here, some children, other grown-ups and some starchy nurses who don't seem to know anything or want to know much, but they are kind and bring Lemonade and food at odd times. There's breakfast early in the morning, which I don't mind because I'm used to waking up on station platforms, but tea is at six pm and we're supposed to go to sleep by seven.

Seven? The night hasn't even started by seven, the Winnies still wailing away. I can't sleep in the middle of the night. I lie awake and watch the rectangular moon shadow move across the ceiling. This place is called Tunbridge Wells and it is one of the hospitals they are now using because the London ones are too full. A doctor came in and told me I was lucky. I don't feel very lucky, but he knows best.

I was found, they tell me, towards midday as firemen were putting out the worst of the fires in that street. I had fallen back down the open manhole and so escaped the worst of the blast. Most of my injuries are from my time in that blistering heat and from my fall. I haven't said that Perce was responsible for a few of them as well. I'm guessing he was blown to bits, as no one could have survived that bomb. I also do not know what happened to Victor Sands and I don't think I ever will know. I like to think he may have got away. I was taken to Whitechapel Hospital and dressed and given blood, and soon after they transferred me here. I am apparently a non-urgent case, with minor fractures, burns and bruises. I've been here for some days.

After breakfast we read or play cards if we can until the nurses come to tuck in the beds and smarten them with hospital corners. The doctors do their rounds mid-morning, checking our charts and asking the odd question. I am, according to them, on my way to recovery, though I still have an awful whistling in my ears and I get sleepy often. Shock is what they call it. It's hard to think straight, which is why I am carrying on with writing this diary. The afternoons are boring and some people get visitors later on. I am told that Ma came with Aggie but I don't remember seeing or speaking to them. The sister says they are coming back.

***

Ma is holding my hand and Aggie is giving me kisses to make me squirm. Ma has buns and Aggie has sweets and all sorts of things and they are planning a picnic here on my bed. It is a long grey Saturday afternoon. Evie is safe, apparently. She and Sands led the missing children out of the underground sewers and tube tunnels to safety. Good girl. She's been released from hospital too, what with everyone being needed for the war effort.

'Is she coming in to see me?' I ask Ma.

'You wait and see.'

'I've had quite enough of wait and see. I want to know now.'

Ma creases up her face, but like a joke. 'Course she is. She's just doing war work today.'

'Is there news about Dad?'

There is a pause and her mouth opens and closes. Suddenly, the tears come fast and untamed. She fusses with her bag and produces a tissue. Choking, she starts to turn away. 'I have to speak to the doctor.'

I tell her. 'Ma. It's all right. I know. I know what's happened.'

'How could you know?'

'I just do.'

Ma kisses me on the forehead. I hold onto her and so does Aggie. We are a sad little knot of people but we are together. I don't cry. No need for more tears, not now.

'Can I see the letter?'

She produces the telegram.

I unfold it, read the cold white strips, and hand it back to her without saying a word.

'He'd be proud of you.' Ma says.

'I know.'

Aggie is picking at the blanket, the bedspread. She's been awfully quiet for her and I reckon something is up. 'What is it Ag? You're dying to tell me.'

'We're going to the country, back with the Perkins family.'

'When you're better.' Says Ma.

'When I'm better.' I say. 'I am awfully tired now though.'

'We'll leave you to sleep. We'll see you tomorrow.'

And they leave, and I do sleep, and I don't dream about Dad, the real ghost.

I have a dream about being in the countryside in the sunshine in the spring.

***

She's here, busying about, being cheeky with the nurses, freckle-faced, lipsticked, her hair done auburn and teased. She wears an olive green dress and it is tight on her. She looks smart, official. She brings a book about planes that I've wanted for ages.

'Well done for rescuing everyone.' I say.

'I was returning the favour. You saved me...'

'Tit for tat.'

'What happened with those nasty Spivs? Or don't you want to tell?'

'They got what was coming. Did Mr. Sands find his son?'

'He checked the mortuaries. Doesn't expect to find anything. He's back at work.'

'And the children?'

'Recovering elsewhere. Most have met up with their mum's.'

'And you?'

She sits on the painted wooden chair beside me and starts smoothing my sheets.

'What about me?'

'Ma said something about war work.'

'That's right Will.'

Another silence.

I've lost.

After all this and being the bloody hero, I've still lost her. I stare at the wall opposite and will myself not to cry and not to hate her for everything and I do hate her but only for being a stupid girl. She is moving beside me, standing to leave. Yes, oh so formal and British. But no… not British and not formal at all. Suddenly she is kissing me on the lips. I sink into her cherry red mouth. I press hard until our teeth click. My arm is painful as I lean up, but I don't care. It is worth it. It has all been worth it. It is an age before she pulls away, but only because she has something to say. She gently chews her lower lip as she considers me.

'Didn't you know then?'

'Know what?'

She rolls her eyes. 'Oh god. Boys.'

'Yes. What about us?'

'Don't you listen to a thing your sister tells you?

'Not really, no.'

'I liked you from the start, silly. You just had no idea how to play the game.'

'What d'you mean – the start?'

'I told Aggie months ago. She spoke to you.'

'You mean… in October.'

'Has the penny dropped now?'

The penny has dropped. 'So… what now?'

'What do you mean?'

'Well, you're going to do war work back in London and they're taking me to the country. When will I ever see you? I want to be with you Evie.'

She frowns slightly. 'I'm not doing war work in London. Never said I was.'

'Then where?'

'It's not just you going to the country.'

'You mean…?'

'I'm joining the Land Girls and staying with you on the farm. After all, we've all got to do our bit, haven't we?'

I lie back on the crisp pillow and gaze up at the ceiling with a smile that will never ever leave my face.

You're right Evie. We've all got to do our bit.

~THE END~

You may also enjoy...

big time

from the author of
sunstroke

marc blake

Lightning Source UK Ltd.
Milton Keynes UK
UKHW030632250920
370514UK00001B/137

9 781789 824049